OTHER BOOKS BY LINCOLN JAMES

VINTAGE THRILLERS •
MODERN NIGHTMARES

<u>Coming Spring 2026</u>

All We Wanted
A Supernatural Thriller

They make your dreams come true. Then you disappear.

Spring Formal, 1982—a weekend of open bars, rented tuxedos, and
bad decisions at a luxury resort in Las Vegas.
But the casino has unveiled something new.
Buried behind the lobby stands a glass display case housing three
mummified figures adorned in gold: a ring, a tooth, an eyepatch.
By day, they're on display.
By night, they hunt.
They slip into borrowed skin.
They feed on desire, envy, regret.
All they need is one phrase.
I wish.
Because in this hotel, dreams don't come true.
They come for you.

<u>**Now Available**</u>

The Ninth Layer
A Claustrophobic Survival Thriller

This wasn't a field trip... It was a burial.

It was supposed to be extra credit.
A simple research descent into the caves beneath Pendleton University.
But the deeper Alex and his classmates go, the stranger things become.
The air hums.
The walls glow.
And the silence feels like it's listening.
Then the lights go out.
And something starts screaming in the dark.
By the time they realize there's no way back up, the ground itself is shifting.
Breathing.
Hungering.
In the dark, they know they're not alone.
And the cave has no intention of letting them escape.

Available in print and ebook.

We Are Human
A Gripping Sci-Fi Thriller

They said it was evolution... He knew it was murder.

In 2040, Tyler Alcaster disappears.
When he wakes, his reflection isn't his own.

His skin is flawless. His pulse is wrong.
His memories—fractured.
They tell him he's special. Reborn. Immortal.
But Ty knows something still hurts. Still remembers. Still dreams.
Now he's trapped in a facility where nothing dies.
The people around him aren't people anymore—
a girl with glass eyes who never blinks,
a woman sewn together like a secret.
They all whisper the same question in the dark:
What are we becoming?
Because immortality isn't a gift.
It's the end of everything human.

Available in print and ebook.

Written Just For You
A Romantic Psychological Thriller

*Some love stories are written in the stars. This one was written in
blood.*

Will wasn't supposed to stay in town. Jean wasn't supposed to meet
him. And the book she gave him? It wasn't meant to be read.
Depoe Bay is a place of whispers—where the fog clings too close and
stories go unfinished. The town says Jean is a ghost, a siren, a memory
that never made it out of the water.
But Will knows she's real. He's seen her. Heard her laugh.
Felt something shift.
And now that he's read her words...He can't let her go.
As the town turns colder, the secrets grow louder—about
the past, the dead, and what love refuses to bury.
Some girls don't make it out of their stories...
But Will's about to make sure this one does.

Available in print and ebook.

All the Time
A Coming-of-Age Sci-Fi Thriller

The past isn't just a memory... It's a trap.

When Carter sets out to reconnect with his dying mother, he never expects to arrive at her house years before he was born. Stuck in the past with nothing but his car, a bag of clothes, and a barely working iPhone, Carter faces an impossible question: how did he get here—
and how can he get back?
Time is slipping through his fingers, and every moment spent in the past pulls him further from the future he's desperate to return to.
Caught between what was and what could be, Carter begins to question if time is something you can outrun...
or if it's already run out.

Available in print and ebook.

The Vanishing Eight
A Pulse-Pounding Survival Thriller

Disappearing was only the beginning.

Eight friends. One missing.
The town of Piedmont had always whispered about them—
too close, too wild, too perfect.
Then Roy disappeared.
Now, Jonathan is racing to hold what's left of their group together.
But the deeper he digs, the more he realizes: Roy's not the first to go missing. And if Jon's not careful...
He won't be the last.

In a town built on secrets, nothing stays hidden forever.
And some friendships don't survive the truth.

Available in print, ebook, and audiobook.

FOREWORD

Content Warning

This book contains scenes of graphic violence, gore, and themes that may be triggering to some readers. These include depictions of grief, trauma, and sadism, as well as physical and emotional harm caused by antagonistic characters. Reader discretion is strongly advised.

A Note on Themes

Devils Like Us delves into the emotional complexities of loss, trauma, and the ways people cope—or fail to cope—with overwhelming grief. The protagonist's journey is one of survival, not only against external threats but also against the internal struggle of processing profound emotional pain. While these darker themes are integral to the narrative, they are handled with care and are not intended to glorify violence or harmful behavior.

If you find any of these themes distressing, please take care of yourself while reading. Remember that it's okay to step away if needed.

Thank you for embarking on this journey with me. I hope the story inspires thought and reflection on the strength of the human spirit, even in the face of darkness.

DEVILS LIKE US

LINCOLN JAMES

Copyright © 2024 by Lincoln James

All rights reserved.

No part of this publication may be reproduced, distributed, or transmitted in any form or by any means, including photocopying, recording, or other electronic or mechanical methods, without the prior written permission of the publisher, except in the case of brief quotations embodied in critical reviews and certain other noncommercial uses permitted by copyright law.

ISBN 979-8-9904966-3-7 (hardcover)

ISBN 979-8-9904966-4-4 (paperback)

ISBN 979-8-9904966-5-1 (ebook)

This is a work of fiction. Names, characters, organizations, places, events, and incidents are either the product of the author's imagination or used fictitiously. Any resemblance to actual persons, living or dead, or actual events is purely coincidental.

Published by Lincoln James

P.O. Box 10660 Page Ave # PO 4034

Fairfax, VA 22038-4034

www.thelincolnjames.com

Edited by E. Lee Caleca

First edition, October 2024

Printed in the United States of America

CHAPTER 1

A MIRAGE OF COMFORT

DAWN SLIPPED in like a thief with a grudge and snatched away the last shreds of nighttime comfort. It draped the room in a stifling blanket of quiet, as if the air itself had thickened, saturated with the weight of unspoken confessions. The silence was a living thing, oozing into every corner, clinging to my skin like a shroud of sticky dread. It seeped into my bones, a venomous crawl that left behind a trail of jagged nerves and icy foreboding.

I jolted upright, my heart hammering against my ribs as if it were trying to break free. A hostage claiming innocence. The remnants of a nightmare clung to me, ghostly fingers scratching at the edges of my mind with a desperate, gnawing hunger, accusing me, insistent in its demand to recall. An inexplicable shiver curled in my stomach, a cold whisper of something sinister lurking just out of sight, waiting to pounce.

The room, once a haven of youthful dreams, was now a prison of decayed hopes. The posters, once bursting with color, had faded into grotesque shades of sickly green. They leered at me. Eyes that once smiled back from a world of imagination now sneered with malevolent glee. The peeling wallpaper and sagging books stood as eerie relics of a past I'd tried to shove into a forgotten corner, where everything that once mattered is broken, no longer relevant in a life such as mine.

I took a deep shaky breath and exhaled slowly, trying to still my racing heart. *It's all good, Jason. Just your mom's place. No need to tweak.* I thought to myself, but the words were swallowed by the oppressive silence. My return home since the start of college felt jarringly alien, a stark contrast to the late-night escapades and frantic study sessions that had become my new normal.

I glanced at the empty pillow beside me, its damp imprint a grim reminder of the restless night that just moments ago had shaken me; something I didn't want to know. Or something I had known that had come back from the place where everything is broken. I didn't want to fit the pieces together. I felt disjointed, uncomfortable. It grated on me, unreal yet as real as anything else.

Harsh sunlight sliced through the window, casting sharp beams that taunted my feeble attempts at finding peace in this cursed place.

For weeks now, these unnatural dreams had plagued me, each one more unsettling than the last. They started innocuously enough, a creeping darkness where nothing ever showed itself. Then came the orange glow—an atomic blaze that didn't burn but felt like knives cutting into my flesh.

Aiight, your move. Face the nightmares again and let them drag you down, or haul your ass out of bed and pretend everything's fine. But deep down, I knew the darkness would follow me, no matter how fast I ran.

With a jolt, I crashed back onto the mattress, yanking the pillow over my face—the moment my alarm clock sprang to life. *Fuck.*

Reluctantly, I heaved myself up again. Brushing my teeth, pulling on my pants—it was all dreary and difficult, like wading through an ocean of muddy dread, a mechanical routine in a life that had lost its sparkle. Every action was an effort to fend off the shadows lurking in every crack. Finally leaving the oppressive gloom of my childhood home, I braced myself to pick up Kimberly from her hotel.

· · ·

Sliding into my BMW E34 was like slipping into a time-traveling coffin, a relic from a forgotten age when reality seemed less tangled. The black leather seats, cracked and weary, wrapped around me like an old lover's embrace, but the persistent shadow of unease gnawed at my insides. The city's labyrinthine streets stretched before me, blurring into a surreal smear of uncertainty. Each turn was a descent deeper into a haze of faded memories, and I couldn't shake the eerie feeling that invisible eyes were watching my every move.

The low growl of the car's engine felt like an ominous heartbeat, echoing the tension coiled in my gut—a grim reminder of the lurking dangers just beyond the edge of perception. The cityscape loomed, an oppressive specter swallowing any hint of hope. Billboards, draped in shadows, loomed like silent guardians, their messages twisted into cryptic warnings that made no sense on the surface. Sure, I was smarter than this, intelligent enough to work this out to be nothing more than my own guilty imagination. Still... there was something that was not imagination. The mind and body played occasional tricks, but the sixth sense did not lie.

As I pulled beneath the hotel's overhang, the dark blue BMW seemed to shrink, a ghost of its former self. The engine's growl was now a mournful dirge, a desperate attempt to outrun the phantoms that danced just out of sight.

Kimberly awaited, an enigma herself, wrapped in contradictions. Her smile, sharp and cutting through the morning haze, was a blade of alluring danger.

Her defiant stride, accompanied by the playful disarray of her chestnut hair in the breeze, seemed to whisper secrets meant only for her ears. Dressed in faded denim shorts and a vintage tee, she exuded a nonchalant coolness. Her eyes, obscured by oversized sunglasses, always held a darkness that slithered beneath the surface. Yet, as she lowered the designer frames from her face, it was her hazel eyes—dancing with an unpredictable glimmer of mischief—that held me captive and sent icy shivers down my spine where there should be none.

Her presence was a magnetic paradox, a blend of salvation and destruction that promised both delirious pleasure and inevitable ruin. As I stepped out of the car to meet her, a shiver of anticipation and dread washed over me. What awaited in the enigmatic embrace of this woman—ecstasy or damnation—was a question I was both drawn to and terrified of answering.

"Hey, stranger!" I called out, trying to keep it light despite the flutter in my chest. Drawing her close, I wrapped her in a warm embrace, planting a tender kiss on her lips. We chuckled, each with our own thoughts about it, keeping secrets that only time, if we had enough of it, would tell.

"Feels like we didn't just share a five-hour flight," she quipped, her sunglasses sliding down her nose to reveal eyes that could ensnare even the most guarded soul. "You ready for today's adventure?"

I laughed, more to ease my nerves than anything. "Excited? Sure, let's go with that," I replied, keeping my tone casual, masking the turmoil beneath the surface. *She doesn't need to know about the latest dream. Let's keep it cool and the momentum rolling.*

A vibrant yellow bandana added an incongruous touch of brightness to her outfit, almost mocking the surrounding gloom I felt. With a quick swipe of shimmery lip gloss, she placed a subtle hint of glamour, a beacon of allure in an otherwise grim landscape. In Kimberly's presence, there was an unsettling blend of laid-back ease and a predatory readiness, as if she was always poised to embrace whatever darkness the day had in store. Her presence was both a comfort and a threat, a reminder that even in the light of day, shadows still lingered.

"Damn, what are you? A trust fund brat?" she teased, her smile cutting through the morning haze with a feral edge. She slid into the car, her presence a potent mix of danger and beauty.

"Yeah, yeah, it totally wrecks my 'bad boy' vibe, I know. Just don't spill the beans back in New York, okay?" I squinted through the grimy windshield, letting the sunlight pierce my tired eyes. My ride was filthy, but a wash was the last thing on my mind. "Besides, looks can be deceiving—especially in this town." I forced a grin, scanning the street, half-expecting villains to leap out and pull us into the darkness.

"Totally. Wouldn't want to mess up your *street cred*," she shot back, snapping her seatbelt into place with a sharp, decisive movement. "So, how are you feeling about this whole... spectacle?"

"Honestly? I'm about as thrilled as anyone can be at 9 AM... I guess," I said, trying to sound nonchalant. But my voice betrayed a hint of anxiety.

The air between us hummed with anticipation, thick with unspoken fears and hopes. "Yeah, coming out to my mom's gonna be a challenge... But hey, it's hard not to want to show you off."

Kim had a resilience I deeply admired, born from her tough Brooklyn upbringing. She wasn't just bubbly and playful; she had street smarts and a sharp mind, studying aeronautical engineering of all things.

Her response was a defiant grin, her messy curls bouncing with each word. "Think she'll like me? I went all out with the '80s look for her," she said, her voice laced with bravado masking the uncertainty beneath.

I couldn't help but smile, a flicker of warmth breaking through the shadows. My hand found its way to the back of her head, fingers tangling in the wild strands, pulling her closer. Another kiss, tender yet desperate, a silent plea for reassurance in the face of uncertainty.

"It looks perfect, babe," I murmured against her lips, my gaze drawn to the dark lenses that shielded her eyes from view. Even hidden behind the tinted glass, I could feel the weight of her stare, the warmth of her presence.

"Besides, my mom's been in sales forever. Even if she didn't like you, you'd never know," I teased, a faint hint of challenge coloring my words. But beneath the laughter, there was a truth we both understood: in the end, all we could do was hold onto each other and hope for the best.

Kimberly and I glided through the sun-blasted veins of North Hollywood in my dated beamer, its engine a rattling beast that felt oddly alive, like it was fighting to be relevant, to survive in a world that did not appreciate relics. Our destination: Pat's Diner, a greasy spoon haunt favored by the Hollywood elite, or so the lore went. Tucked away near the Warner Bros. lot, it was the kind of joint where whispers of celebrity sightings mingled with the smell of sizzling bacon. They only had outdoor seating, and the sun always beat down on you no matter where you ended up. If you got lucky, though, the servers always whispered of the chance to see Julia Roberts or even the illusive George Clooney, if you came at the right time. *But there is never a right time.*

As we wound our way through the canyon roads, the mid-morning sun threw jagged shadows across the cracked asphalt, conjuring an eerie ballet of light and darkness. Kimberly sat beside me. She suddenly seemed like a spectral figure as pieces of my nightmare rushed through me, flashbacks I could not explain. Her face somewhat obscured by her oversized sunglasses, her intention as veiled as her eyes, I couldn't shake the sense of dread at the back of my thoughts, like stinging ants, poking me, prodding me to perdition.

The silence between us grew dense, almost tangible. I flicked on the radio, hoping to shatter the oppressive quiet. Static crackled before settling into the soft, haunting strum of The Smashing Pumpkins. The melody was a balm to my nerves, a bittersweet escape into a realm of neon nights and half-remembered dreams.

I glanced at Kim, her face an inscrutable mask softened by the glow of the music. We danced through the valley's twists and turns, the road a serpentine reflection of the song's ebb and flow. For a moment, the chaos of our mission was a distant memory, replaced by the simple pleasure of shared silence.

But as the last notes dwindled, the radio host's voice sliced through the tranquility. "Aiight folks, that was 'Rhinoceros' by the Smashing Pumpkins, bringing back some memories from the early '90s here on KXV8," he crooned. "Now, let's rewind further with some late '70s disco flair. Here's ABBA's 'Gimme, Gimme, Gimme

(A Man After Midnight),' straight from 1979. Keep it locked, keep it loud, and keep it right here on KXV8!"

With a sudden decisive click, Kimberly cut off the radio, plunging us back into the realm of reality. She turned to me, her gaze penetrating as if searching for the secrets buried behind my façade. "What's going on?" she asked, her voice slicing through the silence like a blade. "You seem a little... wound up."

"Me? Nah," I deflected, though the lie clung to me like a second skin that was a size too small. "Just trying to remember the way... it's been a while since I've been on these roads." But Kimberly's gaze was too perceptive to be fooled.

"Oh, really?" she said, her tone light but her eyes cutting through with a knowing glint. "Didn't bother with MapQuest? Look, I can see when you're spinning out," she added, tapping the dashboard with a smirk. "Ever try and chillax? It might suit you."

I managed a dry laugh. "Yeah. I'll add that to my to-do list right after *'stop worrying about everything.'*"

Anxiety twisted in my chest like a live wire. Mom wasn't awake when I came in last night, and, being the early riser that she was, wasn't there this morning either. The thought of reuniting with her, after so many months, loomed like a shadowy specter.

Kimberly seemed to sense the undercurrent of my thoughts. "You're going to be fine, Jason," she said, her voice soft but with an underlying firmness. "You've got this."

"It's just—," I hesitated, "sometimes it feels like Burbank has this invisible force field. The closer we get, the heavier it presses down on me."

Kimberly raised an eyebrow, her expression a blend of amusement and challenge. "Melodramatic much? And trust me, your mom's going to adore me. I'm *irresistible*."

I chuckled, though it didn't entirely lift my unease. "Yeah, well, you didn't grow up with her. She has this way of making you feel like you're five again, and *not* in the fun way."

"Guess I'll have to work my charm then," Kimberly quipped. "Lucky for me, I'm a pro at it."

I smiled. "Yeah, you've got that part down. Just... steer clear of the nightmares, okay?"

Her expression turned serious. "Fine. But you should talk to someone about them. They're clearly gnawing at you."

I sighed, the weight of my admission heavy. "I know, I know. It's just... complicated. There's so much history here. Sometimes it feels like I'm suffocating when I'm back."

Kimberly's hand rested on mine, grounding and reassuring. "Focus on now, not on the ghosts. You've got enough on your plate without dragging around the past."

I nodded. "Yeah. The present. I can handle that. Besides, I've got you to keep me steady."

"Damn right," Kimberly teased. "Now, quit stressing or you'll end up looking like a prune."

"Okay, okay," I grinned. "Let's get this over with."

Her laughter, light and infectious, cut through the tension like tinker bells in a warm breeze. I watched her, marveling at how she could find joy even in the shadows of her past. Her chestnut hair shimmered in the sunlight that pushed its way around the landscape, and her hazel eyes sparkled with an indomitable spirit.

"Thanks, Kim," I said, my gratitude sincere. "I don't know what I'd do without you."

She flashed a mischievous smile. "Oh, you'd probably just drive in circles, let's be real."

Her joke eased the tension, and we continued in silence, the anticipation building with each mile.

As Pat's Diner came into view, the knot in my chest tightened once more. Kimberly's hand found mine, her touch a silent promise. "We'll get through this, Jason," she said softly. "Together."

Her words, a soothing balm, eased the frayed edges of my nerves. Kimberly had faced it all—drugs, arrests, the dark side of life—and emerged stronger. She wasn't a damsel; she was my steadfast anchor.

I took a deep breath and nodded. "Together."

Pat's Diner emerged from the smog like a faded memory, its neon sign stuttering weakly against the haze. I'd crossed its threshold so many times, each visit warping reality a little more, like stepping into a different realm. But today, with Kimberly by my side, the diner seemed to pulse with a new, ominous energy.

As we parked, I glanced at her, her face a tapestry of intrigue and apprehension. She was my first *serious* college girlfriend, and introducing her to my mom felt like walking a tightrope strung between skyscrapers. One misstep, and the whole precarious charade might come crashing down.

I shut off the engine, the sudden silence hitting like a wall. The air was thick with the gravity of the moment, a palpable pressure that seemed to press against my chest. We exited the car, the slam of the door reverberating through the oppressive heat, a sharp, metallic echo that seemed to distort reality. I locked the car with a decisive click, but the sound seemed out of place, almost like it was mocking our attempt at normalcy.

"You sure this is the right place?" Kimberly's voice cut through the quiet, dripping with skepticism. She stood next to me, her hands on her hips, her eyes scanning the indistinct surroundings with an almost challenging glare. "Because all I see is a mirage and some generic buildings."

"Welcome to LA, sweetheart," I said, forcing a grin that felt like it might crack under the pressure. I slipped on my sunglasses, trying to shield myself from the blinding sun, though it barely touched the growing sense of dread. "Trust me, we're headed in the right direction," I said, my voice betraying the unease gnawing at my core. "Just a few more blocks, and you'll see it."

.   .   .

Returning to North Hollywood for my impending birthday was like being swallowed by the gaping maw of some monstrous entity. The city, once a playground, now loomed as a snare ready to snap shut, its familiar edges twisted into something far more sinister. The diner, which should have been a sanctuary, felt like a predatory trap —an unwelcome pit stop between grueling midterms and the oppressive discomfort of my hometown. I'd tried to delay this return until Spring Break, but my mother, relentless as ever, had denied me that escape.

The morning sun clawed its way through the haze, a cruel spotlight on a stage set for discomfort. The buildings, once stalwart and enduring, stood as weathered sentinels, their facades scarred by the graffiti of forgotten lives. Each step we took felt like a descent into the city's rotting core, the weight of its despair pressing down on us like a suffocating fog.

The air was thick with collective misery, every breath a contest between the sickly-sweet stench of street food and the acrid bite of exhaust fumes. Each breath was a gamble, a spin of the roulette wheel of sensory overload, reminding us that in this city, you took what you were given and thanked your stars if you got something halfway decent. Shadows slithered in the periphery, sinister and elusive, while the glances from passersby felt like daggers, each one a silent judgment from an unseen court.

The weather mocked us, a jarring contrast to the biting cold of a New York February. Here, the locals wrapped themselves in layers of protection, while Kim and I, dressed for a summer's day, stood out in the 65 degree temperature like glaring anomalies. Every lingering stare was a silent accusation, as if I were an impostor in my own city. I wanted to scream, *"I swear I'm from here... just not all the time,"* but the words choked in my throat, sharp as shards of broken glass. We were spectral figures, lost in a sea of indifferent faces and hostile glances.

My hair, the color of a new penny, flared wildly under the relentless sun. Even through my shades, the brightness was a blinding force, compelling my gray eyes into a squint. We shuffled past the bank my mother frequented, a place etched into my memory like a brand, always teeming with the ceaseless churn of city life.

Kim's hand tightened around mine, her voice cutting through the tension with a playful edge. "Why'd we park so far away?" she asked, a mischievous lilt dancing in her tone. "Afraid someone might spot us? Or is this your way of keeping me a secret?" Her teasing wasn't just light-hearted—it had a sharpness that made my cheeks flush, the heat blending with the sun's glare.

"Parking's no better here than in Manhattan, and it's all parallel," I said, forcing a smile that felt more like a grimace. "You take a spot when you see one." Beneath the surface, a coil of dread tightened in my gut. Kim and my mom were eager for this meeting, but I couldn't shake the gnawing unease. I'd always kept my personal life and family separate—no need for anyone to get attached. But with only my mom left and two years of dating Kim, I figured it was time to let the veil slip. We were juniors at Columbia University, and if not now, it was likely never going to happen.

As an architecture student, I found myself staring at the city's face—a mask of weariness marred by time, every crack and flake in the buildings' exteriors echoing the rotting heart of the metropolis. The faded art-deco and Spanish revival structures loomed ominously, their fractured façades screaming from a bygone age, casting a ghastly pallor over the streets. Despite the calendar's insistence that it was 1997, the city clung to its spectral past with the tenacity of a ghost refusing to move on, pounding on an invisible barrier to be recognized.

The sun blazed mercilessly, turning my hair into a halo of blinding light, its rays searing through the cracked pavement as though attempting to incinerate the urban decay beneath. A parking lot sprawled out like a battlefield abandoned by its warriors, strewn with grim relics—chewed-up gum, discarded cigarette butts—that writhed under the oppressive heat. The asphalt itself seemed to exude a fetid sweat, the city's ongoing struggle manifesting in every scalding inch. Horns blared and people surged through the streets in a frenetic dance, the ceaseless rhythm of the urban nightmare.

At the end of the block, a ragtag crew of street performers gyrated on makeshift mats, their oversized jerseys billowing like tattered flags of surrender against the backdrop of crumbling civilization. They danced with an almost manic energy, their movements a jarring contrast to the world's desolate monotony. A small crowd gathered around them, their faces momentarily lit by the performers' chaotic waltz, as though grasping at any chance to escape the grim reality closing in on them.

"Damn, you got street performers here too? Thought that was just a subway thing," Kim exclaimed, her laughter an unexpected melody weaving through the bustling chaos.

"Yeah, cities are more alike than you think," I replied, trying to lighten the mood. "Wanna go check them out? I probably got some spare change."

"We still have a couple minutes, right? I mean, you said your mom was *always* fashionably late." Kim nudged me playfully.

We navigated through the sea of bodies, Kim's face a tableau of conflicting emotions—excitement tangled with apprehension, her chestnut hair fluttering under her bandana like an errant flame. Despite her New York origins, this was her first brush with the California chaos, each new sight ensnaring her in a spell of fascination.

As we neared the performers, Kim's gaze fell upon a more somber scene—a homeless man huddled against a grimy wall, his belongings scattered around him the detritus of a life long forgotten. Kim's eyes lingered and she shook her head slowly, her voice a barely audible murmur. "It's crazy, isn't it? Even out here, people walk right past, like he's invisible. Like he doesn't even exist."

I glanced over, taking in the man's worn clothes and the exhaustion etched deep into his face. "Yeah, survival's a game, I guess," I said softly, my tone reflective. "People get so wrapped up in their own mess that they forget there's a whole world falling apart around them. It's a cruel joke, really."

Kimberly's frown deepened, her eyes flashing with a mix of frustration and empathy. "It's messed up, plain and simple. It shouldn't be this way. Meanwhile I'm sure the performers are making bank."

"Yeah," I agreed, trying to offer a sliver of understanding. "But it's a harsh reminder of how rough life can get. Sometimes, you've just got to claw your way through."

Kimberly nodded, her expression thoughtful yet fierce. "Sure. But it doesn't make it any easier to swallow."

We powered toward the crowd.

"Glad to see you're enjoying the trip, though. Even if we can't crash at the same hotel," I said, attempting a lighter tone. But the weight of my thoughts seeped through, overshadowing any real delight I might have expressed at having her here.

"You bet. Your mom's old school, I get it. And hey, props to her for sorting us out with that flight for your birthday. It's kind of amazing how she's got our backs," Kimberly remarked, her voice carrying genuine appreciation but with an edge of sardonic acknowledgment.

"Yeah, well, after Dad passed, it's been all on her. Guess she wanted to make sure I showed up and didn't drown in the mess," I replied, the bitterness in my voice a faint echo of the loss. Or was it more the obligation I now felt to succeed, to please, to prove.

Pausing for a moment, I let my gaze wander, tracing the contours of the city skyline. My eyes settled on a billboard looming in the distance, its edges frayed and weather-beaten, yet still commanding attention amidst the urban sprawl. "Have You Seen Me?" it read. Missing persons posters plastered across its surface, faces frozen in time, struck me like ghosts from a forgotten past.

Kimberly noticed my gaze and followed it. "Whoa, that billboard's a real piece of work. Check out all those names. It's like an ad for despair."

"Yeah," I said, a hint of a smile tugging at my lips. "It's a gallery of the missing. Do you think they ever get tired of updating it? Do you think they ever find any of them? Alive?"

Kimberly squinted at the billboard. "Who knows, but seriously, some of those names are wild. 'Michael Carnegie'? Sounds like he should be starring in a low-budget thriller."

I chuckled. "And 'Jasmine Dubois'—like she's fresh off a soap opera set."

Kimberly laughed, the sound cutting through the heaviness of the moment. "It's weirdly fascinating, though. At least they're making sure everyone's face is out there. Gives a new twist to the term 'missing person.'"

"Tell me about it," I agreed, my smile fading slightly as I looked back at the billboard. "Just makes me think of the people left behind after someone's gone, I guess. Someone must've cared enough for people to go through all that effort."

The faces haunted me and I looked back at her.

"Honestly, Kim... It's just... been hard to come back. I've set a life up for myself on the East Coast and when I'm back here..." I trailed off, my voice lost in the vast expanse of the hills stretching out before us. "Everything just feels so... raw. Like nothing's ever changed."

Kimberly cut me off. "But that's how life is! Places stay a mess, but we get better at handling it. Still, at least you made the trip; it's gonna be a chill weekend before you hit the big 2-1."

"Sure, like I can't think of anything better to do than spend my 21st birthday with my mom," I quipped, sarcasm lacing my words like barbed wire.

"At least I'm here," Kimberly whispered, her eyes shimmering with an inner glow that mirrored the warmth in her voice. "Por siempre, estaré aquí para ti."

I managed a grin, the kind that didn't quite reach my eyes. "My Spanish might be rusty, but I know when you're laying it on thick," I replied, attempting to deflect my discomfort.

Her laughter, light and melodic, seemed to wrap around us, and she clasped my hand, drawing me closer. "I mean every word, *mi amor*," she said, her smile bright. "I'm here for you—always."

As our lips met, her kiss was a momentary escape, soft and comforting. In that moment, it felt like everything was in place, like the pieces of a puzzle fitting together. Yet beneath that, there was a lingering tension, a reminder of the expectations I felt—both from society and myself. Mom had to meet her; it was part of the script that had been written for us. The lightheartedness was a welcome distraction, but the sense of being trapped in a role I didn't fit lingered in the background.

As we pulled apart, her playful grin returned. "I just hope your mom doesn't mind that you're wearing my lip gloss," she teased, her eyes sparkling.

Our fleeting moment of lightness shattered like glass as the CD player sputtered, its rhythmic pulse jerking into a disjointed cacophony. The sudden halt was jarring, the silence that followed an invasive, alien presence. I caught Kim's eye, and the discomfort mirrored there was almost palpable. As the crowd's energy dissipated, a frustrated performer thumped the boombox, and an oppressive tension thickened the air, as though something was coiling tighter around my chest.

It was a sensation that gnawed at me, primal and unsettling, a venomous snake curling around my spine. I knew Kim meeting Mom was going to be intense, but this was something else entirely—an electric hum in the atmosphere, foreboding and sinister. The city itself seemed to pause, holding its breath in anxious anticipation of impending chaos.

And then, it erupted.

Glass exploded in a shower of dangerous glitter, each shard a sharp whisper of destruction. The acrid bite of gunpowder mingled with the raw, metallic scent of fear, turning the air into a stifling, ghostly fog that clung to my throat. Screams and shouts wove together into a horrific symphony, each note a sharp jab of terror that dug into my bones and refused to let go.

"Get down!" I roared, my voice swallowed by the escalating maelstrom. Kimberly and I hit the pavement with a bone-jarring thud, the impact sucking the air from my lungs. We huddled together, our breaths merging in frantic bursts as we sought refuge from the deadly storm of debris. Around us, chaos spun out of control—screams of agony, the sickening splatter of blood, and the all-encompassing stench of dread.

The crowd surged in a nightmarish frenzy, struggling against the suffocating grip of terror. Time seemed to stretch, each second an eternity defined by the desperate rhythm of survival.

Navigating through the madness, I clung to Kimberly, her voice slicing through the chaos with fierce clarity. "Jason, what the hell is going on?!" Her words cut through the alarms and screeching tires, a sharp plea for clarity amid the dissonance. Her fear was palpable, raw and unfiltered. I pushed her to cover behind a clump of shrubs, bullets in rapid fire around us.

"I don't know! I think it's a damn robbery!" I yelled back, my mind racing in the storm of chaos. "We need to get out of here, now!"

Time seemed to contract, every heartbeat on the crowded sidewalk a thunderous drumbeat of urgency, each heart fighting for itself with no thought to another, with no compass to direct them, a pandemonium of fear. With adrenaline flooding my veins, I dragged Kimberly back, away from the melee.

"Stay low..." I implored.

We moved towards the block behind us, crouching, cutting through the vacant lot that served as a savior, hugging the building next to it, innocents unaware of the peril we faced.

The bank spewed out a flood of terrified faces, contorted in sheer panic. Sirens wailed in the near distance like feral beasts, adding a layer of ominous urgency to the scene. Every instinct screamed survival as we ran.

In an instant, the pandemonium escalated further. Cop cars,

lights blazing like furious, accusing eyes, converged on the scene. Officers, weapons drawn and faces set in grim determination, emerged—a counterforce to the chaos, their presence a harsh promise of confrontation and control.

A crowd had roiled around us, half running away and half running toward, stupidly curious, pushing us, a living, thrashing beast determined to swallow everything in its grasp. I gripped Kimberly's hand like a lifeline, my muscles coiled tight, straining to keep her close amid the storm of panic and dread.

But the surge was insatiable. Bodies slammed together, a relentless assault threatening to rip us apart. And then it happened—the tenuous thread of our connection snapped, devoured by the ravenous chaos.

"Jason!" Her voice sliced through the chaos, a cry of raw determination barely cutting through the pandemonium. I watched helplessly as they wrenched her away, Kimberly battling the sea of bodies like a cornered lioness.

"Kim!" I shouted, fighting the noise. "Hang on!" My heart raced as I tried to push through, bullets hammering into cop cars, each one a brutal reminder of how close we were to disaster.

"Forget it! Get to the diner!" I yelled. My voice strained with urgency. "Find my mom!"

Kimberly's nod was brief but fierce, a silent vow amid the chaos, before she was swallowed up by the storm of bodies.

Alone, I spun, adrenaline scorching through my veins, matching the wild rhythm of the turmoil around me. Determination surged as I bolted, each step a reckless gamble in the deadly game that twisted around me.

Footfalls pounded like grim portents on the cracked pavement, each echo a dark omen of the lurking danger. Gunshots rang out, spectral whispers of doom, as shadows turned into lurking predators in the city's heart.

In the cacophony, screams tore at my senses, clawing at my

sanity. My heartbeat roared in my ears, a frantic drum urging me on. *Faster. Faster.*

Eyes wide and wild, I wove through the labyrinth of parked cars, each a potential sanctuary in the storm. Salvation seemed a cruel mirage, but I pressed on, driven by a desperate hope to find Kimberly in the vortex of madness threatening to consume us.

In the heart of the chaos, amidst the swirling nightmare of flashing lights and tortured cries, it appeared—my beamer, a beacon of relief in the suffocating fog of fear, a lone promise of escape.

Each step toward the car was a defiant roar against the encroaching abyss, a fight for survival in a world gone mad. The primal urgency surged through me, propelling me as if racing not just against mortal enemies but against oblivion.

I hurled myself toward the vehicle, the chaos around me fading into insignificance. All that mattered was getting inside and fleeing this living nightmare.

CHAPTER 2

ANARCHY IN MOTION

CHAOS CLAWED its way through the morning, a relentless beast shredding the thin curtain of calm that once draped over the city. Each thud of my heart crashed against the confines of my chest like a war drum as I bolted toward my car, the world around me dissolving into a frenzied blur of terror and raw adrenaline. Gunshots ricocheted in the distance, brutal punctuation marks in the symphony of anarchy that stalked every shadowed corner and passing car. Yet amidst the chaos, one sound emerged like a jagged note in a twisted melody—a discordant blast of Nirvana from some car's speakers, its ferocity mirroring the storm brewing inside my own mind.

As I staggered closer to my beamer, the realization hit me like a wave crashing against a rocky shore—the music wasn't a distant echo; it was erupting from my own damn car. *What the fuck? I know I turned that damn thing off!*

The air around the car hung heavy with the sharp sting of gasoline and the sickly-sweet tang of sweat. Inside, two figures lounged with a nonchalant menace, their silhouettes etched starkly against the grime-streaked windows, draped in an aura of dangerous apathy. The sirens' mournful wail and the city's oppressive heat only sharpened the edge of impending doom that seemed to curl around me like a tightening noose.

The girl inside had platinum hair, a tarnished halo that framed eyes deep with unspoken sins and secrets. Her face wore a smirk that barely masked the ocean of regrets beneath, her vulnerability hidden behind a façade of defiant bravado. Beside her, a guy loomed large, enveloped in a faded fraternity jacket that seemed to absorb the darkness around him. His gaze was a cold, steely abyss, reflecting the hollow resignation of someone who had glimpsed the void and found it staring back with unblinking eyes. His haunted stare spoke of suppressed fury and a soul worn thin by disillusionment.

My eyes locked onto theirs as the tension in the air grew suffocating. Their clothes, threadbare and scuffed from countless skirmishes, told stories of conflict and survival. Yet beneath their bravado, a shared vulnerability glimmered, a reflection of the encroaching darkness threatening to consume us all.

Their eyes widened to saucers in the dim light of the car's interior as they saw me approach. Without a beat, I lunged, driven by a cocktail of adrenaline and dread. Kurt Cobain's anguished cries erupted from the speakers, a dissonant symphony that underscored my spiraling panic.

"What the hell are you doing in my ride?!" My voice, barely contained, spat out the words, a mixture of fury and fear threatening to burst through the seams. My throat constricted, every beat of my heart echoing in my ears like a drumroll of impending doom. My mind, a frenzied carousel, spun through a panorama of grisly scenarios.

The girl's smirk was a chilling sight, a sinister grin hinting at a reservoir of dark tales left untold. "Surviving, babe. What's it to you?" Her tone dripped with nonchalance, as though she too had stared down the abyss but dared it to blink first.

"I don't give a shit! Get out!"

The man cast a quick, calculating glance between her and me, his demeanor oddly composed. "We're not gonna hurt you," he interjected, his voice a calm amidst the storm. "But we're not leaving either. Not yet. This car is our only way out."

"Bullshit! It's my fucking ride!" My protest erupted, a mix of disbelief and indignation straining against the chaos.

The girl, unfazed, just arched an eyebrow, signaling her partner to crank up the windows. The glass slid up with a final, decisive thud, trapping us in this strange confrontation. The man, sporting a backwards cap, twisted the screwdriver in the ignition, his movements smooth and deliberate. Behind his mask of cool resolve, there was a flicker of regret, but he was resolute. My car had become his ticket, and he was intent on keeping it.

I pounded on the window, the driver's side door handle laughing at my frantic yanks, a cruel tease against my desperate hope of escape. Panic gripped me, icy fingers squeezing my heart as the gravity of the situation heightened.

I fumbled with my keys, their jangling lost in the muffled grunge music blasting from the speakers. My eyes burned into the girl's smirk, her taunting smile stoking the flames of my silent rage as she waved "goodbye."

The engine roared to life, a beast awakened by the thief's command. My pulse quickened. I flung myself at the back door, the lock begrudgingly surrendering to my frantic twist of the key. With a shuddering groan, the door swung open, offering a brief sanctuary inside the car's steel maw. I lunged forward just a split second before the car jerked forward, tires screaming against the gravel. I slammed the door shut. I was now a captive, ensnared by fate's capricious hand, trapped within the accelerating prison of our escape.

Inside, a thick, cloying fog of dread suffocated us as we barreled through the mess we'd left behind. The distant wail of sirens echoed like a mournful lullaby, a grim reminder of the world we were tearing ourselves from.

"Shit, we got company—" the girl snapped, her voice dripping with irritation and barely-contained frustration as her eyes darted between me and her partner. The gravity of our situation was sinking in, dragging us down with it.

"Somebody better tell me what the fuck is happening..." I growled, my voice a gravelly whisper as I sat upright. Outside, the chaos exploded into a symphony of flashing lights and sirens, cop cars circling the bank like predators drawn to the scent of blood.

The man's knuckles turned white as he gripped the steering wheel, his eyes darting nervously to the rearview mirror. "We had no choice," he muttered, sweat gleaming on his brow like dewdrops on a morning leaf. "If we stop now, it's game over. We keep moving. No turning back."

Panic surged through me, a ferocious storm churning in my chest. My heart pounded like a frantic drum. *Jason, what the hell did you get yourself into? It's just a car! You don't even need a car in New York!* But before I could make sense of the chaos in my head, the man's voice cut through.

"Look, we didn't mean to freak you out," his voice wavered, a thread of desperation weaving through the sincerity. "We just needed a ride. We'll be gone soon, I promise," he pleaded, his urgency almost palpable.

"I don't give a damn what you're mixed up in!" I snapped, my frustration raw and electric. "Didn't you hear the gunshots? See the cops? We have to turn around—"

"Yeah, as if!" The girl's voice cut through the air with a biting edge, her tone dripping with defiance. "You think we can risk going back? What if you rat us out?"

"Rat you out? For what? Did you rob the goddamn bank?!" My anger boiled over, the city lights a blurred smear as we sped away.

"Rob a bank? Hell no! We had nothing to do with that mess!" The man's voice was a ragged edge of truth. "We're just trying to escape. We were gonna ditch your car once we were clear. Do whatever you want with it, just—" His voice trailed off, leaving a pleading silence.

"Fuck that! You don't get it. My mom and girl are at the diner. They need me. They need to know I'm okay!" My voice cracked, a raw cry of desperation cutting through the noise.

"And what's in it for us if we turn back?" The man's question hung like a specter, heavy with doubt.

"I don't know! Money? I'll take you to wherever you want after—I just need to get there!" My words spilled out in a frantic rush, a desperate mix of urgency and honesty.

Our eyes met in the mirror, a silent agreement forming between us. In the depth of his gaze, there was no judgment, only a shared understanding of the danger creeping around us. It was like our souls reached out in the midst of our turmoil, finding a strange solace in each other's desperation.

In a jarring twist of reckless abandon, he yanked the wheel, and we careened into a sharp U-turn. I was thrown across the seat, my head smacking against the window. His companion's breath hitched in her throat, her fingers clawing at his arm as if trying to anchor herself in a shipwreck. "What the fuck are you doing?!" Her voice cut through the tension with a raw, almost guttural panic as she stared at him, her eyes wide and unblinking.

He stared ahead, his face a mask of grim determination, his voice scraping out in gritty undertones. "If we go along with this, you won't turn us in?"

"Christopher, are you out of your fucking mind?!" Her words spilled out, a volatile cocktail of desperation and defiance. "Think for once! We're tangled in this mess, and you're making it worse! We can't trust him—this is a nightmare we don't need!"

"For fuck's sake, Nikki! Now he knows my name!" Christopher's voice cracked with a flash of anger, a spark igniting in the dark chaos surrounding us.

"I swear, I want nothing to do with you guys! After this, I'm outtie. I'll wipe the memory," I promised, my voice a thin thread of desperation laced with the bitterness of betrayal and the tantalizing hint of freedom.

In a wordless exchange, the pair seemed to strike a silent deal, their eyes meeting in an unspoken pact. We were adrift together, a fragile flotilla in this storm, heading toward the diner where Kimberly and my mother awaited, their anxiety surely peaking. We barreled past the bank, two vehicles erupting from its lot like specters, a chilling reminder of the dangers stalking us in the shadows.

"Damn, this is seriously wicked," Nikki muttered, her voice seething with a gritty mixture of disbelief and raw adrenaline. The scene unfolded before us like a macabre art installation gone horrifically awry—cop cars, riddled with bullets, littered the street like twisted sculptures. Bodies lay strewn across the pavement, discarded like broken dolls. As the disheveled officers emerged from the wreckage, their gazes locking with ours, Nikki's eyes blazed with a fierce, almost feral urgency. "Get us out of here! Now! Move it!" Her command sliced through the chaos like a jagged knife.

Christopher's foot slammed the gas, the engine roaring to life with a brutal ferocity. We lurched forward, our escape a chaotic ballet of metal and noise. The bank zoomed past us, its grandeur juxtaposed with our reckless flight. He barreled through the red light, the sirens' wails rising behind us, an eerie chorus of relentless pursuit that felt more like a haunting game of cat and mouse.

"Why the hell are we running? We didn't do anything wrong!" I shouted from the backseat, the tension in the car tightening around us like a noose.

"We stole your fucking car and are speeding through a crime scene! We're not stopping!" Nikki's voice was a whip crack of recklessness, her grip on the panic bar bone-white.

"We can't go back home," Christopher muttered as he wrenched the wheel, the car skidding with a jarring lurch.

"Pull over! This is the police!" A voice blared from the pursuing cars, and suddenly, the screech of Hole's "Violet" sliced through the airwaves.

"You guys are insane! Do you even know where you're going?!" I yelled over Courtney Love's angry serenade.

Nikki's jagged hair whipped around her face as she laughed maniacally, rolling down the window like she was inviting the storm to join us. "Who knows, and who gives a damn!" she screamed, cranking up the volume until it roared with a rebellious fury. She thrust her arm out the window, a single, defiant middle finger extended to the chasing police, daring them to catch us.

The world streaked past us in a surreal blur, pedestrians scattering like startled birds. The inevitable jarring impact from behind— our lunacy had caught up with us. Panic surged through me like a jolt of electricity. *Shit, shit, shit!*

"Take this right!" I barked, my voice strained and frantic, squeezed between the two strangers from the backseat. Christopher's eyes darted in the mirror to mine, a silent cocktail of fear and desperate trust. "I know what I'm doing! Trust me!"

Each nerve in my body was aflame as I became the conductor of our chaotic escape, navigating us through a labyrinth of shadowed backstreets. Every turn was a roll of the dice in this twisted game of survival. The car danced with danger, our senses sharpened to the edge of madness.

"Right here, on the left!" I directed, my voice a taut wire of urgency.

"Left or right!" Christopher's shout cut through the din, his voice strained and desperate.

"Just—here! Now!" I screamed over the blaring music, the car skidding wildly through another intersection. "I know this area like the back of my hand!"

"What's your game here? Helping strangers like this?" he spat, his voice a tight cord of distrust.

I fired back, my nerves crackling like live wires. "Is this really the time for questions?!"

His retort was clipped, irritation laced with steel. "If you want me to keep playing your chauffeur—yeah."

I paused, feeling the weight of my choices pressing down like a leaden hand. "I just— I get it, okay? I know what it's like to be desperate to get the hell out. I don't even live here anymore. It's just..." My voice trailed off, swallowed by the dark fog of the morning. "Everything's a mess. Just— Shit! Shit! Go! Go! You've got to beat the light!"

The car lunged forward, defying every traffic law with reckless abandon. The speedometer needle trembled past the danger zone. As we barreled towards a sudden hill beneath the traffic light, the world seemed to tilt, an unsettling dreamscape where nothing was quite right. With a jolt, we launched over the crest, weightless for a fleeting second before gravity yanked us back to the harsh reality. "Fuck! My ride!" I howled, regret and frustration curdling in my throat.

The rearview mirror reflected the police fading into a blur, their pursuit thwarted by our reckless escape. Nikki's laughter cut through the chaos like a jagged knife. "Who gives a shit! We lost 'em!" Her triumphant shout reverberated with a twisted kind of joy.

Christopher, his eyes sharp and intense, adjusted the mirror, locking eyes with me. His gaze was electric, sending shivers racing down my spine. There was something dangerously alluring about him, a charm cloaking a darkness that seemed to seep from the very scar etched into his face. His fraternity jacket hung from his shoulders like armor, a grim reminder of battles fought and lost.

"You're in college, right? UCLA?" I ventured, attempting to bridge the chasm between us. "I'm in a frat too—Pi Kappa Alpha at Columbia back in New York."

"Aw, Jesus, we kidnapped a frat boy!" Nikki's voice sliced through the tension, sharp and biting. She continued, her words tumbling out in a rush like a dam breaking, "Look, it's his dad's! We're—or, were—seniors in high school," she said, spinning around in her seat. Her bleach-blonde hair whipped around her face, brittle and straw-like, while her blood-red crop top peeked out from beneath a worn leather jacket that had seen better days, much like the rest of us.

"No shit! You guys didn't want to stick around a little longer?

Graduation's in, like, three months! Probably would've helped you get outta here–" I shouted, my voice quivering with a fear I could barely mask.

"We're not from *here*," Christopher said, his tone a low, steady murmur as he fiddled with the radio, silencing a commercial. His gaze remained unwavering, fixed on the road ahead.

"Explains why you're lost! Take a right at the sign and it'll get you back on the 405–" I ordered, but Nikki's voice cut through sharply.

"So why are you here? If I had the chance to be in New York City, I'd never leave," she said, her curiosity like a predator circling its prey, her ice-blue eyes gleaming with a sharp edge.

"I..." I hesitated, the lie catching in my throat. I needed something convincing, a distraction from the rising panic clawing at my chest. *Too late.* "I'm visiting my mom. Dad just passed and... it's still a little fresh–"

"No way! Christopher's dad died too. Mom moved on quick, though. New guy's a real asshole," Nikki spat, her bitterness seeping through as her hoop earrings glinted in the dim light, a stark contrast to the grim mood.

Christopher's eyes flicked to the rearview mirror, their brown depths unreadable, like sunflowers beaten by a storm. Our gazes locked briefly, and I saw something haunted in his eyes, mirroring my own fear. The road ahead stretched out, an asphalt ribbon disappearing into the abyss.

"Damn... Sorry to hear that," I said, my voice carrying genuine sympathy despite the surreal and unsettling nature of our conversation.

"That's why we're running away. I'm Christopher, and this is Nicole," he said, his voice firm, scrutinizing my reaction. "But I guess you already knew that."

"I'm Jason. Government name's Jason Murich. You guys come here often?" I tried to inject some levity into the conversation.

Christopher rolled his eyes. "To your car? First time."

"No way, me too!" I persisted, aiming for a lighter tone. "At least you've got good taste in stolen cars. Done this before?"

"I haven't, but Chris knows his way around rides." Nicole's voice was like a blade, cutting through the uneasy atmosphere.

"Dad ran an auto shop. Taught me everything. Mom sold it after he passed," Christopher's jaw clenched, shadows dancing in his eyes. "Good man. You'd have liked him."

"Too trusting," Nicole added coolly. Christopher shot her a sharp look but remained silent.

"And how'd you two meet?" I asked, shifting the focus away from my own discomfort.

They exchanged a look heavy with unspoken grudges and ghostly echoes. Nicole's voice dripped with a mix of affection and venom, a bitter sweetness that barely masked her scars. "Two years ago. We met in school. Bonded over our wrecked lives."

I leaned in, curiosity piqued like a needle pricking a bruise. "So you're not from around here either?"

She shook her head, a smirk twisting her lips into something vaguely rueful. "Nah, my folks and I are wanderers. Military life. Born in Georgia, if that means anything." Her Southern drawl was a flimsy curtain hiding the raw, jagged edges of her past.

"Then... what's got you running?" I prodded, desperate to keep the conversation afloat despite the tension gnawing at us.

"Me? I just *crave* a change of scenery. New faces, new chaos... When Chris decided to bolt, I thought, fuck it, let's hit the road!" Nicole's laughter was strained, an ill-fitting mask over her deeper fears.

As the car veered onto the freeway, a sudden flash of blue lights sliced through the gloom like a knife. The sirens wailed, a banshee's cry that echoed our mounting dread. The lights bathed the dirt-streaked windows in a sickly glow, turning our worst fears into a visceral reality. It felt as though some monstrous beast was lying in wait, closing in, its jaws ready to clamp down around our throats.

"Fuck, they're back–" Christopher growled, frustration and terror lacing his voice.

"Take this exit, I know where we are," I snapped back, my heart drumming a frantic rhythm as the car jerked across lanes.

My ride, a panicked creature cornered by fear, shot down the off-ramp into the city's winding maze. Street signs whirled into a surreal dance of neon and grime, the urban landscape a dizzying hustle of palm trees and asphalt. Every turn was a desperate gamble, the streets devouring our anxiety and spitting it out with the screech of tires and the staccato beat of our pounding hearts.

The city roared around us, a beast of metal and decay, when suddenly a flicker of refuge appeared through the storm of chaos—a dim beacon in the urban landscape.

"Quick, reverse down that street you just passed! It's a garbage alley; they won't find us here," I urged, my voice a rasping plea as I pointed to a narrow, hidden passage, a secret artery in the city's flesh.

The car groaned in reluctant agreement, its tires screaming as we slithered into the alley, a dark vein in the city's underbelly. They fought against the jagged asphalt, howling in protest before finally falling silent, the sound becoming swallowed by the city's ravenous maw. The air was thick with the stench of rot and lost hope, a pungent reminder of decay.

Smoke from the adjacent restaurant curled into grotesque shapes, twisting and writhing in the sunlight, casting long, distorted shadows on the hideaway's crumbling walls. They danced like tortured spirits, reflecting our own anguish. Time slowed to a creeping crawl, each second a torturous weight pressing down on us, squeezing the air from our lungs in the suffocating embrace of the alley's overhang.

We huddled together, the three of us, in that oppressive silence. The outside world faded to a distant hum, leaving us cocooned in a fragile stillness. The heavy silence wrapped around us like a grim shroud, a fleeting illusion of safety amid the encroaching shadows.

CHAPTER 3
WHISPERS IN THE ALLEY

WE CROUCHED in the domineering shadows cast by the rusted awning, feeling more like prey than people, quivering rabbits in range of the fox. The air was thick, reeking of rot and despair. The morning sun struggled in bright patches to pierce the dense veil of pollution, casting a sickly, oppressive glow in the near atmosphere. The stifling heat was suffocating, making each breath a struggle against the decay that surrounded us. The walls leaned inwards, pressing down with a malevolent weight, as if the city itself sought to trap us.

Every sound was amplified, from the distant wail of sirens to the drip of water from a broken pipe. The stench of urine hung heavy in the air, mingling with the acrid tang of exhaust fumes from passing cars—a noxious cocktail that assaulted our senses. Graffiti-covered walls rose ominously on either side of the alley, their vibrant colors muted by a layer of grime, faded remnants of a lost world. Each spray-painted tag told a story of the city's tumultuous past, a history written in layers of paint and forgotten dreams.

The distant wail of sirens echoed through the labyrinthine streets, a haunting melody that underscored the immediate threat bearing down on us. Police cars nearly discovered us twice, their flashing lights casting ominous reflections on the walls. Christopher,

Nicole and I huddled closer, our faces etched with fear and anxiety. The tension was palpable, each second stretching into an eternity as we anticipated the next close encounter with danger.

As we hid in the alley, my mind churned with thoughts of betrayal and survival. Paranoia gnawed at me—*could I really trust them?* Every action, every word from my companions seemed laced with potential deceit. Every instinct screamed at me to run, but something in their eyes—a shared desperation—kept me rooted in place. For now, I had no choice but to rely on them, even as doubt coiled around my heart like a serpent, squeezing tighter with each passing moment.

Each second of silence stretched like a sinister countdown to our inevitable discovery. My breaths came in ragged, uneven gasps, each inhale a struggle against the dense, suffocating air that seemed to press in from all sides. The alley walls loomed closer, shadows whispering dark promises of impending doom, mirroring the turmoil inside me. Memories of past betrayals and traumas flared up, their scars etched deep into my psyche, carving distrust into my very soul.

We held our breath as one last police cruiser crawled by, its sirens blaring in sync with the pounding of my heart. The sound filled my ears, the rush of my own blood nearly deafening. *Was it the adrenaline? Was I about to pass out?* My mind raced to my mom and Kim, tucked away in that godforsaken diner. *Stay alive, Jason.* I thought to myself. *You got this. You're almost home free.*

And then, mercifully, the cruiser rolled past. I let out a slow, shaky exhale, turning to my motley crew of sort-of-criminal comrades. The weight of our predicament pressed down on me, heavy as a lead cloak.

"So, you guys trust me yet or what?" I murmured, my voice barely audible. The fear in their eyes mirrored my own, a silent acknowledgment of our shared dread. *How much longer could we pull this off?*

Nicole shifted in her seat, her sharp features momentarily illuminated by a sliver of sunlight piercing through the suffocating smog. "Yeah, it's complicated," she murmured, her voice a brittle blend of defiance and raw vulnerability, a storm lurking behind glassy eyes. Her fingers drummed an erratic beat on the armrest, betraying the tempest within. Tension crackled between us, an unspoken conflict simmering just beneath the fragile façade of our tentative alliance. I could almost see her hidden resentments, shadowy phantoms lurking in the periphery. It felt like she wanted to trust me, to let me in, but the ghost of betrayal hovered, keeping her shackled. Our relationship was steeped in a desperate craving for connection and a paralyzing fear of deceit, trust and suspicion playing a game of chess... black queen, white knight... every interaction stippled with apprehension.

"Well, that was fun! If you don't mind, I'm gonna check out that payphone up the street." She nodded in its direction. "See if Stacy has some news for us."

"Not happening, Nik. Our train leaves in two hours—we gotta keep moving." Christopher's voice sliced through the thick, oppressive silence like a jagged shard of glass. His eyes flitted nervously, scanning the alley's shadowy depths, fingers tapping a staccato rhythm on his knee. Despite his veneer of calm, his body language screamed tension. He was a coiled predator, every muscle taut and ready to spring.

"No duh, Chris. Like you can tell me what to do?" Nicole's retort was razor sharp, her determination a steel barrier against the encroaching risks.

Christopher's shoulders slumped in reluctant surrender, a weary sigh escaping his lips as he killed the car engine with a twist of a screwdriver, the motion swift and practiced. His eyes flickered with concern as they tracked her. "Just be quick. We can't afford to get caught."

"It'll take a minute, tops," Nicole replied, a mischievous glint dancing in her eyes. She slipped out of the car, vanishing into the alley's murky maw, swallowed by the shadows of cement dust, smog, and the remnants of lives disposed in a collective pit, where despair reigned supreme and the homeless found hope in a discarded pair of oily trousers.

The car door's click echoed eerily in the confined space, almost drowned by the city's ambient noise. The distant growl of traffic and the muffled murmur of pedestrians wove a soundscape that felt disconcertingly intimate, enclosing us in our clandestine bubble. The caustic scent of gasoline mingled with the bitter tang of morning coffee, a sensory reminder of the world just beyond our precarious haven—a world brimming with danger and uncertainty.

A thrill of excitement surged through me, an electric jolt entwined with the constant undercurrent of fear. The anticipation of what lay ahead was intoxicating, a potent blend of excitement and dread that blurred the boundaries between reality and nightmare. The allure of the unknown was almost irresistible, pulling me deeper into the chaotic whirlpool of our fractured existence. *But there was still the diner*, I reminded myself.

"Who's Stacy?" I ventured, the question hanging in the air like a whisper in the woods just before dark, when shadows start to dance and you're not quite sure if you're alone or if something is lurking just beyond the trees.

"She's Nikki's best friend. Never liked me much, but she's skipping class today to help us cut loose." Christopher's response was as flat and unyielding as the dusty alley we were parked on, a road that seemed to stretch into infinity, or maybe nowhere at all. His eyes never left Nicole, trailing her every move with a kind of dogged determination that could either end in triumph or disaster.

"Solid. Mind if I sit shotgun?" I leaned forward, a subtle grin spreading across my face. The old leather seat creaked under my weight, and the sun's rays slipped through the windshield, casting a net of dappled shadows across Christopher's face, making him look like a man caught in the middle of a ghost story.

"It's your car, isn't it?" Christopher said, a hint of flippancy in his tone. His fingers tapped out a restless rhythm on the steering wheel, like he was playing some hidden, frantic tune only he could hear. Satisfaction surged through me as I climbed over the console, feeling like a kid sneaking a peek into the forbidden parts of his father's study, a place filled with secrets and untold stories.

"Don't forget it," I chuckled, our shoulders brushing in a brief moment of shared warmth. "So, what's a place like you doing in a guy like this?" I joked. But my words hung in the air, heavier than they should have been.

Christopher's face remained a stone mask, eyes fixed on the road ahead, on Nikki. His fraternity jacket hung loose over a fitted white tee, and his baggy blue and white track pants looked like they held stories of their own, stories that might be whispered in dark corners or screamed in the dead of night.

"Why are you being so... cool with us? With... everything?" Christopher asked, genuine curiosity breaking through his stern facade. The morning light highlighted his uncertainty and a flicker of hope, like a candle in a storm, fragile but determined.

I settled into the plush passenger seat, the scent of leather thick and enveloping, almost suffocating. I turned to face him, the weight of his question hanging heavy between us. "Listen, like I told you," I began, my voice softer than intended, "I know what it's like to want to get out. I've never stolen a car, but... I know desperation." I met his gaze, searching for a flicker of understanding, a spark of shared pain. *Maybe he's not used to someone being nice to him. Maybe he's not used to kindness at all.*

"Look," I continued, my words spilling out, each one carrying a piece of my soul, "I... I guess I... never really felt like I fit in here. Sure, I had friends and everything, but... California's never held much appeal for me. If my parents– I mean... my mom... wasn't here, I'm not sure I'd ever come back." I paused, the silence stretching out, my vulnerability hanging in the early morning light like a ghost, a specter of my past haunting the present. "Besides, I need to keep an eye on my ride, don't I?"

Christopher's expression softened, a flicker of something raw and unspoken dancing in his eyes, and for a moment, the oppressive air around us seemed to lighten. "What about you? What are you running from?" I asked, my voice barely piercing the thick fog of our shared silence.

"I... I got tired of my stepdad hitting me," Christopher replied, his tone flat and hollow, the words drenched in a heavy, unbearable history of bruises and broken bones. "After my dad died, home wasn't the same. So I figured... fuck it. I'm getting out. And making my own home somewhere else."

Jesus. His words were a punch to the gut, resonating with a painful, inexplicable familiarity. *That's... heavy.* The silence stretched between us, taut and fragile, as the world outside continued its indifferent dance. In the distance, Nicole spoke on the payphone, her back turned. The sun's rays caught her leather jacket, turning it into a beacon of defiance. The flannel tied around her hips and the high-waisted jeans clinging to her legs added to her rockstar aura, a lone figure standing against the bustling backdrop of a city that chewed up and spat out the weak.

I groped for the right words, something to keep the fragile thread of conversation alive, something that might help him unravel his pain. But the words eluded me, slipping through my fingers like sand. I reached out, hesitated, then withdrew my hand. A silent understanding passed between us, a ghostly whisper of shared torment filling the space.

"Just... thanks for helping," Christopher finally broke the silence, his voice a mix of gratitude and weariness. He glanced around the car's interior, the tension lifting like a dissipating fog. "Can't see anyone else being this chill about it."

"What, most people wouldn't be cool with a couple of teenagers jacking their car and leading them on a police chase? *Wild,*" I joked. The lingering tension wavered, momentarily broken. Then, like a rare bloom in a desolate wasteland, a smile curled at the corners of Christopher's lips. A small, fragile victory in the midst of chaos. *Hell yeah, I finally managed to do it. Made the fucker smile.*

"You're the one who threw yourself into a moving car," Christopher quipped, his tone teasing, a spark of life returning to his eyes.

His gaze shifted from Nicole to me, the shadows of worry giving way to a glint of amusement. "You've got some guts, I'll give you that."

"Yeah, well, living in New York does that to you," I let out a nervous laugh, the sound hanging in the air like a ghost, haunting but brief. "And you never would have made it without me," I quipped. The shared humor eased the weight of the situation, if only for a fleeting moment. "What made you turn the car around? Why help me? Seems like you guys were pretty set on getting outta Dodge."

"Listen, we might've looked like monsters in the moment, but we are who we choose to be. Like you, I know desperation when I see it. Nik might not understand my choices, but we're not bad people."

"Yeah, well. She's definitely something," I laughed. "What's her deal? She seems pretty *go-with-the-flow*. You guys been planning this for a while?"

Christopher's chuckle echoed in the car, a mix of amusement and tension that bounced off the dimly lit walls. "'Go-with-the-flow,' huh? Don't think she's ever been called *that* before..." His words trailed off, lingering like smoke in a closed room, heavy with unspoken meaning.

"Honestly, Jason, this was all her idea. Just took me saying yes. She's used to moving around, and... really, I think she's ready for something new. She calls it a 'change of scenery,' but I know it's more than that."

I prodded, my curiosity a relentless beast in the dim confines of the car. "What about your friends? Everything you're leaving behind?"

"I— I don't think Nikki cares much about that. Everyone's replaceable to her."

"Damn, that's one way to roll... Must be tough to make friends when you're always on the move," I mused, watching the tension in Christopher's knuckles tighten on the wheel. "You must have something special about you, though—serious staying power. Only known you fifteen minutes, but I'd say you're a standup guy." My words dripped with empathy, a silent balm in our conversation. "Seems like she wouldn't take this leap without you."

Another faint smile crept onto Christopher's face, but his gaze remained distant, fixed on a horizon only he could see, perhaps wondering if what I'd just said about him might one day be true. He seemed choked up, as if grappling with an uncertain future. "I hope you're right," he murmured softly, his voice barely audible. "Home's a dead end for me. All I got is Nicole, and that's enough. Our homes are both messes. Her parents are both workaholics, and frankly, we don't even think they'd notice if she was gone. She's never had anyone there for her, so she acts like she doesn't need anyone... like she doesn't care." He continued, his eyes locked onto the payphone. "But she's deeper than that. And I'd do anything for her." His brown eyes met mine, a plea for understanding passing silently between us. "Now it's your turn. What's your deal?"

"Me? Well, there's not much to write home about. Lost my old man two months back—cancer. Mom's holding down the fort solo now, booked me a ticket back for a few days. I'll be 21 this week-end, but honestly, can't imagine my birthday being any more... *exciting*... than today's been." The words hung heavy in the air, sarcasm laden with loss and longing, a snapshot of a life marred by sorrow.

"Damn, happy early birthday..." Christopher's voice carried a weary resignation, regret flickering across his features. "A bank robbery, grand theft auto..." He paused, grappling with the weight of his words, drawing in a breath. "Hopefully, your birthday's *less* eventful."

His gaze, heavy with remorse, met mine, searching for absolution. "You don't hate us, right? For... all this?" The words hung in the air, heavy with guilt and uncertainty that mirrored my own.

"Scout's honor," I replied, my voice betraying a hint of self-consciousness amidst the chaos. *I've never been a scout, but that's what they'd say, right? God, you're a dork.* Despite my internal derision, the futility of my words was palpable.

I sighed, the sound carrying resignation as I turned to face him fully. "Trust me. This is some shit you two pulled me into, but it'll make one hell of a story to tell my mom, Kim, and the boys back home."

Despite my attempts at levity, Christopher's expression remained grim. He struggled to maintain his composure, his gaze fixed on Nicole across the road, silently seeking reassurance. Suddenly, his façade crumbled, and his hands fell to his face in defeat.

"I– I'm sorry, man. This is just a lot," he admitted, his voice frayed like the edges of a worn-out photograph that had been mishandled for decades. He turned to face me, and for the first time, I saw the raw exhaustion that haunted his features, his eyes betraying a vulnerability that twisted my gut. "Things were supposed to get better after I turned 18, but... they didn't..." His words spoke of broken dreams and a future gone awry. "I– we– never meant to pull you into this. The plan's already falling apart..."

My mind scrambled for something to say, but words felt like a foreign language. I couldn't grasp what he was enduring, what pushed him to such an extreme; something gnawed at him from the inside. And damn it, I cared.

I placed a steady hand on Christopher's back, trying to offer some semblance of comfort. He flinched, sucking in a sharp breath, his composure cracking for a split second. With a quick, frustrated motion, he tore off his cap, running his fingers through his tousled light brown hair before jamming the hat back on. His eyes drifted beyond the windshield, lost in the labyrinth of his thoughts.

"Hey, it's cool," I said, my voice softer. "I can't say I get it all, but I'm here. And, honestly, you've got a knack for making life interesting. Besides, you're cute. Makes it hard to stay mad at you." I chuckled, giving his knee a playful pat, trying to cut through the tension. A faint smirk tugged at his lips before he looked back at me.

"I just... I haven't slept," Christopher admitted, his voice gritty with exhaustion. "We caught a late bus down here from Big Bear last night, and it's all been a mess since." He rubbed his hands over his face, weariness etched into every line. "Do you think, uh– Can– Can you tell me what college is like? Doesn't look like I'll get the chance now, after all this." He gestured vaguely to the sky, as if searching for answers among the stars.

A chuckle escaped me, mingling with the distant hum of passing cars. My eyes wandered to Nicole as she replaced the payphone receiver, her movements erratic.

"Shit, I wouldn't go that far... You can always get a GED, look into trade schools," I offered, knowing Christopher wasn't really seeking advice. His eyes drifted, searching for something in the urban sprawl around us.

"Well, uh... college beats high school any day. It was *my* escape. Football, grades, girls... did what I had to. College was freedom. Frat parties, stumbling to class... finally got to be myself. Left my hometown and all its baggage behind."

"But why ditch *Hollywood* of all places?" Christopher's question was sharp, his curiosity almost desperate, as if seeking validation from a stranger.

"I just... I don't know." I hesitated, feeling his gaze cut into me. Under his scrutiny, I felt naked, my soul laid bare. A silent understanding passed between us, unspoken words thickening the air. "Had to figure out who I was, who I wanted to be. NoHo, Burbank, 'Hollywood' —seems big if you're not from here. But the longer you stay, the smaller it gets. Had to get comfortable in my own skin, so I left, went as far as I could." My voice trailed off into a new uncertainty that crept in like a shadow in a film noir, silent, sinister and unexpected, compelling me to turn around in my mind's eye to look at the past, the shadows left behind... the nightmares.

"So, who are you then?" Christopher's question pierced my privacy, suddenly, disquieting, causing my heart to stutter in my chest.

"I'm... still figuring that out, I guess." A faint smile tugged at my lips, but underneath, vulnerability gnawed at me, a reminder of my mom, Kimberly, the diner, and the long road ahead.

Christopher's eyes locked onto mine, a silent exchange of understanding, a brotherhood of sorts, passing between us like a ghost flitting through the dark corners of an abandoned house. *Damn it, Jason, way to make a fool of yourself. Did you pluck that line from a fortune cookie? Why are you saying all this?* A knot twisted in my gut, tightening with each heartbeat as I braced myself for his reaction.

But in that fleeting moment, our gazes collided, then he glanced away, a hint of amusement curling his lips like the playful dance of a malevolent spirit.

"You know, Jason, I think I might *actually* like you," Christopher confessed, his hand languidly draped over the steering wheel, the faint creak of the relic's engine a backdrop to his words.

"Well, damn. I'd hope so," I started, a nervous chuckle escaping me, caught off guard by his unexpected honesty, unsure how to navigate this uncharted territory. "I mean, I let you steal my ride." Outside the car window, Nicole's Doc Martens tapped against the pavement as she made her way back towards us, silently observing our exchange.

"And you didn't hear it from me, but I think Nikki likes you too," he revealed, his tone solemn yet tinged with a subtle warmth. "She's rough around the edges, but trust me, it's her way of saying she respects you. Don't take anything she says too hard."

A surge of camaraderie washed over me as I leaned closer to him. "Don't worry, I won't say shit," I grinned. His finger traced his lips making the 'zippered' motion as he stole a sideways glance at me.

"If it means anything, I think I like you too." I continued. "Maybe we'll look back on this and laugh one day. You'll have to give me a call when you get to... wherever."

"We're heading East, as far as we can go. Maybe check out the monuments in DC, and hit you up once we make it to New York," Christopher replied, his guard finally easing from under the weight of our shared adventure.

A chuckle escaped my lips, anticipation coursing through my veins as I gripped the oh-shit bar, ready for whatever lay ahead. "Sounds like a plan to me, as long as you don't mind crashing in a dorm."

As the tension in the car eased, Christopher turned to me with a curious expression.

"Hey, man, I've been meaning to ask," he began tentatively. "Remind me of your girlfriend's name?"

I blinked, momentarily caught off guard by the question. "Oh, Kimberly?" I replied, a faint smile tugging at the corners of my lips as I thought of her. "Yeah, she's studying with me back in New York."

Christopher nodded, a contemplative look crossing his features. "Kim, huh? She must be something special if you're willing to brave all this chaos for her."

"Yeah," I chuckled softly, the warmth in my voice masking the unease bubbling beneath the surface. Kimberly was incredible—strong, supportive, everything I should want. But the image of her, smiling and unaware, clashed with the facade I maintained. "She's pretty rad. Always has my back, you know?"

A silence settled over us, the hum of passing cars filling the void. I glanced at Christopher, noting the way his expression had shifted. *Was he seeing through me?*

"What about you guys? Got any last names? Feels like we're there already," I said, attempting to steer the conversation away from my own insecurities.

Christopher hesitated, meeting my gaze before revealing, "I'm Christopher Charleson, and that's Nicole Parce," a nod indicating his companion. "Pleasure to meet you, Jason 'Government Name' Murich," he added, a sense of camaraderie threading through his words, solidifying our newfound connection in the quiet of the car.

"Likewise—now I'll know who to blame when the cops come asking about my stolen car," I joked.

My thoughts drifting back to Kimberly.

Society had painted the picture of a perfect couple, and I'd stepped into the frame without hesitation. Yet, sitting next to Christopher, I couldn't shake the feeling that I was living someone else's life. Kimberly deserved the truth, but the weight of expectations pressed heavily on my shoulders, keeping the facade intact.

Outside the windshield, my attention was quickly drawn to an unfolding scene. Through the dirty glass, Nicole leaned casually against the weathered brick wall of a bustling restaurant, morning sunlight casting a golden halo around her slender figure. Beside her, a figure with greasy waves of blond hair leaned in close, his animated gestures capturing my focus.

"Oh snap, check it out—looks like your girl's got company," I remarked, pointing towards Nicole. Christopher's eyes widened, knuckles tightening on the steering wheel, a tense silence descending over us like a heavy veil.

"Shit," he muttered quietly. In a sudden, swift motion, Christopher yanked open the driver's side door, the metallic protest echoing in the car's confines. The door swung wide, flooding the interior with the hot morning air, carrying the scent of asphalt and exhaust. Despite the urgency, I remained frozen, hand gripping the door handle tightly.

In that suspended moment, time seemed to slow to a crawl, each passing second stretching into eternity as I remained rooted in the passenger seat. My gaze fixated on the ignition, the dashboard a jumble of buttons and dials, a silent testament to the chaos that had engulfed us. My fingers absently traced the outline of my keys in my pocket, their weight a tangible reminder of the power they held—the power to escape, to disappear into the urban sprawl of Los Angeles and leave Christopher and Nicole behind.

But as the weight of those dangerous thoughts pressed down upon me like a suffocating blanket, I hesitated, torn between instinct and morality. The allure of freedom beckoned, promising relief from the turmoil and uncertainty that gripped us. Yet beneath the surface, a nagging voice whispered of loyalty and obligation, urging me to stand by my newfound companions in their hour of need.

With a heavy sigh, I tore my gaze away from the ignition, forcing myself to confront the harsh reality of our situation. Christopher and Nicole had taken a chance on me in a world fraught with danger and betrayal, risking everything for someone who might turn them in. To abandon them now would be an act of cowardice—a betrayal of the fragile bond that had formed between us in the crucible of our shared experience.

With a resigned sigh, I shook my head, casting aside the fleeting temptation like a discarded cigarette butt. Whatever lay ahead, I would face it alongside Christopher and Nicole, come hell or high water. Because in the end, we were all just scarred souls searching for a way out of the darkness, clinging to each other in the hope of finding a sliver of light in the vast expanse of the unknown.

And so, with a reluctant resolve, I released my grip on the door handle, the metallic clang of the latch reverberating through the car. As I finally stepped out onto the pavement, my gaze fixed on Christopher's determined form as he strode purposefully towards Nicole, ready to face whatever lay ahead.

CHAPTER 4

THE DESCENT

IN THE MORNING heat's oppressive silence, Christopher's voice broke the stillness like shards of glass underfoot. "Yo, what's your damage, man?" His words hung in the air, charged with an electric tension, as though the world held its breath, waiting for the storm to break. Nicole and the man faced each other, their movements synchronized, bodies coiled like springs, anticipating the inevitable clash.

"There you are!" Nicole's voice dripped with sarcasm, each word a venomous caress. She turned back to the man, her grin a jagged edge, arms crossed in a defiant display. "I told you to back off, didn't I? Maybe you need a hearing aid or something."

"This poser hassling you, Nicole?" I cut in, my voice sharp with a protective edge as I stepped beside Christopher. The alley, a narrow strip of decay and grime, was alive with the stench of old beer and rot. Adrenaline surged through me, each heartbeat a drumroll heralding the clash to come. The man's eyes flitted between us, a predator sizing up its prey. Christopher and I exchanged a look, silent but resolute: we were braced for whatever might emerge from the shadows.

"What's your problem, huh? Got something to say?" Christopher's voice was a rumble of restrained fury as he closed the distance, his words punctuating the air with palpable threat.

In a swift, practiced motion, the man revealed a switchblade, its cold gleam a silent promise of pain. He brandished it with a sneer, the blade catching the dim light, a small, deadly sliver of malice. "Looks like you're my problem," he spat, his voice a snake's hiss, thick with menace. "Why don't you just let me and the lady continue our conversation."

My heart pounded, a relentless drum that threatened to drown out everything else. The man's gaze was a cold, calculating vise, locking onto mine and sending an icy shiver through my veins. Every instinct screamed for action, for escape, for anything but standing still. Yet I forced myself to remain composed, muscles taut, every sense sharpened for the moment that might come.

Nicole's voice, wavering despite her attempt at calm, sliced through the tension with a defiant edge. "Might want to chill out, there, Tough Guy. Don't you know how to pick your battles? 'Cause this one's way outta your league," she shot back, her eyes darting between the looming threat and Christopher.

The shadows around us seemed to breathe, warping and stretching, amplifying the pervasive dread. My heart thudded, a frantic rhythm that drowned out reason, as panic clawed at my sanity. The alley constricted, its walls pressing in, the darkness hungry for our fear.

Christopher, his jaw clenched in a grimace of fear and resolve, fought to steady his breathing. Vulnerability gripped us, a tightening vice that made every breath a struggle. Despite Nicole's plea, the man remained a frosty specter of menace, a smile curling his lips as if mocking our terror. "You think you're special? People like you don't fit in here. You're just asking for trouble," the man hissed. The alley, a claustrophobic labyrinth of brick and shadow, closed in around us, its darkness eager to devour.

But Christopher, unyielding, surged forward, his movements a fluid dance of necessity and defiance. His muscles tensed, fists clenched, his eyes locked onto the looming threat. He moved with the grace of someone accustomed to the harsh ballet of confrontation, a deadly elegance.

The man's confidence faltered only momentarily as Christopher's fist connected with a sickening crack, a brutal symphony of bone meeting bone. The assailant staggered, blood trickling from his split lip, surprise flashing briefly before a savage rage replaced it. He spat blood, his eyes burning with murderous intent.

"Boys!" The man yelled, his voice slicing through the thick tension with a harsh boom that echoed off the brick walls. The sound was an ominous prelude, a herald of what was to come. Then, from around the corner, they emerged—specters summoned from a malignant abyss. Four figures that moved with an eerie swiftness, their presence a chilling shroud over the already dim alleyway.

TIME TWISTED LIKE A PRETZEL, folding in on itself as if in anticipation of the evolving chaos. Reality wavered and rippled, like I was looking through a water glass. Everything in slow motion. The gang advanced with a creeping, deliberate menace, eyeballs bulging like drug-addled youths. But these were men, fully fleshed out, hands balled into fists and ready for a rumble. Their steps echoed like the distant drumbeats of an impending storm. Slowly, the three of us exchanged glances with one another, before turning back to them.

The ringleader, the man Nicole had been speaking with, took us in like a predator stalking its prey. His greasy hair framed a face marred by a jagged scar that twisted his features into a grotesque mask, a thorn that had altered him. Or maybe he did the altering. Dressed in a battered leather jacket that spoke of many past skirmishes, he radiated an unsettling dominance, the heavy chain necklace around his neck swinging with every step, as if mocking the very air with its weight.

Beside him loomed a hulking presence, slowly walking towards us, his muscles undulating beneath a canvas of ink. A serpent coiled up his arm, its eyes locking with his in a silent, predatory dance. His slicked-back hair and scarred hands told tales of a past soaked in violence, a silent testament to his raw, unsettling power.

On the opposite side, a wiry figure skulked with a twitchy unpredictability, his wild hair and nose ring giving him a manic edge. His bare chest, covered in crude, frenetic tattoos, suggested a life lived in the throes of unrestrained chaos. No, these were prison tats. 1488: the signature of a white supremacist Nazi inmate. His jittery, restless energy crackled like static, a walking time bomb poised to detonate.

Behind them, a colossal shadow of brutality loomed, a walking storm barely contained by tattered flannel. The sleeves were cut off, revealing the notorious 5-point crown. The Latin Kings. One of the biggest Hispanic gangs in the US. *But they were based out of Chicago. What was this guy doing here? And with a Nazi? And why did I know this information?*

My mind was truly spinning fear rose a hundred-fold. We were not dealing with wanton street thugs, and by the looks of these guys, we were about to be obliterated. I needed to use my brain, my smarts. *Hey, it worked in the movies.*

The brute's muscles strained against the fabric of his crude shirt, as though they might burst free, itching to see more violence, a vampire thirsting for lifeblood. His heavy boots stomped with a thunderous echo, a grim prelude to the storm brewing within him. Blood-stained bandages wrapped around his limbs, each a mute testament to his insatiable thirst for conflict. My mind wandered to Little Red Riding Hood: the wolf's mouth in a snarl, dripping with saliva, pointy teeth bared. I shook myself.

And trailing in their wake was a figure cloaked in darkness, a spectral silhouette wrapped in black. His hood pulled low, shrouding his features in obscurity, he moved with a ghostly silence that prickled the skin. Sunken eyes gleamed with a feral hunger, and the occasional flash of metal hinted at hidden blades, lying in wait for their chance to strike.

. . .

In that narrow alley, enveloped by shadows that seemed to seep from the very essence of their being, they formed a tableau of nightmarish terror. Their collective presence was a chilling reminder of the abyss of human depravity, a scene plucked from the darkest corners of the mind, one that most people didn't even believe existed outside of the cinema.

"What do you say now, Doll? Still think I don't know how to pick my battles?" The leader shot a devilish smirk.

Nicole, raising an eyebrow, edged closer to the man with a predatory elegance that sliced through the dim alley like a knife. "Oh, sweetie..." she began, a storm of fury in a delicate frame. Instantly, her strike, sharp and precise, found the leader's groin, a jarring crack reverberating through the narrow space as he collapsed, his weapon skittering away to the indifferent pavement.

"I'm nobody's *doll*." She gleamed, standing above his doubled form. "And next time, don't be such a dumbass," she growled, her voice a gritty snarl with a smirk that dared him to try again. But beneath her bravado, fear was a shadow, tangled with the adrenaline racing through her veins.

Christopher, tethered to her by fate, stumbled along, Nicole's hurried steps weaving their desperate escape. "Time to bounce," she snapped, moving swiftly toward the car, her words cutting through the tension like shards of glass.

"You bitch—" The leader's voice, a raw snarl of hatred, sliced through the alley's fog. His eyes, twin fires of rage, scorched through Nicole, sending a shiver of dread slithering down my spine. The early morning quiet was shattered by his roar, a jagged symphony of menace that unsettled the city's fragile calm.

His gang, a pack of hungry wolves, shifted restlessly. The tweaker, an unsettling wraith cloaked in malice, grinned with a sadistic edge. "Man, I dig a girl who's got some fire!" he jeered, his voice dripping with venom. "What should we do, boss? Want us to go after her?"

"What the fuck do you think?" the leader choked, regaining his stature.

Christopher, his knuckles white with tension, shrugged off Nicole, his words a desperate plea against the encroaching storm. "How 'bout you just fuck off, huh?! We didn't do shit to you," he said, but the weight of his plea was swallowed by the unrelenting sea of hostility.

"Chris, just shut up!" Nicole's voice, a sharp, scathing command, was drowned out by the leader's harsh laughter, a grating sound that gnawed at their frayed nerves like rust on metal.

"You think you can order me around, pretty boy? You—" The man shook his finger at Christopher. "You made me *bleed.* This ain't over— not by a long shot," he spat, his words punctuated by a brutal punch that sent Christopher crashing to the ground with a sickening thud. The others began a merciless tirade of kicks and punches until Chris just lay there, motionless. Perhaps lifeless.

Shit. Shit, shit, shit, you idiot!

Nicole's gasp reverberated through the alley, a raw, primal wail that mirrored the chaos and terror churning within me. In that moment, her wide, terror-stricken eyes reflected my own rising panic, a visceral echo of the danger closing in.

"Chris!" I screamed, rushing forward, but Nicole's arm held me back. Her eyes shot at me, mouthing "don't." The weight of the situation pressed down like an oppressive shroud, suffocating my resolve with its relentless gravity. Every nerve flared with a storm of fear and adrenaline, a maelstrom of emotions whirling within the claustrophobic alley.

Blood dripped from Christopher's battered form, each drop a grotesque jewel against the asphalt's dark sheen, his pallid skin almost translucent in the harsh alley light. We were ensnared in a nightmare, outmatched and cornered in a grim dance with fate. *I gotta do something.*

The man with the snake tattoo stood over him, his knuckles cracking with the foreboding rhythm of an executioner's gavel. His eyes glittered with a cold, predatory hunger. "Think you're tough, huh? Some *hero*." His voice was a sinister whisper, the promise of violence curling around each word.

Suddenly, Christopher's instincts flared, pushing him into a frantic, futile struggle. He threw himself to his feet, his fists thrashing at the tattooed man, but finding only the void. The man moved with a serpentine fluidity that bordered on the supernatural. Like a big cat playing with a beetle. A calculated sidestep sent Christopher staggering, his path curving perfectly into the brute's waiting grasp. With the ease of a puppeteer controlling his marionette, the brute's gargantuan hand seized Christopher's neck, lifting him into the air like a rag doll.

Time seemed to stutter, each second stretching into an eternity of thick, oppressive tension. The alley was a cauldron of acrid sweat and raw fear, each breath a battle against the crushing weight of impending doom.

I couldn't look away. I pushed harder against the force of Nikki's outstretched arm, her eyes darting to mine. But I didn't care. We might not know each other, but we knew where our loyalties laid. And I was done watching this.

"Aw, he still thinks he has a chance..." The brute's voice rumbled like distant thunder over Christopher, a harbinger of the storm breaking. His fist surged forward, a juggernaut of fury. But before the blow could land, I hurled myself at him, tackling his side and sending Christopher sprawling to the ground.

Scrambling up, I clutched Christopher with a desperate grip, our combined urgency propelling us toward the car that seemed to taunt us with its nearness. Each step was a struggle, the distance mocking our frantic pace.

"Nicole! The car! Now!" I screamed, dragging Christopher alongside me. She nodded, turning on her heel. Instantly, I threw open the driver door. My heart pounded. *We're so close. The diner. Escape. We're nearly there.* But before I could throw myself inside, the hooded figure emerged from the shadows, swift and predatory, a specter of malevolence, slamming it with a deafening clang, sealing us within the alley's putrid, unfeeling embrace.

"You're not going anywhere..." The man whispered from the void below his hood.

AND THAT WAS IT. We were trapped. The brick walls loomed like jagged teeth, scraping against our shoulders, eager to pull us further into their grim maw. The gang encircled us, their smiles wide and hungry, like wolves scenting their prey. Panic coiled within me, its icy fingers tightening around my throat, each breath a desperate fight against encroaching darkness.

We were the eye of the storm, cornered by the tempest's full fury. With no escape, despair gnawed at my insides, urging me to fight against the encroaching void.

The men closed in, their eyes gleaming with a malevolent light, their grins widening like predatory masks. The alley was thick with the stench of sweat and fear, mingling with the distant hum of the city, a world oblivious to our dire plight. My heart pounded a frantic rhythm, desperation clawing at my mind as I searched for any hint of salvation.

Then, a flash of metal glinted in the murky gloom – a manhole cover loose from its intended purpose, the hole open and inviting. It shimmered like a lost coin in a shadowed sea, promising a glimpse of salvation against the encroaching void.

The air buzzed with a frenetic, almost electric desperation as we circled the obstinate hatch. "Christopher, get in!" I shouted, my voice slicing through the oppressive stillness. Christopher, quick as a flicker, was by my side. Fate was urging us down into the unfathomable depths.

Nicole, however, wasn't ready to plunge blindly into the abyss. "Whoa, whoa, whoa! Slow your roll!" she shouted, her voice a sharp jab in the heavy air. "We have zero clue where this thing goes!" Her impatience and sharp edge made her anxiety clear, her voice dripping with a mix of frustration and fear.

Christopher's response was an urgent, unyielding force. "What, you'd rather stay here?!" he shot back through gritted teeth, keeping his eyes on the predators. Their eyes locked, and with a resolute nod, Nicole descended the ladder first, her movements cautious but firm. The gang's predatory presence loomed closer, basking in our ludicrous attempt at a desperate escape.

Christopher's eyes connected with mine, a silent lifeline passing between us, laden with unspoken promises. "You next – I'll hold them off," he said, his voice steady but edged with urgency. I hesitated, my face a mask of determination, but his gaze held a firm resolve. "Go!" he urged, his voice insistent. I nodded, steeling myself for the plunge into the waiting dark, the acrid scent of the underground seeping into my senses as I left the simmering surface behind.

Climbing down the ladder felt like grasping at a live eel, squirming and slippery in my hands. I landed in a hurried slide onto the damp, grimy concrete, standing beside Nicole as we gazed up at the hole in the ground. The stench of rot and decay scratched at my throat, its acidic taste growing with each inhale. *Sure, anyplace is better than up there, but...*

In a matter of seconds, Christopher came barreling down the ladder, before jumping a few rungs short of the floor. His feet slid on the concrete, falling into mine and Nicole's waiting grip, but his arrival was marked by the mocking laughter of the gang above.

"Yeah? Is that how it's gonna be? Just gonna run? Hide?!" The leader's twisted taunt boomed from above, his features obscured by the sunlight as he peered down at us. "Well, I really hope you enjoy your time. And above all else," he paused. "I hope you like the fucking darkness." He cackled loudly, a cruel symphony echoing off the sewer walls, before replacing the sewer cover with a grating push.

As we huddled in the oppressive blackness, the air grew denser, colder, punctuated by the distant drip-drip of water – a mournful melody winding through the gloom. Each droplet added to the relentless, echoing soundtrack of our entrapment, a grim reminder of our precarious fate.

Beside me, Nicole's frustration crackled like static. "I had this shit under control, Chris," she snapped, her voice rough and laced with a rebellious edge as we stared into the yawning dark, the terror of the unknown curling around us like smoke.

"Don't you dare make it seem like I'm the one messing up here." he ended.

CHAPTER 5

SCREAMS IN THE DARKNESS

FOUR FEEBLE BEAMS of light sliced through the oppressive darkness, descending from the finger holes in the manhole cover above. They cast an otherworldly glow on our anxious faces, the faint illumination playing tricks with the shadows. The narrow corridor pressed in on us like the walls of a forgotten tomb, the darkness a suffocating prison. The moisture-slick walls, adorned with patches of oozing moss and grime, shimmered ominously, the air thick with the metallic tang of old blood. *Human blood? Rats, more likely.*

Each step resounded with a wet squelch, the sound an eerie counterpoint to the relentless dripping of unseen water. Murky streams wound their way beneath our feet in a sluggish flow, adding to the tunnel's chorus. Everything echoed in a haunting rhythm, amplifying the sense of creeping dread.

Nicole, her arms folded defiantly, stood stubbornly, as if to say, *now what?* Even in the stygian blackness, the resolute slap of her platform sneakers against the sodden ground resonated with a fierce determination.

"So, what, we're just gonna stand around? What about the train?" Nicole demanded, her voice cutting through the silence. Beneath her facade of bravado, a tremor of fear threaded through her words. My thoughts, tangled and frantic, kept circling back to Kim—the way she smiled, that goofy yellow bandana she wore... The image was a punch to the gut, a reminder of the life I was supposed to be living, the life I had promised her. *Damn it, Jason. You should've been with her by now.*

"Fuck the train, Nik! What happened up there?" Chris interjected sharply, his frustration flaring in his gaze. His usual calm was now laced with irritation and concern. "Fuck, I think I have a broken rib," he mustered, clutching his side. The tension between us crackled like static, mirroring the storm within me. As Nicole bristled under Chris's scrutiny, I could see the unspoken history between them—years of shared pain and loyalty—that only added to the heaviness of the moment.

My heart pounded in my chest, each beat a reminder of the dual lives I was leading. Kim's face seemed to blur with Nicole's intensity, the contrast between them a cruel reminder of my fractured reality. Here I was, caught between the urgency of the present and the promise of a future I wasn't sure I could achieve or even wanted anymore.

"He saw me at the payphone, asked for my number. No need to freak out over nothing!" Nicole shot back, her tone sharp and dismissive, challenging Christopher.

Christopher's voice, edged with worry, cut through the rising tension. "Yeah? And what if Jason and I hadn't been there? He didn't take your rejection lightly—"

Nicole's frustration erupted like a volcanic blast. "I'm not used to being followed down alleys!" she snapped, her voice reverberating in the confined space. "If your *buddy* hadn't led us there, we wouldn't be in this mess."

"I'm not the one dodging the cops," I interrupted, trying to defuse the situation. "Sorry I didn't lead us to the Miami of hiding spots—"

"You can talk to the fucking hand, whoever you are!" Nicole snapped, waving me off dismissively.

"Leave Jason out of this!" Christopher's voice boomed, his frustration clear. "You turned us into criminals, Nik! If it weren't for you, I wouldn't have stolen that damn car."

As Chris's words cut through the chaos, I couldn't help but think about Kimberly waiting somewhere, wondering if she'd ever made it to the diner, her trust in me unshakable despite the uncertainty. And Mom. Waiting, wondering if my failure to appear was intentional, a snub. *What am I doing? What am I becoming?* The weight of my indecision felt like a physical burden, pulling me down into the mire of my own making.

But Nicole remained unwavering. "Without me, Chris, you'd still be getting beaten every damn night! I saw your potential. Don't screw this up now."

"Damn it, Nikki! You almost screwed us over! Look around, we're in a damn sewer! You wanted out of Big Bear so bad, you didn't care where we ended up. We could've been busted!" Christopher's frantic gestures mirrored the chaos inside him.

Nicole's face contorted with anger and hurt. She took a step forward, her voice breaking through the din of their argument. "You think I wanted this— to be stuck between two worlds?! To have to fight every day just to survive, only to find out that the world you wanted to escape from is still dragging you down?!"

The declaration hit like a sledgehammer, momentarily silencing the argument. Weak tears fell from her haunted eyes, then fell in a deluge, uncontrolled, admissible like an eye-witness testimony in the court of life. They reflected a deep internal struggle, a battle of loyalties and survival.

As I stood in the dim chamber, the tension in the air was palpable. Their voices clashed, echoing through the tunnel—a haunting reminder of the bitter arguments from my childhood. My father's stern voice seemed to linger, his judgment ever-present.

I clenched my fists, guilt twisting in my stomach. His disapproval felt like a ghost, haunting every shadow and harsh word. *"Man up. Caring doesn't get you anywhere,"* he'd say, his disappointment palpable.

But now, I was grown. My heart raced as I grappled with his expectations and my own desires. *Quick, Jason. You gotta find a way out of the nightmare they dragged you into.*

"What happened on the call—with Stacy?" My voice sliced through the thick tension, sharp and unyielding.

"Yeah, Nikki, spill it. How deep are we in this shit?" Christopher's frantic gestures stilled, his eyes wild with anxiety.

"Oh, and now you care about Stacy? Instead of ranting about the goons upstairs—" Nicole's retort was a razor, cutting through the air.

"Nicole, get to the point. How much trouble are you in? I need to know." My voice remained firm, measured, a steady anchor in the storm.

Nicole's gaze dropped, shoulders slumping as if bearing the weight of the world she lived in. She took a deep breath, turning to Christopher. "We're... we're in deeper than I thought," she confessed, her voice barely a whisper.

Christopher's eyes locked onto hers, urgency in every question. "What's wrong? What happened? What do our parents know?" His voice softened with concern, anger melting into worry.

"Chris, I... I haven't been completely honest," Nicole admitted, her words trailing off, lingering in the air like a haunting melody. "Our parents know everything. I didn't think we could make it on our own, so..."

A pregnant pause filled the space, tension coiling tighter with each passing second. Christopher's gaze bore into hers, his voice steady and controlled. "Nikki, what did you do?"

The admission hung between them, taut like a wire stretched to its limit. Tears streamed down Nicole's cheeks, her facade crumbling under the weight of her confession. Each drop a testament to the fractures in their plans, the shattered dreams of a life they so desperately sought.

"I... I took things," she confessed, her voice a fragile whisper in the heavy silence. "Valuables, from my parents' place. Watches, jewelry, pieces of our family history... all stuffed into my bag. I thought... I thought we could sell them, start fresh in D.C., away from this mess."

I felt the urge to comfort her, but I restrained myself, knowing it wasn't my place. I glanced at Christopher, finding him frozen in disbelief. His face was a mask of shock, every muscle tense as if gripped by unseen forces. The woman he cherished was unraveling before him, her words cutting deep, each syllable an agonizing echo in the cavernous tunnel. Like me, he was caught in a heist he hadn't bargained for, a pawn in someone else's escape plan.

Nicole's sobs pierced the silence, a symphony of despair echoing through the room. "I just– I wanted this so badly, Christopher. We were so close–" she choked out between sobs. "There's no turning back now. It's D.C. or handcuffs. That's all we have left. The charges are pressed."

In the dim, dank chamber, an oppressive hush settled, as if the very air conspired to suffocate us. The duo before me crumbled like old limestone worn by relentless rain, their despair palpable. Nikki's sobs punctuated the silence, their rhythm blending with the steady drip of water from corroded pipes reverberating off the slick walls, amplifying their torment until it filled every corner of our underground sanctuary.

Christopher moved forward with a determined stride, his hand resting gently on Nikki's trembling shoulder. "You should've trusted me, Nik," he murmured, his voice a soft caress against the heavy silence. "We could've made it, damn it. I had a plan, a place for us in New York City." His eyes flickered with a glimmer of hope, briefly piercing the darkness that surrounded us.

"I'm not too sure how Columbia would feel about harboring fugitives in my dorm room... but hey, desperate times," I quipped, my attempt at levity falling flat in the oppressive atmosphere.

"Listen, Chris," Nikki interjected, her voice thick with tears, the weight of their predicament bearing down on her. "We have to get out of California— now. No more waiting around," she urged, her words echoing in the stagnant air, a stark reminder of time slipping through our fingers.

Before she could finish, a sound more sinister than the darkest recesses of our nightmares tore through the stillness.

A primal scream erupted, its anguished cry slicing through the moist atmosphere of the sewer. The sound reverberated off the slimy walls, sending shivers down our spines. It seemed to emanate from all directions at once, a spectral lament that pierced the very fabric of my soul. The scream pressed down with a suffocating grip, as if the darkness itself had coalesced into a malevolent force, ensnaring us with icy tendrils that constricted our chests and stole our breath. A real-life fun house of fright.

The cacophony twisted and distorted with each echo, forming a haunting chorus of terror. Born from the depths of despair, its primal anguish felt otherworldly.

We stood, transfixed, as if the very air had turned to ice, trapping us in a tableau of fear. The metallic scent of rusted iron intensified, mingling with the haunting echoes, signaling imminent danger.

"What the fuck..." I stammered, my voice barely more than a whisper, struggling to articulate the shock that gripped me.

"Nah, nah– Alright, screw this place. We're outta here," Christopher declared abruptly, his voice edged with frantic urgency as he bolted for the ladder. The sewer walls seemed to close in, their cold, damp surfaces pressing against us, eager to trap us forever in this subterranean nightmare.

Each tentative step toward the ladder felt like a gamble with fate. The rungs were slick and treacherous beneath Christopher's trembling hands. With every upward movement, the air grew thicker, oppressive, laden with the whispers of the damned.

Christopher pounded his fist against the stubborn sewer cover, a futile gesture against the unyielding metal, its unmoving form a cruel testament to our entrapment.

"They must have put something on top of it to keep us from pushing it open," he screamed back at us.

Another scream shattered the oppressive silence, a primal wail echoing through the confines of our underground prison. The sound was born of despair, a symphony of anguish that reverberated through the narrow tunnel, amplifying our own terror. It was as though the darkness itself had found a voice, a howl of agony that clawed at our senses, driving us further into the depths of madness. My heart thundered in my chest, our breaths ragged and shallow, the weight of our predicament suffocating.

"Jason, I need your help!" Christopher's voice cut through the thick air like a blade, urgency palpable in every syllable, digging into my core. Rushing to his side, I strained to see through the dimness, his silhouette stark against the faint light filtering through the manhole cover. His lean figure strained against the unyielding metal, each breath a labor against futility.

I grasped at the icy rungs, the chill sinking into my skin. Each attempt to move the cover felt like battling the world's weight, our fists pounding in the oppressive darkness. Sweat and grime streaked down my face, unnoticed as I focused on our Herculean task. Yet, despite our efforts, the cover remained unmoved, mocking our struggle, despair creeping in.

But we couldn't quit now—not with so much on the line.

Above, laughter dripped venom, a cruel reminder of our captivity. "Want out already?" The taunting voice echoed off the dank walls. "Send up the girl, we'll let you out."

"Go fuck yourself, asshole!" Nicole's defiance roared from below, cutting through the darkness. Christopher and I exchanged glances.

My father's memory clawed at my mind, the grief of his death mixing with the danger we faced. Every moment with Christopher intensified the conflict within me. His eyes mirrored my own turmoil —loss, helplessness, and the shadows of fear.

"Too bad! Looks like you're stuck for the night," the taunt slithered down to us, deepening our despair. The shifting shadows above swallowed the light, casting us further into uncertainty.

The realization hit me with a sickening thud—*the sadistic bastard was standing on it!* Then chaos erupted: glass shattered, metal groaned, and my car's alarm blared a cacophony of fury. The tunnel seemed to close in, the walls eager witnesses to our doom.

As we faced the destruction, my father's expectations and my desire to protect my newfound companions felt like competing weights on my shoulders. I could feel his disapproval mingling with the urgency of our predicament, making every decision feel like a tightrope walk between honoring his legacy and embracing the reality of our situation.

Think, Jason, think... Urban engineering and civil planning. I got a C in that course... but LA was a big unit. If there's really 17,000 miles of underground pipes here... There must be a way out.

A third scream pierced the air, snuffed out in darkness, leaving eerie silence. Chris and I shared a glance, eyes betraying primal fear, understanding whispered. Nodding, we flung ourselves back down the ladder.

Metal bit into our palms, sewer chill seeped into our bones with each plunge. Our frantic descent mirrored our racing hearts. Each echo peeled back sanity, revealing festering fears.

The sewer lived, malevolence feeding on terror, growing stronger. Shadows menaced, sounds doomed us, the abyss deepened, minds teetered on madness.

"Look, we need to find a different way," my voice cut through the oppressive air, sharp and commanding. Urgency laced my words as I locked eyes with Chris. "If we stay here, whatever's lurking will catch up," I pressed, desperation tinged with a flicker of hope.

"There's gotta be another exit," Chris pushed on, dread and determination mixing in his tone. The darkness seemed to press closer, thick with unseen threats.

I nodded grimly, my eyes reflecting our shared fear and resolve. We had no choice but to push forward, defying the encroaching darkness.

Nicole's fear broke the silence. "Where do we go? Who knows

where that scream came from!" Her panicked gaze darted around the dim tunnel, fear palpable in every jittery movement.

"We need to keep moving," I asserted, the echo of that chilling scream still haunting my thoughts. Decay and dampness hung heavy in the air, each breath a struggle.

"But what about your car? My bag—" Nicole's plea trembled in the echoing darkness, her voice a stark contrast to the oppressive surroundings.

"Didn't you hear them? My car's wrecked. We follow these tunnels out—LA River, ocean, anywhere but here," I snapped, determination cutting through the gloom.

"Jason's right, Nikki. It's our best shot," Chris's voice wavered slightly, almost lost in the growing sounds of approaching footsteps. The ominous rhythm echoed through the tunnel, danger drawing closer with each passing second.

"We gotta move—now!" Christopher's urgency rang out, a beacon amidst the suffocating darkness.

Darting into the blackness, the oppressive void swallowed us whole as the echoes of the footsteps grew louder and more menacing. Each step seemed to lead us deeper into an abyss where time and space twisted into a nightmarish labyrinth.

The chill in the air bit deeper, the walls closing in like the embrace of the damned. Every step echoed with the pulse of malevolence, a reminder of the horrors lurking in the shadows, waiting to consume us whole.

CHAPTER 6

THE WEIGHT OF GUILT

IN THE CLAMMY recesses of the dank tunnels, our frantic footsteps echoed, swallowed by the yawning abyss of darkness that devoured any semblance of direction. Each splash of our sneakers mingled with the distant drip of water and the sinister rustle of unseen creatures, weaving a discordant symphony of dread.

The memories of my father's demise clawed at me like a ravenous beast. His voice, a grim echo, constantly haunted me with unfulfilled duties. He had been a stoic figure, a man of few words but profound wisdom. Each failure felt like an act of betrayal against his silent legacy. The night he passed away replayed in my mind like a cursed reel—the phone call, my mom's tear-soaked voice, the rhythmic beep of the heart monitor slowing until it flatlined.

I remembered our Sunday park rituals, rain or shine. He'd sit on the bench, eyes crinkling with pride as I played. *"You're gonna be somebody, Jason,"* he'd rumble, his voice a low growl. *"But don't let others drag you down."* Those words, now a shackle around my soul, seemed to tighten with every misstep, every missed chance. The weight of his expectations was an anchor dragging me into a bottomless abyss of despair. Guilt, thick and suffocating, cloaked me like a leaden shroud.

Each twist in the labyrinthine passages felt like a step further from redemption. I remembered failing my architecture midterms, my professor's disappointment a mirror to my father's imagined scorn. My relationship with Kimberly was another knot in this web of failures—forced, strained, void of the passion I pretended was there.

The pressure to fit societal molds was a relentless vice. I'd always been the golden boy, the one who could do no wrong. But beneath the polished facade, I was crumbling. The suffocating expectations, the push to succeed, to be the perfect son—it was a trap. Kimberly, the epitome of societal approval, was a costume I wore to perfection. Our relationship was a staged performance, draining me with every passing day. Each misstep, each missed chance, was another stone added to the crushing weight of my regret.

The air thickened with each step, the stench of decay a tangible presence. Walls slick with grime seemed to sweat in the dim light, a testament to years of neglect. The muck clung to my shoes like a malicious force, threatening to pull me into the abyss.

Red eyes gleamed in the shadows, the rats' ominous gaze a chilling reminder of the peril encircling us. Each breath tasted of decay, a nauseating brew that tainted the very air we struggled to inhale.

Moisture seeped into our clothes, a clammy embrace that chilled us to the bone. Every amplified sound bore down on us like a heavy weight, threatening to crush our spirits. The darkness seemed alive, a malignant entity reaching out to ensnare us in its grasp, dragging us deeper into its insidious depths.

The tunnel stretched before us like the intestines of some ancient beast.

We trudged forward, stumbling through the labyrinth of shadows, our hearts pounding in terrified unison, drowning out the echo of our frantic footsteps.

"Okay... so this is officially the worst day ever," I said, attempting to lighten the mood despite the fear gnawing at my insides. "Anyone else feel like we're stuck in some messed-up horror flick? Because I'm starting to think this is one big, twisted set-up."

Nicole shot me a look that could cut glass, her sharp features catching the dim light. "Jason, stop clowning around. We need to get out of here, like, yesterday."

"Right, right, focusing. But seriously, if a monster jumps out, I'm totally blaming the rats."

Christopher's voice cut through the oppressive silence like a rusty blade. "Jason, get it together. We're almost there."

"Yeah, sure, almost there. Almost where, exactly? Into the giant rat king's lair?"

Nicole's retort was sharp, her determination a steel wall against the looming risks. "Jason! This isn't a joke!"

"Okay, okay! Just trying to keep things light. But come on, we need a plan. These tunnels stretch out for miles."

"We keep moving. No breaks. We can't let that thing, whatever it is, catch us," Christopher's voice was strained, eyes darting nervously. His fingers tapped impatiently.

"Got it. Keep moving. No stops. And if anyone spots a map, let me know. Because right now, this place feels like a never-ending nightmare."

Nicole's tone softened, but there was still an edge to it, a hint of fear beneath her tough exterior. "Just... stay close, okay? We can't afford to lose anyone."

"Don't worry, I'm not planning on getting lost in here. Besides, where would I get lost to? It's like one direction, either way. This isn't Scream. Let's just hope we can bounce before someone, or something finds us."

But as the words left my mouth, our steps abruptly halted. In the dim light, a massive tangle of debris loomed ahead, a precarious barrier of unstable rocks and twisted metal partially blocking the tunnel.

"What the hell are we supposed to do now?" Nicole's voice shattered the eerie silence, reverberating off the jagged tunnel walls like the screech of a tortured soul.

Christopher's grip was iron, pulling her away from the rubble that seemed to pulse with a life of its own. His voice, strained and clipped, cut through the darkness. "We keep moving, Nikki. No other choice. Reverse course. Back the way we came."

Tears glinted in her eyes, her once-steady facade crumbling to reveal raw, unfiltered fear. I stood apart, a shadow in the backdrop, wrestling with the jagged edges of guilt and envy. Guilt for trespassing on their fragile moment of despair, and envy for their unspoken connection that spotlighted the emptiness gnawing at my own core. I wished I could be as open, to unmask my fears with such abandon, but the specter of rejection and my father's unyielding expectations shackled me.

"I'm done with this shit, Chris," Nicole's voice wavered, trembling as she slumped beside a fallen beam, her body a shivering echo in the stifling gloom.

Christopher's gaze was a lighthouse in the abyss. "I know, Nikki. Me too. But we've got each other. We'll find a way out." His touch was a thread of warmth in the cold, a fleeting comfort in the oppressive darkness.

"We shouldn't have come down here," Nicole murmured, her words dissolving into the shadows. "Leaving Big Bear was a mistake."

Christopher's eyes, steadfast and fierce, met hers. "I know it's terrifying, but we can't stop now. There weren't any other paths for us back home, and there sure aren't any others here."

"Yeah, guess I missed the memo about an earthquake," I quipped, attempting to pierce the thick tension with a sliver of humor. "Maybe there's a hidden exit? Like in Indiana Jones?"

Nicole's gaze was sharp, cutting through the dark. "Jason, this isn't some fucking movie!"

"I get it, I get it," I said, a forced grin tugging at the corners of my mouth. "Just trying to crack a joke. What if we try that gap over there?"

Christopher's resolve hardened, a glimmer of hope in his eyes. "Jason's right. It's our only shot. We're here now. If all else fails, we continue to head back the other way."

"Alright, team," I said, trying to infuse the moment with a sense of strange camaraderie. "Let's find our exit and escape this nightmare. And remember, no secret handshakes with rats, got it?"

A hesitant smile flickered on Nicole's lips, a brief respite from the encroaching dread. "God, you're such a dork."

"Hey, *you* kidnapped *me*. I'm *your* dork. At least until we're out of this mess. Now, let's move before this place gets any weirder." I reached out to pull Nicole to her feet, the grip of the darkness tightening around us as we stepped forward.

We edged closer to the wreckage, the tunnel's suffocating grip tightening around us like a vice. The jagged shards of debris formed a maze of perilous angles, a sharp-toothed beast waiting to tear us apart.

"Ready? Let's slither through," Christopher's voice cut through the oppressive gloom, steady yet taut with the same unease that coiled in the air. He moved first, his body a reluctant serpent wriggling through the narrow, menacing gap, brushing against the unstable shards that groaned in protest with each shift.

Nicole followed, her movements less fluid, her body contorting as she tried to navigate the treacherous space. "I'm right behind you!" Her voice was taut, straining to keep up with the pace.

I squeezed in behind her, the narrow confines pressing against me with a claustrophobic grip.

But in an instant, the debris shifted. Nicole's progress slowed, her panic growing. "I— I can't move! It's too tight!" Her voice was a strangled wail, her shoulders wedged tightly between two massive pieces of rubble. She looked back at me as she struggled, a sharp edge of debris grazed her cheek, slicing through the skin with a painful, vivid streak. Blood trickled down her face, a stark contrast to the grime and darkness.

"Nicole, breathe!" I shouted, trying to keep my voice steady despite my mounting anxiety. My hands bled scraping against the sharp debris looking for purchase as I clawed desperately at the rubble.

Christopher's voice came from the other side, now tinged with an edge of panic. "Jason, we need to get her out now!" His tone was urgent, a plea that cut through the growing tension.

"I'm trying!" I shouted back, my own voice trembling with the weight of fear. The space was so tight I could barely breathe, let alone move. The oppressive darkness seemed to close in around us. Then, the echo of footsteps grew louder, a relentless reminder of the unknown danger that lurked just beyond our reach. *It's coming.*

The sound reverberated through the tunnel. The heavy, hurried steps were closing in, their echo a chilling reminder that time was running out. My breathing grew ragged, my chest tight as if the walls themselves were pressing in on me.

"Hold on, Nikki! We're getting you out!" My hands pressed desperately against her leather coat and the debris, trying to create more space. The jagged edges of the rubble sliced into my palms, each movement sending fresh waves of pain through my hands. Nicole's face dripped with blood from wounds she didn't know she'd acquired, a raw, painful sight. Her eyes were wide with terror, her struggle a raw, desperate attempt to free herself from the vise-like grip of the rubble.

"I can't... I can't!" Nicole's voice was a desperate cry, the fear in her tone a stark contrast to the steely resolve I was trying to muster. Her face was contorted with pain, the blood mixing with tears and grime.

Christopher's voice cut through the chaos, a lifeline in the encroaching panic. "Jason, just a little more! We can't let it catch us!"

The footsteps were a thunderous roar that threatened to drown out everything else. The oppressive darkness seemed to press closer, wrapping us in a shroud of impending doom. My hands trembled, scraped and bleeding, as I pushed against Nicole's back.

"Pull her!" I yelled, each movement a desperate attempt to free Nicole from her prison.

With a final, gut-wrenching shove, I managed to help her inch forward. The debris groaned and shifted, protesting our efforts with a deep, resonant creak. As Nicole emerged from the tight space, she let out a pained gasp, collapsing to the muck-ridden ground. I squeezed through the gap behind her, reappearing on the other side into the tunnel's grim embrace. A sudden puff of smoke exploded from the falling debris, a cloud of dust and ash erupting into the narrow space. It billowed around us, swirling and adding a surreal haze that briefly obscured our view.

"Thanks, Jason," she panted, her voice a shaky whisper of gratitude, her eyes reflecting both relief and the pain of her injury.

"Don't mention it. We need to get out of here before our... *friend...* catches up," I said, my breath coming in short, uneven bursts, my voice strained. My hands were raw and bleeding, the sensation a reminder of the desperate effort it took to free her.

Christopher looked back at the narrow gap we had just squeezed through and let out a relieved sigh. "There's no way it can make it through that. We've got a chance."

But as if to mock his words, a leather-gloved hand shot through the debris, fingers grasping hungrily at the air. It was a ghastly, surreal sight, emerging from the smoke and shadows like a specter of doom.

"Run!" Christopher shouted, his voice breaking into a panicked edge as the hand clawed at the debris, trying to widen the gap.

We broke into a sprint, our breathless and disheveled forms pushing forward with a new surge of adrenaline. The oppressive atmosphere and the imminent threat that pursued us clung to us like a shroud, urging us onward.

Our only hope was to stick together, to push forward despite the looming threat, and to find safety in the shadows of the sewer. The journey ahead was fraught with danger, but in the midst of our shared terror, the bond between us grew stronger, a flicker of hope, human at its core.

Hope is the human spirit, I remembered one of my professors saying. *For without it, we should all perish.*

With each faltering step, the darkness coiled tighter around us, a beast hungry for our fear. The tunnel breathed its putrid stink, exhaling a chill that clung to our skin and turned our own breath into ghostly wisps. The walls, slick with dampness, scraped against us like reluctant lovers. A dismal drip of water provided a sinister sound-track, echoing in the labyrinthine dark, where we wandered like lost souls.

Rot festered in every corner. The stench of putrefaction, rat feces, and stagnant water was a visceral slap, seeping into our clothes and hair, an olfactory terror. Footsteps echoed behind us, a grim drumbeat heralding our doom, as if the very walls conspired to choke us with their malice.

Shadows twisted and wriggled like living nightmares, flickering in and out of existence. The metallic tang of fear was palpable, a sickening taste that clung to the back of my throat. My heart pounded like a caged beast, every thud a desperate plea for escape. I reached out for Chris and Nicole, but the shadows had swallowed them whole. Panic clawed at my chest, rendering me breathless.

"Chris? Nicole?" My voice was a fragile whisper, swallowed by the ever-encroaching void. The tunnel yawned before me, a ravenous maw of darkness. I took a hesitant step forward, my breath hitching as the suffocating stench of death thickened. Every instinct screamed retreat, but I forced myself onward, clinging to the memory of my father's voice, urging me to face the abyss with courage. *But fuck, it was so impossibly hard.*

A sudden rustle broke the oppressive silence, a faint movement in the dark.

In the subterranean void, where shadows held dominion and silence reigned, terror gripped me like a predator's jaws. Then, a sudden, icy jolt yanked me backward, a spectral hand seizing my shirt and dragging me into the cold, uncharted abyss. My heart thundered, frantic, desperate for release.

Before a scream could escape, a rough hand clamped over my mouth, silencing me. The touch was familiar, urgent in its intensity. I felt Christopher's presence materialize from the gloom.

"Shh! Chill out," Christopher's voice cut through the darkness, commanding and firm, a beacon in the encroaching chaos.

With swift precision, he guided me into a narrow offshoot pipe, its claustrophobic confines pressing in on us, the cold metal a harsh reminder of our vulnerability.

"Damn, Chris," I gasped, struggling to steady my breath. "You really know how to make an entrance, huh."

Christopher's eyes flickered with a tense smile as he scanned the dark beyond. "We're safe here for now. Stay quiet, stay sharp."

"Yeah, quiet as a mouse," I murmured, the humor of my words sinking into the oppressive silence, falling flat.

The tension in the cramped pipe was a living thing, thick and oppressive, pressing down with every shallow breath. The only thing that came to mind was a scene from It, and I prayed we wouldn't be devoured alive. Huddled in our fragile sanctuary, I wondered how long this slender thread of safety could hold against whatever was following us.

The air was thick with dread, a stifling shroud woven from our collective fears. Shadows danced on the damp walls, where flickers of light played tricks on our eyes. The stench of decay mingled with the sharp metallic tang of blood.

We stood on the edge, hands clamped over quivering mouths, trying to silence the terror that threatened to drown us. My own blood lingered on my lips—my hands burned with pain, probably already on their way to gross infection. Each breath was a struggle, a battle against the oppressive weight of our predicament. Water seeped rhythmically from the curved pipe above us, its relentless drip a metronome for our mounting anxiety.

In the dim, I met Nicole's eyes—two dark pools reflecting our shared terror and defiance. A silent pact formed between us, a vow against the encroaching darkness. Beside her, Christopher stood as our lone beacon, his presence a flicker of hope amid the shadows. Despite the despair, there was a spark of resolve—we would find a way.

Footsteps reverberated through the tunnel, a sinister rhythm that pulsed through the silence. Each step was a tremor, a signal of the menace closing in. The vibrations of approaching dread were almost palpable.

"We've faced worse," I said, my near-silent voice an anchor amidst the rising panic. "Stay alert. We'll get through this."

Nicole's breath caught, her eyes narrowing as she processed the gravity of our situation. "Do you really think so?"

Christopher's jaw tightened, his gaze piercing through the darkness. "We have no choice," he said, his voice a low growl. "We fight together."

There must've been something wrong with me. Or maybe I was just blessed with seeing humor when I face danger because again, It came to mind. Here we were, staunch kids ready to battle the colossal unknown, the giants of fear, the monstrous being that grew larger in our minds with every passing moment. I nodded, the resolve in my chest solidifying, forcing the fear to recede. "Together," I promised, a mantra against the looming danger.

Then, emerging from the enveloping darkness, two figures appeared—a living nightmare. The man was a shadowy blur, an embodiment of malevolence that suffocated the air around us. Old fears resurfaced, memories of past confrontations with trembling hands and a heart brimming with courage.

As I stole a glance at Christopher and Nicole, I saw them holding hands. Christopher's grip was firm around Nicole's, a tangible link of solidarity. Then Nicole's other hand entwined with mine, a silent gesture of shared resolve. We stood in this grim reality not just as individuals, but as a united front against all comers. Her chin was raised in defiance, though her hands betrayed her with a slight tremor. We had faced adversity before, but this—this was a realm of terror unlike any other.

CHAPTER 7

THE ABYSSAL CALL

TIME DRIPPED LIKE THICK, viscous tar, each second bleeding into the next, trapping us in an endless spiral of dread. The darkness laid its cold breath on us, whispering secrets of despair. The walls, narrow and suffocating, pulsed with a sinister energy, their rough surfaces closing in with each heartbeat, making it feel as if we were being swallowed whole.

The figures ahead stood like twisted shadows, their forms indistinct yet menacing. Their stillness was deceptive, a prelude to the inevitable. Though their steps had ceased, the memory of their relentless pursuit echoed within the tunnel, a haunting rhythm that merged with our own racing pulses. Every beat of our hearts seemed to amplify the spectral footsteps, casting a chilling pall over our fragile sanctuary.

We stood frozen, ensnared by a potent blend of terror and a faint, flickering hope. The darkness embraced us, a shroud of concealment. Silently, we pleaded with the unseen forces of the tunnel, hoping they would keep us hidden, protect us from the malevolent presence that lurked just beyond the veil of shadows.

But fate, that merciless puppeteer, had other designs. As Nicole's grip tightened on my hand, I felt the weight of my father's disappointed gaze, a spectral reminder of the admiration and respect I owed my newfound companions, despite the risks we faced. I vowed silently to protect them, to prove my worth not just to myself, but to the memory of him.

Nicole's breaths came in ragged gasps, each inhalation a desperate battle against the oppressive weight of the tunnel's atmosphere. Her wide eyes darted around our cramped refuge, pupils dilated with terror, scouring the shadows for any sign of impending danger.

In the dimness, their gazes pierced through the gloom like shards of obsidian, each glance a cutting edge slicing through the eerie stillness and homing in on us with chilling precision.

"Come out, little ones," the woman's voice purred through the silence, smooth and serpentine, as if it slithered through shadows with a practiced grace. Her tone was rich with a velvety menace, each word dripping with a promise of dangerous allure. It was a voice that could tempt and ensnare, drawing you into a web spun from forbidden desires and dark fantasies. Yet beneath the seductive veneer lay a cold, calculating malice, hinting at ancient horrors and concealed threats that promised nothing but dread. The stillness was pierced by her voice like a blade through silk, shattering the quiet with its ominous, enchanting edge.

"Olly olly oxen-free," the male voice called out, dripping with a casual, mocking charm. "We know you're hiding somewhere in that pipe. It's kinda adorable, really. Think you can keep playing hide and seek with us?" His tone was smooth, taunting, carrying a sinister edge that suggested he was toying with us, savoring our fear. There was an easy, almost lazy menace in his voice, as if he were confident of his dominance and relished the terror he was about to unleash.

My heart hammered against my ribcage like a frenzied bird desperate to break free, each beat a frantic plea for escape. Every nerve in my body screamed, senses sharpened to a razor's edge, picking up every distant drip of water, every scuffle of rat feet, every subtle shift in the dark, every whispered menacing threat.

My palm, pressed against the rough, damp pipe, felt the jagged rusted texture scraping against my skin. It was as though the very pipes themselves screamed for mercy, bearing silent witness to the unyielding cruelty of our predicament, not unlike their own, trapped in the bowels of the city.

Nightmarish visions pirouetted behind my closed eyelids, grotesque and taunting. Nicole's grip on my hand tightened, her knuckles white. I could feel her pulse, a mirror of my own, racing and frantic, and the chill of her sweat-soaked palm against mine.

"Well, we could always drag you out," the woman's voice cooed, its soft, serpentine cadence dripping with a twisted delight. "But where's the thrill in that? No, no, let's savor this dance a little longer." Her tone lingered in the stagnant air, seductive and chilling, as if drawing out our suffering was a pleasure she relished.

In that harrowing moment, Christopher and I shared an unspoken pact, forged from raw courage and the promise of sacrifice. His sense of loyalty burned within him like a fire, a relentless, consuming flame. His resolve was unwavering, a testament to his unyielding pursuit of what was right, no matter the danger. With a silent nod, he positioned himself between Nicole and the looming threat.

"Fine," Christopher's voice sliced through the oppressive silence like a surgeon's blade through flesh. "We'll come out." Each word was laced with steely resolve, his jaw clenched, defiance etched into his features like a stone carving.

Before I could step forward, my eyes shifted to Nicole. She stood frozen, wide-eyed with terror, silently begging me not to leave her alone in the dark. I dropped her hand, but without a word, she lunged forward, her fingers trembling as they clutched the fabric of my shirt, her grip desperate and pleading.

Our eyes met, and in that silent exchange, volumes were spoken. She implored me to stay, her lips forming a mute plea for protection.

I hesitated, torn between shielding Nicole and confronting our tormentors. Her fear was suffocating, a visceral weight that pressed down on my chest, but the necessity to face our adversaries overrode my heart's paralysis. Every instinct urged me to honor her plea, yet I knew shielding her from the looming threat was paramount.

"Nicole," I murmured, my voice a faint whisper in the oppressive darkness. "Trust me. We'll be back. Stay hidden, okay? They may not know there's 3 of us."

The grim reality of our situation loomed large.With a heavy heart, I gently loosened her grip from my shirt, offering a fleeting, reassuring smile that faltered at its edges, betraying my own apprehension.

Pressing a finger to my lips, I urged her to remain silent, to stay concealed until the danger passed. It was a promise, a vow to return unscathed, though uncertainty lingered heavily in the air.

Reluctantly, I pulled away, the warmth of her touch like a haunting memory. With one last fleeting glance, she crumpled to the ground, shielding herself in the shadows. As I followed Christopher, my resolve hardened, each step a defiant march toward the unknown.

The tunnels yawned before us, their mouths wide and hungry like the gaping maw of some subterranean beast. The slick, clammy walls glistened with a sinister sheen, illuminated by the faint, sickly light that barely pierced the suffocating darkness. Fuzzy green mold clung to the decaying structural concrete of the pipes, its twisted tendrils grasping like parasitic fingers. The mold seemed to pulse, breathing, casting grotesque shadows that writhed and twisted along the walls like tormented specters.

The air was a stifling miasma of decay and stagnant water, an oppressive exhalation from the tunnels themselves. Each breath was a struggle, the atmosphere thick and cloying, pressing in from all sides. The smell was an abominable cocktail, a vile blend of rot and despair that assaulted our senses. It mingled with the acrid stench of fear-sweat, forming a rank fog that clung to our clothes and seeped back into our pores. It wasn't merely a smell; it was a palpable, malevolent force that clawed at my sanity and gnawed at the edges of my resolve.

Fear clutched me with icy talons. Ahead of us, a grotesque assembly of humanity waited, their faces twisted into masks of malice. Each figure seemed to meld seamlessly into the shadows, their features obscured by the gloom that enveloped them. Yet, even in the dim light, the malevolence emanating from their presence was tangible, a force so oppressive it seemed to seep into the very walls of the tunnel. *This was their turf.* They closed in, a suffocating presence, their forms looming over us like vultures forming a nightmarish tableau.

The figures encroaching upon us bore the scars of their malevolence like badges of honor, their twisted forms a hideous mockery. The sound of their footsteps reverberated off the damp walls with a hollow thud, each footfall a macabre dance of death that echoed through the tunnels, a haunting melody of impending doom that set our nerves on edge.

And then she appeared.

The woman emerged from the shadows like a specter conjured from my darkest nightmares. Her skin, a rich mahogany marred by scars, each laceration a testament to the pain and torment she had both endured and inflicted. Her presence was suffocating, an aura of malevolence warping the very air around her, making it difficult to breathe. She moved with a predatory grace, eyes glinting with sadistic delight, and as she drew closer, the malevolence intensified, like a storybook seer, the embodiment of some primeval being.

Her lank hair cascaded in midnight curls, framing her face in a halo of darkness, stark against the pallor of her scarred bony flesh. Eyes like pools of obsidian, black and fathomless, peered like a blind cave animal with an intensity that gave me chills, They bore into me, exposing the raw fear thrumming beneath.

I tried to scream, but my voice caught in my throat, choked by the suffocating grip of terror. Panic surged within me, a primal instinct, yet my body remained paralyzed. Every movement she made, every twitch, every breath, every bit of spittle that flew from her sharpened teeth, echoed in the madness that surrounded us.

And then she smiled.

"Well, well, what have we here?" Her voice slithered through the shadows, a velvet purr laced with a dangerous edge. Her crimson lips twisted into a smile that was more cruel than comforting, a smirk that promised a symphony of suffering. She took in the scene with a gaze that was both piercing and predatory. "Oh, it seems we've stumbled upon a little love affair," she cooed, her tone dripping with mockery. "How adorable."

My face flushed, a mix of anger and embarrassment surfacing. "We're not—" I began, but the words caught in my throat, unable to fully defend the truth or dispel the uncomfortable truth that her words hinted at.

The woman's laughter cut through my protest, sharp and mocking. She took a step closer, her gaze never wavering from me. "Such fire in your eyes. I do enjoy a bit of drama. But let's not get too distracted. Where is the girl?" Her voice shifted to a cold, predatory whisper, a palpable threat lingering in the air. "Tell me now, or this little game of yours will become quite... unpleasant."

"She ran. Outpaced us," Christopher's voice rang out, a beacon of defiance amidst the encroaching gloom. "It's just Jason and me."

The woman's laughter pierced the stillness like a dagger, a chilling reminder of our precarious position in this twisted game of cat and mouse. She licked her lips hungrily, her gaze fixing upon me with a predatory gleam. Her sleeveless, form-fitting bodice of weathered black leather hugged her torso, adorned with tarnished silver studs. The leather bore the marks of countless battles, scars and scratches weaving a tapestry of suffering across its surface.

She stepped out of the shadows like a wraith, her lower half swathed in a cascade of frayed filthy denim that clung to her slender legs like a second skin, the faded black hue making her look like she had been fashioned from the darkness itself.

Around her neck hung a pendant fashioned from bone, its

grotesque form a grim representation of the souls she had claimed in her relentless pursuit of pleasure. Rings of tarnished silver adorned her fingers, each one a trophy won in some unholy war fought in the shadows. These weren't just accessories—they were markers, signposts along the road of her damnation, each one a testament to a life snuffed out, a dream extinguished.

But it was the details that truly set her attire apart. Leather straps crisscrossed her chest and arms, their buckles and clasps gleaming in the dim light like instruments of torture. Chains dangled from her waist, their links clinking softly with each step she took, a haunting melody that carried the weight of her sins, each link a soul trapped in her web.

"Mmm... Jason," the woman purred, her voice a dark, honeyed caress that sent a shiver racing down my spine. The tall man's silent gaze held me captive, a lurking threat cloaked in his unnervingly calm smile. The woman's eyes, gleaming with a sinister sparkle, turned toward Christopher. "And who might you be?"

"I'm not telling you shit," Christopher spat back, each word a bullet of defiance. His stance was firm, but I noticed the tremor in his hands, the fear clawing its way through his bravado.

"Aw, but isn't that the fun of it?" the woman cooed, her eyes alight with a twisted delight. "There's nowhere for you to hide, darling. These tunnels stretch on forever. Even if you think you can escape... we'll find you. And you'll be oh-so sorry you didn't play nice." Her voice, with its smooth, honeyed Missouri accent, was a sinister promise, a velvet glove hiding a razor-sharp threat. "You see, you two... you're mine now. Soon enough, you'll learn exactly what that means."

Her laughter ricocheted off the damp walls, a chilling symphony that underscored her power. Each word was a dagger, twisting deeper into our fear, manipulating us like marionettes in her macabre performance. The air grew thick with dread.

"Who are you?" The question spilled from my lips, a desperate plea for understanding amidst the chaos, but beneath it simmered a rage threatening to erupt. "What do you want from us?!"

Her smile stretched wider, revealing teeth as sharp and numerous as a predator's. "What do we want? Oh, my little pet... you'll find out soon enough," she crooned, her eyes twin voids devouring the light. "As for why... it's simply in our nature to seek out fresh company."

Her gaze sharpened, curiosity mingling with cruel amusement. "But tell me, why didn't you follow my cries? Most people, they rush to save a 'lost soul,' thinking they're heroes. But not you. How... intriguing."

Christopher's jaw clenched, a glance at me before he spoke. "We had enough for one day. We're not like most people."

"Indeed," she mused, her fingers trailing over the bone pendant at her throat. "Not like most people at all. You might just be more entertaining than the others."

"That's enough, Misha," the man cut in, his voice smooth as silk but edged with a dangerous undertone. His calm exterior masked a chilling menace, a subtle warning hidden in his words. His auburn hair, slick and immaculate, framed a face that was both unnervingly beautiful and marred by scars. The light played tricks with his features, casting an otherworldly allure that was both captivating and horrifying.

His icy blue eyes glowed with a malevolent intensity, burning with a fire that seemed to see right through you. They were the windows to a soul teetering on the brink of darkness, where unspeakable horrors whispered just beyond the edge of sight.

Dressed in a mix of rugged denim and sleek leather, his attire was a paradox—part elegance, part survival. The tailored leather jacket fit him perfectly, its pristine condition starkly contrasting with the raw scars that peeked from his collar, each one telling a twisted tale of madness, a map of his dark and labyrinthine mind.

Standing beside Misha, he was a shadow among shadows in a world long devoid of sanity. Their connection was evident, forged in shared pain and pleasure, but his presence hinted at something far darker—a palpable stench of malevolence that seemed to taint the air around him.

An instinctive dread coiled in my bones, a primal warning. He wasn't just her companion; he was a living nightmare, an embodiment of humanity's deepest fears.

His smile, sharp and cruel, twisted like a blade. "Welcome to our world, beauties," he drawled, his voice dripping with malicious delight. "Let's see how you handle it."

His voice slithered through the air, a serpent's hiss weaving a web of deceit and dread around us. He was a maestro of manipulation, orchestrating chaos, and we were mere pawns in his malevolent game.

Terror coiled around my chest, squeezing the air from my lungs. Each breath was a battle, a frantic struggle against the choking grasp of fear. Yet, amid the chaos, one thought flared with a harsh intensity: *Nicole's safety was all that mattered. If even one of us could claw our way out of this nightmare, the sacrifice would be worth it.*

In the stillness between Christopher and me, a distorted symphony of emotions played out—desperation, grim resolve, and a haunting resignation to our inevitable end. We were tethered by fear, an unspoken pact to face the encroaching darkness together. As I braced myself for the excruciating choice that lay ahead, the weight of our shared doom draped over me like a suffocating shroud. *I wasn't ready for this.*

CHAPTER 8
THE DEVIL'S PLAYGROUND

THE DEMONIC DUO forced Christopher and me deeper into the darkness, the tunnels gaping like the maw of some ancient, slumbering beast. The abyss seemed to swallow all feeble light that dared to filter in from above, mocking our hesitant steps and snuffing all hopes of escape. *What did they intend to do with us? If they wanted to kill us, wouldn't they have done it by now?* Nicole's image flickered in my mind, a ghostly silhouette sketched against the darkness that coiled around us like a living thing. Each step felt like a clumsy waltz along the precipice of madness, her presence a faint, flickering beacon in the all-consuming void. As we descended, hope was a frail ember, threatened by the encroaching shadows. Doubt clawed at my resolve, a relentless parasite gnawing at the edges of my sanity.

"Christopher," I murmured, my voice barely above a whisper amidst the oppressive silence. "Do you think Nicole got out?"

The air was thick with a weight that pressed down on us, distorting the already stale breath we fought to draw. Nicole's escape seemed less a possibility and more a cruel jest whispered by the darkness. Each echoing footfall was a mournful dirge, resonating with the despair festering in my heart. I pressed my scraped hand against the slick, clammy wall, struggling to steady myself.

"Nicole? How sweet. Is that your little friend?" Misha cooed, her voice dripping with venomous amusement. I bit my lip as Christopher shot me a fierce glare. *Damn it, Jason. No names!*

"No," Christopher replied, his voice cutting through the darkness like a blade.

"Oh, come now, sweetheart," Misha purred, her tone a silky caress veiling a sharp edge. "Why be so shy? We're all friends here, aren't we?"

"Silence suits me just fine," the man drawled, his voice smooth and laced with mocking charm. "But don't worry, we'll find her soon enough. Or maybe she'll find us first. Little Nikki, are you out there? Come out, come out wherever you are!" he taunted, his voice echoing with a chilling, almost playful menace through the labyrinthine tunnel.

"Don't listen to them!" I screamed, my voice shredding as I shouted. "Keep running! Find a way out!"

"What you don't understand, darling," Misha laughed, her voice a twisted melody of sadistic delight, "is that there's no escape from this place. We know every inch of it. And you've just waltzed into our little playground."

The man's voice oozed with theatrical menace. "You see, this place is not just a maze; it's a trap. And *everyone* who comes here finds themselves... thoroughly entertained."

Misha's voice turned smoother, more intimate, as though she were confiding a dark secret. "It's rather thrilling, like a game—except the stakes are a bit higher. In our little playground, there are rules. And you're already breaking them by helping someone escape. Naughty, naughty."

The man's laughter was a sultry, sinister sound, dripping with satisfaction. "But the best part? The game only ends when we say it does. And oh, we do love to drag it out. It's so much more entertaining when you're squirming."

"We'll see about that," Christopher spat, his voice sharp with anger.

"See, that's the spirit!" The man's voice dripped with mock admiration. "I do love it when people try so hard. It's like watching a kitten batting at a mouse. You're so close, yet so far. Just remember, the more you struggle, the more you reveal yourself. And the more fun I have."

"So why don't you just relax and enjoy the show?" Misha purred, her voice a velvet-lined poison. "It's going to be a long, dark morning, and you're the stars of our little production. Make it interesting! After all, the more entertaining you are, the more likely we are to keep you around for the grand finale."

The man's voice grew softer, more seductive, as if drawing me into a false sense of security. "But don't worry, sweetheart. We'll have plenty of time to get to know each other. I'm quite looking forward to it."

As we ventured deeper into the tunnel, it felt like the walls were closing in, squeezing the life out of the air. The scent of musty earth and rot was overwhelming, mingled with a sharp, metallic tang that gnawed at my senses. Flickers of light from storm drains and manhole covers cast grotesque, writhing shadows on the slick, moss-clad walls. They seemed almost alive, twisting and contorting as if eager to swallow us whole.

Christopher's breathing was ragged, his eyes darting everywhere with a mix of terror and determination. I could see his brain working in overdrive. The tunnel stretched endlessly before us, a merciless maze with no clear path to salvation. "Keep your eyes peeled for anything, any sign of an exit. And remember every turn," Christopher whispered, his voice barely audible but sharp in the oppressive silence.

"Already on it," I replied, my voice trembling like a fragile leaf in the wind. "But every damn wall looks exactly the same."

"Well, what did you expect?" The man's voice oozed from the darkness, silky and sinister. "A luxury suite? Trust me, you'll get used to the stench. Till the rain comes. Then it's just a delightful mix of blood and *rot*." His laughter slithered through the tunnel, a chilling melody of malevolent amusement.

"You know, it's almost poetic," Misha's voice drifted through the gloom, smooth and mocking. "Here you are, stumbling through our maze, while your precious *Nicole* is out there, playing a twisted game of hide and seek with devils like us."

"I wouldn't be too confident," Christopher snapped, his frustration palpable. "We're not the type to just roll over and die."

"Ah, there it is again!" The man's voice slithered into the room, a sultry whisper tinged with perverse satisfaction. "Your defiance—it's what makes this all so deliciously thrilling. And don't fret about your little friend. She's probably got the best seat in the house for all this drama. Wouldn't want to miss the show, would she?"

Christopher and I exchanged a heavy, knowing look, the silence cocooning us in its suffocating embrace.

"Tell me." Misha's voice was a dark, velvety caress, laced with malicious desire. "Does the darkness feel more intimate now? Think of it as a love letter from us to you, penned in shadows and despair."

My stomach churned, my face reflecting Christopher's silent horror. *These people are fucking crazy.*

"Aw, don't look so glum." The man's voice dripped with faux sympathy, like honey laced with venom. "Even if you don't find your way out, I assure you, you'll have plenty of fun. We always do."

Doubt clawed at us, a relentless companion whispering that our quest might be futile. Nicole, a girl I barely knew, didn't strike me as the type to seek help from the cops. I hoped she somehow escaped, somehow found a lifeline, but the grim reality of our predicament pressed down on me.

The tunnel devoured sound with a ravenous hunger, our footsteps swallowed into ghostly echoes that twisted and slithered through the cavern. The walls, slick and clammy, seemed to inhale our presence, their damp surface reflecting the dim light of passing manholes. Silence hung like a thick, suffocating fog, amplifying each drip from unseen pipes above, each drop a morose countdown to an unseen fate. The intervals between drips stretched into an oppressive infinity, the quiet pressing against our eardrums, heightening the tension with every heartbeat.

Flickering light filtered through storm drains and manhole covers, casting fleeting, grotesque shadows that danced along the moss-covered walls. I knew any cry for help would be swallowed by the city's all-encompassing everyday noise.

Every inch of the tunnel exuded an aura of ancient malevolence, as if the very walls were pregnant with dark secrets, eager to trap unwary souls. It stood in stark contrast to the world above, where sunlight and open skies felt like distant myths, lost to the endless darkness. As we ventured deeper into the abyss, the cavern seemed to tighten its grip, pulling us toward whatever unspeakable horrors lay in wait.

Christopher's voice shattered the silence, laced with defiance. "Who are you?" His demand for answers cut through the oppressive stillness, daring the shadowy figure before him to respond.

The man leaned back, his posture relaxed but no less intimidating. A smirk played on his lips like a man with a secret, a full house; someone who knew he would win regardless of what the other guy had. "We're the ones who got bored with the ordinary. We were once like you—innocent, naive. But those days are long gone, sweetheart. We've evolved."

Misha's voice slithered into the conversation, smooth and hypnotic. "We'll introduce you to pleasures and pains that dance on the edge of your wildest dreams. If you're willing, you might just find yourself a cherished place among us.

My disbelief broke through in a stammer. "So... vampires?"

The man's grin widened, amusement dripping from his words. "Vampires? Oh, darling, you think you've figured it all out, don't you?" His tone was mocking, almost flirtatious.

"You avoid sunlight, hide in sewers, prey on people from above... Sounds like a solid guess, right?" I pressed, grappling with the surreal, buying time, hoping against all odds for some miracle.

The man's amusement faded into a more serious, almost pitying expression. "We don't hide, kid. And this isn't some fairy tale. We're as real as you are—just a bit more... advanced." He gestured casually with a hand as he stepped through the murky water, his boots sending ripples that splashed up around us.

"If you're not vampires, then why live down here? In the sewers?" I asked, my curiosity piqued.

"Up there, life's a relentless agony," The man replied, his smirk both seductive and sinister. "But down here, with us, it's a... different kind of paradise. All it takes is a little submission, and you'll understand."

"You're monsters," I spat, the word barely audible in the stifling atmosphere. My voice trembled, fear and defiance fighting for dominance in a game I knew I could not win.

"Monsters?" The man chuckled, a rich, velvety sound that sent shivers down my spine. "To some, perhaps. But to those we've taken from the surface, I'm their savior. They see me as a beacon of hope, as long as they endure the transition."

Misha's voice was a sultry whisper, dripping with allure. "Oh, sweet Jason, up there you're a ghost—discarded, abandoned by a society that doesn't care. But here, we offer a family, a purpose— everything your world cruelly denies them. You're not just given a place; you're given a new identity."

Christopher stepped forward, his eyes a battleground of anger and fear. "And what if we refuse to join your twisted family? Are you going to kill us?"

The man tilted his head, his smile taking on a patronizing, almost affectionate quality. "Refuse? Oh, sweetie, you don't understand. You don't have a choice. Out there, you're just pawns, easily replaced. Down here, you can be reborn, part of something far greater."

I exchanged a resolute glance with Christopher. "We won't be part of this... whatever *this* is. We have lives, people who care about us."

A dark chuckle rumbled from the man. "Care? They care until you step out of line. Believe me, the moment you're no longer useful, they'll toss you aside like yesterday's news. Here, the outcasts, the misfits—they find solace, away from the harsh, judgmental eyes of your so-called society."

"And when you find us no longer 'useful'? What then? You're no better than anyone else, up there or down here. At least up there, in the real world, we can make our own choices. You talk about submission like you're the devil's pawn. But even the devil gives us a choice."

Misha glided closer, her gaze intense, almost intimate. "Think about it, Jason. Out there, you're living a lie, hiding from who you truly are. Down here, you can embrace the freedom you've been too afraid to seek. I once thrived on adoration, but when I was transformed, I discovered what true freedom really was."

A chill ran down my spine as her words hit too close to home. "Freedom? This is a nightmare!"

The man's eyes narrowed, his voice dropping to a seductive whisper. "A nightmare that offers salvation. Above ground, you're lost, stumbling in darkness. Here, you can be found, embraced by the true light."

Christopher's voice shook with suppressed rage. "We won't join you. We won't be part of this madness."

The man's gaze turned steely, his voice a low, dangerous growl. "Then suffer. In time, you'll come to understand what you've rejected."

Misha's hand reached out, almost touching my face before I recoiled. "The choice is yours, Jason. Join us willingly, or be dragged into enlightenment kicking and screaming. I was once like you, until *Darren* showed me the way." She gazed at her companion with a mixture of longing and reverence. "*He* taught me that true freedom lies in surrender."

My heart pounded as her obsidian gaze locked onto mine, the weight of our predicament crashing down. "Never."

Darren's lips curled into a sinister, almost playful smile. "We shall see, boy. We shall see. The darkness always reveals what the light hides."

This is what hell must be like. These... creatures... had all the earmarks of it. The opposite of heaven. Salvation, submission, the dark revealing truth like the light of God is supposed to do. What the...?

Panic slithered through my veins, each heartbeat a jagged, discordant note in the symphony of terror that threatened to drown my thoughts. The darkness pressed in, a suffocating blanket of dread that seemed to pulse with a life of its own. My mind clawed at the black void around me, desperate for an escape that felt as distant as the stars in this cavern of nightmares. *We had to get out.* This hellish realm of shadows and malice was closing in, and every second seemed to stretch into eternity.

We had been moving steadily, deeper into the bowels of hell. My sense of direction was lost but I knew that any manhole would lead me to the city, somewhere, anywhere. I hoped Nicole had found the courage to find a way out.

Darren loomed over us, his presence suffocating and oppressive. The scent of decay mingled with the fetid dampness, thickening the air until it was almost tangible. His footsteps were a rhythmic drumbeat, each step resonating with a finality that seemed to tighten around me like a noose.

My eyes darted around, searching for a glimmer of salvation. They landed on the glint of a Bowie knife strapped to Darren's belt, its blade reflecting the dim, sickly light with a promise of pain. My heart pounded in sync with my frantic footsteps as I edged closer, my shoulder brushing against the clammy, slick wall, the cold seeping through my clothes.

But Darren seemed to notice my distraction. He paused mid-step, turning his head slightly, his eyes narrowing with an amused curiosity. "Ah, I see something's caught your attention," he said, his voice smooth and velvety, laced with a hint of amusement. "You've got that look, like you're plotting your grand escape."

"Please, just let us go." I forced the words out, my voice trembling despite my best efforts. "All of it, this place—it's Hell."

A slow, dark smile spread across his lips, his eyes gleaming with a cold light. "Hell? Now, that's a bit melodramatic, don't you think? I prefer to call it... an opportunity." He drew closer, his gaze flicking to the knife. "That old thing? Not just for decoration. But it's clear you have a taste for the dramatic."

His tone was casual, almost conversational, but the underlying menace was unmistakable. He moved closer, his presence becoming more oppressive with each step. "You think you can just grab it and bolt?" he drawled, his voice silky and dripping with mockery. "How charming. But here's a little secret, sweetheart—nobody walks out of this place alive. Not unless I say so."

Before I could react, his hand closed around my wrist with a vice-like grip. "No! What are you—" I cried out, struggling futilely. His strength was overwhelming, a crushing force against my frantic attempts to escape his grasp.

He leaned in, his breath a hot whisper against my ear. "Did you honestly think it would be that easy? Look at me, Jason."

Inches apart, his icy blue eyes bored into mine, before locking onto my scraped hand. The blood had begun to coagulate into a brown gooey reminder of the barrier we'd crawled through. Again, I thought of Nicole. Then Kimberly. I whimpered ever so slightly, my breath catching in my throat. Christopher laid a hand on my shoulder, Misha yanking him back.

A predatory grin twisted Darren's lips as he drew the knife from his belt with a smooth, deliberate motion. The blade gleamed wickedly in the faint light. "This blade isn't just a tool. It's a symbol. And right now, it's a promise— a promise to make sure you understand exactly what it means to be trapped here."

I clenched my fist, tightly, trying to shield the stinging wound, but his hold was relentless. He pried my fingers open one by one with a nonchalant brutality, each movement deliberate and controlled. "Let go!" I shouted, my voice cracking, but it was no use. His strength and the casual cruelty in his eyes made it clear he reveled in my desperation.

"Don't bother," he said softly, his voice a dark, seductive murmur. "The more you struggle, the more fun it gets. And I do love a good show."

Without hesitation, he pressed the blade into the already bleeding scrape, carving deeper into my palm. The pain was immediate and excruciating, a searing fire that seemed to rip through flesh and bone. A scream tore from my throat, raw and unrestrained, as the blade sliced with brutal precision.

He didn't stop. He traced a crimson trail from the webbing between my fingers down towards the wound, each cut a deliberate act intended to cause agony. Blood flowed freely. Weak tears blurred my vision as my screams echoed off the walls, mingling with Darren's sinister laughter. His voice, dripping with malice, added a chilling layer to my torment. "You'll remember this," he taunted, his tone dripping with sardonic delight. "Every defiance, every struggle, shall be baptized in this pain."

Out of the corner of my eye, Christopher's face was a mask of desperation. His voice cracked with raw intensity. "Let him go! I'll fucking kill you if I have to!" His frantic pleas cut through my agony, each word underscoring his helplessness as he reached out, restrained by Misha, trying to bridge the gap between us.

Darren's gaze flickered to Christopher, a smirk widening. "Yeah? And what makes you think you can stand a chance, pretty boy?" He chuckled darkly. "You think you can save him? That's adorable."

He continued his cruel work, each slice of the blade a calculated act of torment. His enjoyment grew with each moment of suffering he inflicted, feeding off the helplessness that radiated from me and Christopher. I struggled frantically, but his grip remained unyielding.

"Stay still, kid," he whispered, his voice a taunting murmur. "You wouldn't want me to slip and make this worse, would you? Might lose a finger—"

"I said leave him the fuck alone!" Christopher shoved Misha aside and lunged forward, his voice cracking with desperation, but Darren sidestepped effortlessly, his movements fluid and predatory.

With a flick of her wrist, Misha produced another blade, its edge catching the dim light in a menacing glint. The coarse blade pressed to Christopher's neck, drawing thin streams of blood.

"Ah, now, that wasn't very wise, was it?" Misha purred, her voice a seductive hiss. "You see, darling, we could end you right here... but where's the fun in that?" Her tone was laced with dark allure, a twisted charm that made her threat all the more chilling as she pressed the knife deeper into his throat. "We have so much more to explore together, don't we?" Her words wove a sinister promise of torment, as the tunnel became a stage for their dark, macabre play.

"He's quite the feisty one, isn't he?" Darren sneered, his eyes glinting with amusement. "You've got spunk, I'll give you that."

Darren glanced back at me, his smile widening. "See that? Your knight in shining armor is here to save you. How sweet." He leaned in closer, his breath hot against my ear. "But we both know how this ends, don't we?"

Christopher strained against Misha's grip, his eyes blazing with fury. "You bastard, I'll—"

"Shh," Darren interrupted, placing a finger to his lips in a mocking gesture. "No more empty threats. Just enjoy the show."

With a final, cruel twist of his wrist, he inflicted one last cut, stepping back to admire his handiwork. "There we go. A masterpiece of agony."

Christopher's cry ignited a fleeting hope within me, even as danger loomed. Time seemed to stretch endlessly, each heartbeat a reminder of my dilemma. The weight of Christopher's safety was a burden I couldn't ignore.

I was torn between my deep, genuine attachment to someone I barely knew, and the expectations from my father who would condemn it. *He's not worth it! Think of your future!* I could hear him screaming. The internal conflict was suffocating, each moment intensifying my desperation. *Fuck it, Dad.*

"I– I'll do whatever you want," I croaked, my voice shaking. "Just — please, stop hurting him."

Darren's smirk widened as he watched my struggle. "Now that's the spirit!" he crowed, lifting my restrained hand with a cruel flourish. He used it to clap with his own, the motion making the pain in my gushing palm sear through my body. "Go on, then, Misha. Put him down," he commanded, his voice slicing through the air. "If the kid's still itching for a peek beyond the veil after this, that's his problem." His words dripped with an icy indifference as he surveyed Christopher with eyes as dead as a winter night.

Misha's hesitation was palpable. She squeezed Christopher's arm, tightening the blade against his neck, her eyes darting between him and Darren with a flicker of inner conflict. The air crackled with electric tension, her furrowed brow a map of her turbulent thoughts.

"Don't keep me waiting, Misha," Darren drawled, a hint of impatience creeping into his voice. "Our other guest is eager to comply. Let's not *spoil* his moment of bravery!"

With a reluctant sigh, Misha released Christopher, who crumpled onto the filthy ground, trembling from his ordeal. His neck leaked a sickly crimson, his eyes darting between me, Misha, and Darren in a desperate dance of confusion.

Darren relinquished his hold on me, and I staggered back, clutching my battered hand where his fingers had left a brutal imprint. The blade, now smeared with my blood, glinted with a sinister gleam, its malice mirroring my plight.

"This is just the beginning," Darren murmured, his voice a chilling whisper. "Consider it the opening act of your metamorphosis. And let me tell you, you've played your part *admirably*."

He moved closer, eyes alight with dark amusement. "Pain is just... a doorway." He flicked his hand in the air, his tone oddly conversational. "A gateway to something far more... sinister. And you, my friend, are about to step through."

Christopher, his body wracked with anger and fear, tried to rise, but Darren raised a hand to halt him. "Ah, ah, ah. Patience, pretty boy. Your time will come soon enough. For now, just watch and learn."

Seeing Christopher on the ground, I extended my other hand toward him. He looked up, relief and desperation mingling in his gaze. His grip was firm as he pulled himself up from the muck, his movements urgent yet cautious.

The instant he was upright, Christopher enveloped me in a tight embrace, trembling with relief and lingering dread. "Thank you," he whispered, his voice choked with emotion.

"Like you wouldn't have done the same," I quipped, a frail smile weakly spreading across my face. His warmth against my neck was a stark contrast to the icy dread pervading the cavern, offering a fleeting respite from the looming terror.

Misha's expression was unreadable, while Darren's eyes narrowed in displeased contemplation of the unexpected display of emotion. "Enjoy your reunion while you can," he sneered. "It won't last. There's still much more to come."

His words hung in the air, thick with promises of horrors yet to come. The atmosphere was charged with an oppressive weight, and as I stood there, trembling and wounded, I couldn't shake the sinking feeling that this was only the prologue to a nightmare from which I might never awaken.

CHAPTER 9

LABYRINTH OF NIGHTMARES

A THICK, suffocating fog of malevolence settled over us, a miasma so dense it felt like a physical weight pressing down on my chest. We were ensnared in a nightmare where the boundary between reality and horror dissolved into a grotesque blur.

Their true nature had been laid bare, stripped of pretense. It was a grotesque display, a grim tableau of depravity that mocked our futile resistance. Every glance into their icy, empty eyes revealed a yawning void, a chilling abyss that seemed to swallow all traces of empathy. The darkness was not merely present; it was an active force, taunting us with its insatiable hunger.

The pleasure they took in our suffering... the twisted delight in our torment were reflected in their bodies, which bore the marks of their malevolence—scars and bruises, each a trophy of their relentless thirst for power and dominance over those weaker than themselves. Facing such relentless cruelty, hope felt like a distant, flickering flame, tiny, struggling to exist, teetering on the brink of extinction.

Yet even as despair clawed at my soul, a sliver of defiance flickered within me—a stubborn ember of resistance against the encroaching dark. It was a whisper of courage, a silent vow to fight back against the consuming void. Each step forward was a step towards that frail light, a desperate attempt to cling to hope amidst the overwhelming odds.

Our survival hinged on this—on standing firm against the relentless wave of oppression. I caught Christopher's eye, a silent exchange of resolve passing between us. We had to resist, to find strength in unity, for surrender would mean a fate far worse than death. We were too far into this to back down, bound by a shared determination to overcome, no matter the cost.

Darren and Misha dragged us along, their grip unyielding, the damp air of the tunnel closing in around us. Each step echoed with a foreboding resonance.

Misha's voice sliced through the darkness, dripping with a venomous sweetness. "How's that hand feeling, darling?" she purred, her tone laced with a twisted kind of tenderness. "It's almost endearing, your stubbornness."

Darren's voice joined in, a chilling grin spreading across his face. "Adorable, really. But so utterly pointless. You haven't the faintest clue about what's coming."

"Well why don't you share it with us," Christopher mocked, "so we can anticipate the joy you're going to bring us."

Darren showed no sign of surprise or anger. He just huffed out a low growl.

We needed to find a moment, a crack in their control.

"You know," Misha continued, her voice smooth and conversational, "we haven't had this much fun in ages. It's rare to find prey that actually tries to fight back."

Darren's laugh was a hollow, echoing sound that sent a shiver through me. "I do enjoy the chase," he admitted. "But it's the endgame that excites me. The moment their spark fades from their eyes."

Christopher's grip tightened, his gaze fierce and determined. He mouthed, "Get ready."

Darren's voice took on a mocking lilt. "Oh, what's the matter? No witty comebacks? You were so full of fire a moment ago..."

A surge of defiance welled up inside me, sharp and clear. "You're underestimating us," I said, my voice unwavering despite the fear clawing at my insides.

Misha's laughter was cruel, mocking. "Oh, we don't underestimate you. We know *exactly* what you're capable of. And it won't be enough."

And then it happened.

In an instant, hope flared—a fork in the path winking with uncertain promise. "Now!" Christopher's voice, taut and frayed with desperation, shattered the silence. He lunged forward, his body a coiled spring driven by raw survival instinct, a defensive linebacker pushing for the glory of the last play.

A primal roar erupted as Christopher's shoulder crashed into Darren's torso. Darren's skull serendipitously slammed into the wall; the impact was so hard it reverberated through the tunnel as the pipe twanged in protest. He hit the ground as Misha lunged.

Instinct took over as my senses sharpened to a razor's edge. In one desperate, fluid motion, my elbow drove into Misha's nose. The sickening crunch of bone echoed through the tunnels like a morbid requiem.

"We need to go!" Christopher's voice cut through the tension, urgency dripping from each word. I gritted my teeth against the pain as he seized my hand, yanking me into motion. We shot forward, propelled by an equal measure of terror and hope. My injured hand throbbed with every step, the pain searing with each movement. The blood loss sapped my strength, but the fear driving us pushed me onward like ancient man running from a primeval beast fight or flight.

Darren's voice slithered through the darkness, taunting and menacing. "Now that's how I like it!" His laughter followed, chilling and almost playful. "We own this place, and you're just another piece of prey. Keep running, little rabbits. Make us work for it!"

Adrenaline crackled, electrifying our senses as we tore through the grimy passage. Every footfall pounded loudly, a relentless drumbeat of impending danger.

Misha's agonized cries, a twisted ballet of pain and pleasure, spurred us on. The air buzzed with tension, our breaths ragged and uneven, hearts drumming a frantic rhythm against the encroaching doom.

The air thickened in our lungs, every breath a struggle against the mounting dread. Shadows leaped and writhed on the walls, reaching out like groping hands, eager to swallow us whole.

With every reckless twist and turn, urgency fueled our flight, our bodies pushed to their limits. The labyrinth closed in around us, the path ahead swallowed by creeping shadows.

Behind, the pounding footsteps of our pursuers grew louder, chains clanking with a metallic rhythm that drove them on. Fear gnawed at the edges of our sanity, a relentless predator at our heels.

Each step was a battle, each breath a struggle against the encroaching pain and despair. Darren's mocking laughter echoed through my mind, a cruel reminder of the torment awaiting us if we faltered. We pressed on, driven by a primal urge to survive as the underground maze conspired against us.

As we rounded another corner, Christopher's urgent whisper cut through the chaos. "Keep going, Jason. We're almost there. Don't look back."

I nodded, forcing myself through the pain and fatigue, eyes locked on the path ahead. The voices of Darren and Misha faded, their presence a lingering threat in the darkness.

We had to keep moving. We had to survive.

We plunged deeper into the cavern, and the shadows seemed to writhe and coil, as if plotting against us. The darkness was a living thing, wrapping itself around my mind, distorting reality, feeding my paranoia. Every rustle, every flicker, felt like a prelude to something monstrous waiting just beyond sight.

The air clung to my throat, sour and choking. Each breath was a gasp of decay, a reminder of how far we'd strayed into this forgotten hell. Questions buzzed in my head like angry wasps, each one sharper than the last. *What secrets lurked in this darkness? Were we in danger, or mere pawns in some twisted game beyond our grasp?*

Dread became a physical thing, gnawing at my stomach, suffocating me with its weight.

"What... what the FUCK is happening?" The words escaped my lips in a desperate whisper, torn from my throat amidst the ragged cadence of my breaths. Each syllable hung heavy in the air, pregnant with the weight of our uncertain fate. I dared not raise my voice, afraid to provoke whatever lurked in the dark.

"I don't know, fucking drug addicts? We're not sticking around to find out," Christopher snapped, his voice sharp with urgency.

Every sound was amplified, every shadow stretching grotesquely, mocking us. Reality seemed to warp, twisting into shapes that taunted us with their inscrutability. Yet amidst the chaos, a stubborn flicker of defiance burned within me, refusing to be consumed by fear.

"Come on, there has to be something!" I murmured urgently, my voice a tense whisper barely audible over the ominous echoes. "There's gotta be a way out!"

I forced myself to scan the passing surroundings, seeking any sign of escape—a ladder, a manhole, anything. But the silence was a void, an abyss of uncertainty stretching endlessly before us.

As we barreled through the smothering blackness, an eerie hum slithered into my ears—an unsettling, guttural murmur that twisted and contorted with every step. I skidded to a halt, straining to decipher the distorted sounds.

"Wait. Wait, wait, wait." I jabbed my hand out to stop Christopher, my whisper barely cutting through the thudding pulse of my heart. "You hear that?" My voice trembled.

Christopher's face tightened in a grimace, eyes wide and fearful. "Voices... They're in front of us," he muttered, his voice cracking with dread.

"Shit, they're getting louder!" I hissed, trying to pierce through the shadows to find their origin.

We pressed ourselves against the icy, damp wall, the cold seeping through our clothes like a creeping disease. The voices sharpened into a malicious clarity, slicing through the silence with venomous intent.

"They think they can play games with us and get away," one voice seethed, dripping with spite.

"Yeah, let's show them what happens when they mess with us," another voice growled, punctuated by a sinister, bone-chilling laugh that wormed its way into my bones.

Christopher's grip on my arm tightened painfully, his eyes mirroring the dread that clutched at my heart. "We've got to find a way past them," he rasped, urgency threading through his voice.

I nodded, pivoting, our footsteps urgent and uneven. But as the sound of distant chains reached my ears, the grim realization crashed into me—we were trapped down here with not just one group of pursuers, but two. The tunnel constricted around us, a sinister maze of darkness and dread, closing in with each step.

The silence returned, oppressive and thick, broken only by our ragged breaths and the ominous murmurings of the gang. Time felt like it was slipping through our fingers, the darkness thickening with every step, as if the walls themselves conspired to swallow us whole.

"Stay close," I whispered, urgency threading through every syllable. "We'll find a way out."

Then, as if conjured by our fears, a voice slithered through the murk. "Well, look what we have here. Lost your little boyfriends?"

"Fuck off," Nicole's voice sliced through the gloom, sharp and defiant. "There's worse shit down here than you assholes."

Another voice laughed, cruel and mocking. "Oh really? Think you're tough without your backup?"

"Trust me, I can handle all of you," she snapped back, her tone dripping with scorn and reckless bravado.

"Oh, I'm sure you can," the first voice taunted.

A piercing scream ripped through the tunnel, Nicole's cry a jarring mix of rage and desperation. The sound was followed by a sinister, echoing chuckle that coiled around my spine. My heart raced as I shot a frantic glance at Christopher.

"Nicole?!" Christopher's shout cracked with raw terror.

"Nicole! Where are you?" I cried out, my voice tinged with desperation as it ricocheted off the labyrinthine walls.

Her screams faded, growing more distant and strained, until they abruptly ceased, leaving behind a suffocating silence that seeped into my very marrow. Chris and I exchanged a look, our eyes wide with shared horror, a silent testament to the nightmare unfolding around us.

CHAPTER 10
PATH OF THE DAMNED

WITHOUT HESITATION, we sprinted toward what we prayed was the source of Nicole's scream, our footsteps echoing like gunshots against the slick, damp floor. The tunnel stretched endlessly before us, each second dragging like a lifetime. The walls seemed to close in, the air thick and stifling. We rounded a bend, and there it was: a ladder, the manhole above, its cover parted, its metal surface gleaming ominously in the dusty sunlight.

We skidded to a halt beside it, our breaths coming in ragged, desperate gasps. Beneath the rungs, a pool of fresh blood was spreading, its dark crimson hue a grotesque contrast against the damp, gray stone. The sharp, metallic scent of blood mixed with the musty odor of the tunnel, made my stomach churn. Cold dread seeped into my bones, paralyzing me with an icy grip. A single hoop earring lay in the blood.

I dropped to my knees, fingers trembling, stopping short of touching it. Memories of Nicole flooded my mind, her laughter, her spirit. *What happened?* The cold metal earring clashed painfully with her warmth.

"Shit..." I whispered, barely audible over my pounding heart.

Blood-streaked and shaking, my hand closed around the earring. Our eyes locked, shared resolve passing between us.

"There's a trail—" Christopher's voice cut through, tight with grim determination, snapping me from my daze. "Come on, we have to follow it!"

Sure enough, blood marked a path from the manhole cover, vanishing into the tunnel's darkness. Christopher bolted ahead, veering sharply right. Caught off guard, I hesitated. "Chris, wait!" My shout echoed off stone walls, but he didn't look back. The darkness swallowed him, his figure disappearing into the abyss.

"Chris!" I yelled again, met only by silence. By myself, I faced a choice: follow him into the unknown, or escape alone.

The blood path would be there when I got back. I could find help...

The distant sound of water dripping mixed with the occasional scurrying of unseen vermin. *Pursuit it is.*

But beneath the cacophony of my hurried steps, another sound pierced the air—a chorus of agonized screams, distant yet unmistakable. The gang's voices, twisted with fear and pain, sliced through the silence like a blade, sending a shiver down my spine.

What the hell was that? My eyes widened in alarm. *Did Chris find them? Is he alright? In danger? Or was he already dead?*

I shook my head, trying to banish the thought. The screams echoed in my ears, a haunting reminder of the lurking dangers. But I couldn't afford to dwell on it, not with Nicole's life hanging in the balance.

As I rounded another corner, a scream tore through the air, chilling me to the core. *Christopher.* I sprinted toward the sound. My heart pounded, fear propelling me forward.

I found him sprawled on the ground, his face pale with shock. The gang's ringleader lay beside him, his torso shredded and limbs splayed unnaturally. The man's lifeless eyes stared blankly at the ceiling, his once-menacing features now a grotesque mask of agony. His leather jacket, a symbol of dominance, was torn to shreds, deep gashes and puncture wounds marring his flesh. The jagged scar on his face mocked his demise, a cruel reminder of the violence that consumed him. Blood pooled around his form, staining the ground a sickening crimson, as if the earth itself recoiled from the horror.

I rushed to his side, pulling him to his feet. "You okay?" I asked, concern tight in my voice.

Christopher looked down at the ringleader's body, face pale. "Fuck, they killed him!" he whispered, shock and horror in his wide eyes.

We stood there, the reality sinking in. The man in the alley who had terrorized us now lay dead at our feet, a victim of something far more brutal. The gravity of it pressed down on us, but we knew we couldn't stay.

"Come on, we have to keep moving," I urged, squeezing Christopher's arm. He nodded, and we pressed on through the blood-soaked tunnel, the weight of what we'd witnessed propelling us forward.

Within a few steps, more bodies littered the path, each more mutilated than the last. *Their deaths were monstrous.* The hulking figure with the serpent tattoo lay sprawled against the wall, his muscular frame torn apart by some savage beast. The wiry figure, once full of volatile energy, now lay twisted and broken, his wild hair matted with blood and his chest riddled with wounds. The behemoth of brutality, who had once suffocated Christopher with his presence, now lay motionless, his tattered flannel soaked in blood. The shadowy figure, once draped in darkness, now lay exposed under a beam of light from a sewer cover, his hood drawn back to reveal a face contorted in agony.

As we stepped over the bodies, a weak voice broke the silence. "Help... me," it croaked. I spun around to find the hulking figure with the serpent tattoo still clinging to life, his body ravaged but not yet claimed by death. He reached out, his bloodied hand grabbing Christopher's ankle with a desperate grip.

Christopher knelt beside him, his expression a mix of horror and pity. "Who did this?" he demanded, his voice steady but tinged with emotion.

The dying man's eyes fluttered open, filled with pain and fear. "Monsters... in the dark," he rasped, each word a struggle. "Help... me..."

"We can't just leave him here," I uttered, my voice trembling.

"We don't have a choice," Christopher replied, standing. The man's grip tightened, but Christopher shook his leg free. "He won't survive. We have to find Nicole."

I nodded, my heart heavy. The man's pleas haunted me as we pressed on, our footsteps echoing against the walls, mingling with his dying breaths. The darkness closed in around us, chilling the air.

Each step was a violation of the unseen boundary between the living and the damned. Our feet, coated in thick, sticky blood, slipped across the grotesque canvas of the ground. The echo of our footsteps mingled with a haunting symphony of dying screams that wove through the stifling air. Darkness wrapped around us, a living entity with fingers of shadow pressing against our skin.

"What could've done this?" My voice quavered, a fragile thread of disbelief in the suffocating gloom. The scene played over in my mind like a grotesque art piece, with the gang members now consumed by the clutches of something far more sinister.

The blood trail snaked deeper into the winding labyrinth, the walls closing in as though the earth itself was conspiring to crush us. We had no choice but to press on; Nicole's life was the only thing that mattered.

Our progress was a defiant rhythm against the encroaching dread. The tunnel twisted like a serpent, the air thickening with a palpable malevolence. Darkness wasn't merely an absence of light; it was an entity, breathing heavily down our necks. But retreat wasn't an option.

Before us yawned three tunnels, each a gaping maw of foreboding. Christopher stopped, his gaze darting between the options.

"Which one? One, two, or three?" His voice was taut, a barely restrained snarl of urgency.

I squinted into the shadows, my gut churning with unease. "I don't know— There's blood everywhere."

Christopher's jaw was set in a grim line. "One," he said, his voice slicing through the oppressive air with steely resolve. We plunged into the left tunnel, the darkness tightening its grip around us like a vice.

Minutes dragged into an agonizing stretch as we twisted through the labyrinth. Just as doubt began to claw at my sanity, a chilling realization hit me.

The open manhole loomed ahead, its grimy surface a sickening reminder of where we had started—where we'd found Nicole's earring. My spine prickled with icy dread. *What the hell—?*

"We're going in fucking circles!" I howled, the realization freezing my veins.

Christopher's face, usually a mask of control, was now a mirror of my own panic. "Shit, we went the wrong way!" he yelled, desperation slicing through his voice. "We need to go back—try another tunnel!"

I stopped abruptly, breaking away from Christopher's frantic energy. His eyes flitted between me and the echoing footsteps that grew closer, relentless and heavy with the sound of clanking chains.

"What the fuck are you doing?" he demanded, his voice a jagged edge of concern and scorn. "Are you losing it?!"

The footsteps grew louder, each hollow thud and splash reverberating through the tunnel like a ghostly dirge. The clinking chains sounded like the rattling bones of some spectral predator, an ominous harbinger of the doom that trailed us.

"Chris—we have a way out! We have to try!" I pleaded, pointing toward the exit. "We can't keep running!"

"And what, leave Nicole?! Even if we try it, look where that got her! Jason, we don't have time. We have to keep moving!" His voice was fierce, but beneath the anger lay raw fear. "Those twisted fucks know these tunnels better than anyone. We gotta go!"

I glanced up, straining to catch the faint glimmer of sunlight filtering through the manhole. My heart thundered, adrenaline turning my hands into trembling, useless things. My vision wavered, reality's edges blurring under the weight of dread. Doubt gnawed at me like a feral beast. *Could I trust this man with my life? Were we just trading mine for hers?* "Chris, you need to face it. We don't know if Nicole's even alive anymore. She might be—"

"No!" Christopher interrupted, his eyes blazing with a wild, desperate fire. "You don't know that! We can't just give up! Please, she's all I have!"

His words struck me like a physical blow. The anguish in his eyes was palpable, his entire existence tethered to Nicole's fate. His plea sank into me like lead, and for a moment, my resolve wavered. I took a ragged breath, the gravity of our situation crashing over me.

"Jason," Christopher continued, his voice breaking, "I can't let her die down here."

The weight of his words settled in my chest like a heavy stone. I looked at him, his face a portrait of raw determination, and realized that he wasn't just fighting for survival—he was fighting for the last piece of his world.

I nodded, a terse motion before he seized my arm. With a shared resolve, we burst into a frantic sprint, our legs pounding with desperate, furious energy. The tunnels twisted and contorted around us, but we kept our eyes locked ahead, racing against the echoing footsteps, the rattling chains, and the encroaching darkness. Fear and hope clashed within me, each step a testament to our will to endure.

Every breath was molten fire, scorching our lungs as if we were inhaling the flames of some unseen inferno. Our legs felt shackled by invisible chains, each step a defiant rebellion against the oppressive gravity of fear. Sweat blinded me, warping the serpentine path ahead, yet we pressed on, pursued by a menacing force that seemed to seep through the walls themselves. This chase wasn't just a race against time; it was a visceral clash with a relentless nightmare, a Groundhog's Day of the macabre. The slick stone walls of the labyrinth reverberated with our frantic footsteps, each echo an ominous reminder of the darkness clawing at our heels. Darren's sinister laughter, like shards of broken glass, punctuated our desperate flight. I knew he wouldn't play nice this time.

Christopher's gaze met mine, a silent communion of dread and resolve. We had to return to the fork and make a different choice. We continued to follow the circle, knowing it would bring us to the split; the blood-soaked ground beneath our feet became a grotesque reminder of the danger closing in. Each turn was a gamble and the odds were in favor of the house.

But stopping was not an option. Fear and determination blended into a volatile cocktail, propelling us through the suffocating gloom. Each fleeting second brought us closer to our goal, yet the uncertainty of what lay ahead diminished the odds with every step.

The fork reappeared, a grim crossroad suspended in the void. Christopher hesitated, his face a canvas of raw anxiety, then turned to me with a voice barely a whisper of sanity. "Your call."

I nodded toward the right-hand tunnel.

"Why that one?"

"It has more blood than the other one."

And with that, we plunged into the third tunnel.

Then, like a lone candle flickering in a cavernous black void, there was a glimmer of hope. A steady flow of air, and a faint, elusive beacon of light danced in the distance, teasing us with the possibility of escape.

"Chris, is that—" I panted.

"Daylight," he whispered, his voice a fragile thread of hope.

"Of course! The tunnels would have to open up and empty into somewhere!"

Our eyes, starved for brightness, latched onto it, and our hearts, burdened with dread, dared to believe that maybe, just maybe, we could break free from the labyrinth's suffocating grasp.

We pressed forward, the light expanding with each step, the darkness beginning to falter. The labyrinth seemed to writhe in frustration, its passages contorting in mockery of our desperate flight. Each step was a battle against the encroaching shadows, our breaths ragged, reverberating off the cold stone like a dirge. But we weren't out yet. The maze was still alive, waiting for its moment, a malevolent entity savoring our struggle.

But that fragile glimmer of light was our salvation. It was the promise of that elusive light that urged us onward, a desperate chase through the eternal night of the underground.

CHAPTER 11

GUTTURAL PLEAS

AS CHRISTOPHER and I sprinted toward the distant, flickering light, an unsettling shroud of dread enveloped us. The stench—an almost palpable rot—intensified, clawing at our senses. Christopher's clenched jaw betrayed a maelstrom of anxiety, a mirror of my own internal chaos. I sensed that Nicole weighed heavily on his mind, but something else was there. It was like he couldn't look at me. I couldn't tell if it was regret for dragging me along through this nightmare, or if underneath his strong bravado, he was really just a scared little kid.

Nicole's image, fragile yet hardened, lingered in the recesses of my mind, trapped in the claustrophobic confines of a shootpipe. How she trembled, the girl I barely knew, shaken to her core. Thoughts of Kimberly, and the worry she and my mother must be shouldering in my absence, gnawed at my consciousness, too. Was I destined to become another faceless victim of the city's brutal landscape, or would I transform into something monstrous, an abomination beyond comprehension?

The shadows surrendered slowly to the encroaching daylight, each step feeling like a knife slicing through the fragile fabric of our sanity. The possibility of escape seemed tainted, threatening to leave Nicole behind, a sacrificial offering to the darkness. Christopher's eyes, pools of dread, mirrored my rising guilt with an unsettling clarity.

In the suffocating dampness of the tunnel, every breath was a struggle against unseen horrors, but now the air seemed to lighten, just a bit at first. Yet the decay that permeated the air, a rancid miasma that seeped into our skin, had left a greasy, nauseating residue. The stench of rotting flesh mingled with the metallic tang of congealed blood, a grotesque blend that made each inhalation a battle. My throat burned, the taste of decay a vile presence on my tongue. Goosebumps prickled like braille on my skin as we got closer to freedom and help. But the overwhelming fear that saturated the air, pervading every inch of the tunnel, still gave me a stifling sense of dread.

Come on, we must be close! Where's the exit? And where are we about to end up? My thoughts roared as my stomach twisted in agitation, each stride intensifying the churn in my gut.

The stench grew heavier and heavier, a tangible force that clawed at our senses. We were trespassers in a realm where time had stopped, where echoes of suffering clung like specters to the shadows. The floor, a gruesome mosaic of gore and viscera, silently testified to the atrocities committed in this forsaken place.

Then, suddenly, our progress was halted by an unexpected horror.

Corpses, both fresh and desiccated, lay in grotesque heaps, their vacant eyes staring into nothingness, mouths frozen in silent screams. Flies buzzed over them, as maggots squirmed through eaten pores. Death itself seemed to block our path, with the faint light of day seeping through above the festering pile. Each jagged incision, each twisted limb, whispered unspeakable secrets, stirring the darkest corners of our minds.

In the oppressive murk of the chamber, Christopher's voice cut through the silence, ragged and strained. "We... we need to get past them." He gagged, his face draining of color. "Got any ideas?"

I looked at him, my stomach sinking further. *Jason, are you really going to do this?* With a shuddering breath, I reached for a rigid, outstretched hand, yanking it from the pile. The corpses above shifted, a nauseating movement, but remained unmoved.

"I... don't know what you want me to do," I admitted. The stench was overwhelming, threatening to pull my insides out.

"Think we can climb over them?" Christopher's voice was fraught with desperation. I returned to him with a blank stare, before turning back at the pile.

"You're fucking kidding," I shot back. "Shit, ladies first."

Gripping my shoulder, Christopher planted his foot into the pile, the sickening crunch of bone reverberating. Vomit surged in my throat, but I swallowed it, the acidic taste merging with the noxious stench.

Christopher paused. "Did you hear that?" His voice trembled with unease.

I nodded, fear coiling in my gut. "Yeah, man. This is a bit much for me."

"No, listen," Christopher's eyes widened in fear. A distant, rhythmic thudding echoed from the earth's bowels. I edged closer to the pile, each step deliberate, my heart pounding.

"Yeah," I whispered, masking the terror that gnawed at me. "What is that?"

Suddenly, a faint, desperate voice pierced through the bodies. "Help," it whimpered.

In a frenzy, Christopher leapt from the pile and crashed into the murky ground beside me. Together, we wrenched at the bodies, pulling until the top layer collapsed. Pain radiated through my hand with each movement, the webbing between my fingers stinging relentlessly. Each effort sent sharp, searing pain up my arm and into my spine, but we couldn't stop. Steadily, blood dribbled out the wound, mingling with the foul grime. I clenched my jaw, the ache a brutal reminder of my vulnerability.

As we scrambled atop the corpses, the source of the unsettling noise emerged—a ghastly apparition. Yet nothing could prepare us for the sight laid bare: a cavernous passageway, its vastness defying reason, yawning open before us.

THE ROOM we stumbled into felt like a grotesque departure from the familiar stench of the sewers. It was cavernous, dominated by the harsh, rhythmic clatter of industrial machinery. Large, rusted pumps lined the walls, their metal surfaces encrusted with grime and age. The room's layout created a labyrinth of obstacles—overhead pipes, clunky machinery, and steel grates formed an intricate maze of barriers. Moisture dripped relentlessly from the ceiling, pooling in the cracks of an uneven floor—a grotesque mosaic of ancient bricks and crudely poured concrete. This chamber felt like a mausoleum for the city's forgotten detritus, a testament to a bygone era now consigned to oblivion.

The room was dominated by a colossal, industrial fan, its grimy blades turning with an unsettlingly deliberate slowness. Behind a heavy iron grate in the ceiling, the fan's movement was more a taunt than a comfort. Shadows from the blades sliced through the dimness with a predatory grace, creating an eerie ballet of light and dark as a shaft of blinding daylight pierced through gaps in the grate. The contrast was jarring—an almost hallucinogenic clash between the dim, oppressive gloom of the sewers and the harsh, surreal clarity of sunlight above.

Underneath this monstrous fan, Nicole was suspended, her body swaying gently in sync with the fan's slow, metronomic rhythm. Chains bound her wrists, their metal links catching the harsh daylight in a cruel display of glint and glitter, like serpents gnawing at her flesh. The sight was a gut-punch, a visceral blow that left me reeling.

And then I noticed the others.

Hanging in grotesque array around her were more victims, their bodies in various stages of horrific decay. Some barely clung to consciousness, heads drooping as crimson dripped in slow, relentless streams from their tortured limbs. Others were unnervingly still, their pallid faces locked in grimaces of eternal agony, their skin peeling away in the oppressive, fetid air.

In the shadows, amidst the grotesque tableau, a face flickered in recognition—a face that had haunted the missing persons billboards. The sight twisted my insides into knots as a horrifying realization sank in. These bodies bore the marks of a macabre feast—skin stretched tight, some missing organs, leaving hollow, lifeless husks dangling in the heat. It was as though some insidious force had consumed them, leaving only these spectral remnants to sway in the stale, rancid breeze.

Christopher and I approached Nicole tentatively, uncertain if we would find salvation or damnation in her presence. Our footsteps echoed softly against the decrepit walls, Chris' eyes betraying a mix of emotions dancing like specters in the gloom—relief, sorrow, and a dread anticipation of what lay ahead.

"Christopher," I murmured, barely more than a breath. I paused, pointing to the man chained to the wall. "Look."

"What? Do you know him?" Christopher's eyes darted to where mine were fixed.

"Not exactly, but—" I faltered, grappling for coherence. "He's... Mike Carnegie. His face is everywhere, he's a missing person. I— I think they all are."

From the shadows, a raspy plea emerged, barely cutting through the relentless drone of the fan. A slight shuffling—another lost soul, moaning with cracked lips, a desperate whisper in this forsaken place.

A shudder rippled through me, the full weight of their anguish crashing over me like an unforgiving tide. They were more than just casualties; they were ghastly monuments to the terrors hidden in this desolate realm. Each faint cry, each ghostly visage etched into the dimness, stoked the burning resolve within me.

"We can't just leave them," I whispered, the words heavy with despair.

"Jason," Christopher's voice sliced through the gloom, steady, though his emotions choked his words. "I'm only here for Nikki."

I wrenched my gaze from the tormented souls, caught between dread and an overwhelming compulsion to intervene. Every muted cry gnawed at my conscience, but Christopher's words rooted me to our mission.

The clang of chains against stone reverberated like a grim requiem as we edged closer to Nicole. Christopher's approach was deliberate and hesitant, his hands shaking as he reached out towards her.

Her chains jingled softly, blending with the fan's low, mechanical growl—a dissonant symphony that merged with the occasional drip of water echoing from hidden pipes. The fan's blades cast flickering shadows over her, weaving a grotesque tapestry of light and darkness that twisted with each rotation.

With every step, the severity of her plight became starkly apparent. Her clothes, once vibrant, now hung in tatters, drenched in a chilling tapestry of blood. The crop top was soaked through, clinging to her like a macabre second skin, its crimson stains a silent testament to her torment. Her jeans, shredded and grimy, were splattered with the dark, drying pools of her blood, whispering of a desperate struggle against unseen horrors.

A sharp pang of sorrow struck me at the sight of her accessories— a hoop earring, once a symbol of defiant spirit, now dimmed and tarnished; a choker, once a mark of her freedom, now a cruel mockery of her captivity.

"Nik," Christopher breathed, his voice a trembling wisp, like a ghost lost in the smoky haze of despair. His fingers, pale and unsteady, parted the tangled curtain of her hair, revealing a face marred by brutal captivity. "We're here. We found you."

The silence that followed was a heavy, smothering shroud.

"We need to get her down," I croaked, my voice swallowed by the cavernous void around us.

Christopher's eyes, dark wells of anguish that fought back tears, remained locked onto Nicole's fragile form. The fractured light seeping through the grate painted his face with shadows of grim determination, etched deeply by desperation and weary resolve. Together, we moved in a grim ballet, working to sever the chains that bound her, each metallic link echoing like hollow notes in the oppressive quiet, punctuated only by the languid creak of the fan blades above.

As we struggled with the restraints, the tormented cries of other victims bounced off the walls, their faces flickering with desperate glimmers of hope. Each clasp we freed seemed to drain a piece of our own strength, but Christopher's resolve remained as unyielding as the iron chains.

"Just... one more," he murmured, his voice strained, a fragile thread stretched thin by emotion.

The sound of chains clinking against stone was a haunting, dissonant lullaby, a grim rhythm to our desperate struggle. Amidst this agony, a quiet solidarity emerged—a shared burden of guilt and sorrow that seeped into the very walls.

Christopher cradled Nicole's bloodied form, her breaths shallow and ragged, each exhale a whisper of fading life. Her eyes, once fierce and fiery, now held a resigned, bitter glimmer as they locked onto his.

"Crazy seeing... you here," she rasped, her voice a fragile echo that barely rose from her lips, a bitter smile curling them.

"I'm so sorry, Nikki," Christopher choked out, tears streaming down his face in rivers of anguish.

Her trembling, ghostly pale hand brushed against his cheek. "Should be," she murmured, her voice barely a breath. "You know how much I... hate the dark."

Tears fell unchecked down Christopher's face. "We're getting you out of here," he vowed, his voice breaking under the weight of his promise. "I swear."

With a final, shuddering sigh, Nicole's hand slipped away, her eyes closing in a haunting silence. Christopher held her close, his sorrow palpable, an overwhelming tide of loss and regret.

"No—no, don't leave me, Nik, please," he choked out, his voice a fragile thread strung with grief. "Please, I love you..."

But she was gone.

The void left in her absence was a chasm of unspoken words and shattered dreams. As Christopher gently laid her down, silent sobs wracked his body, a broken rhythm to the cruel ballet of fate and fleeting human hope.

Christopher hovered above her, his anguish melding with the discordant symphony of moans and the rattling breaths of those barely hanging on. His eyes, a morass of desperation and shattered dreams, were fixed on her still form. I moved closer, my heart sinking under the unbearable weight of the loss he must be feeling. Inside, I cried for him... and for her. Bonnie and Clyde. Doomed from the beginning.

The sunlight began to wane as thick, foreboding clouds rolled in above, obscuring the fragile beams of light with a shroud of darkness. Nicole's vibrant spirit felt like a ghost haunting the dim space. I fumbled through my pocket, fingers brushing against the cool metal of her missing hoop earring—an emblem of her fierce defiance. The earring sparkled dully in the dim light, a flickering reminder of her once-burning fire.

Kneeling beside Nicole, I gently laid the earring in her open palm, the coldness of her skin biting into my fingertips. Her fingers remained frozen around the trinket, a chilling testament to a life that had been extinguished far too soon.

"You didn't deserve this..." I whispered, the words barely piercing the heavy silence.

Christopher's fists were clenched tight, his knuckles pale against the darkness. The silence was shattered by the raw force of his grief.

"I'm going to fucking kill them!" His voice roared through the chamber, a terrifying blend of rage and heartbreak, eyes blazing with an almost supernatural intensity as he faced the encroaching dark.

"Where are you, you sons of bitches! Come the fuck out!" He pleaded with the darkness.

I stepped in front of him, my hand firm on his shoulder. "Chris, we need a plan," I said, my voice a desperate anchor in the storm of his emotions. "We need to find where they're coming from, where their exit is."

His gaze was a storm, breaths coming in ragged, uneven bursts. "I don't give a damn about their exit," he spat, shaking off my hand. "They took her. They're all going to die."

"But if we find their exit," I persisted, my voice a steady current against his tempest, "we can escape this nightmare and save the others. This is bigger than us—"

"They're dead weight. All of them," Christopher cut in sharply, eyes cold with unyielding resolve. "It's just us now."

With a sudden, almost mechanical determination, Christopher pushed past me, his jaw set in a grim line. Ignoring my stunned stare, he advanced toward the adjacent tunnel, each step a defiant echo against the oppressive darkness.

"Chris," I called out, my voice barely cutting through the eerie hum of distant machinery. "Where are you going?"

He turned, eyes meeting mine with a silent promise and a spark of feral intensity. "I dragged you into this hell. I'll get you out. And I'll take out as many of those motherfuckers as I can along the way."

His words hung in the air, a challenge and a vow that ignited both dread and a flicker of hope within me. I watched him slip into the shadows, merging with the encroaching darkness that seemed to pulse with a life of its own.

Alone now with Nicole's lifeless form and the distant cries of other victims, a fierce resolve took root within me. Christopher was right—we had to do something. We had to end this. With a heavy heart and a steely determination, I prepared myself.

We were driven by righteous vengeance, an inferno that burned like the archangel Michael leading the armies of heaven.

AND SO WE WENT, deeper into the bowels of the sewer system. The air thickened once again. But this time, we at least half knew what to expect. We took a new path, homing into a sound that seemed to mutter in the near distance, a vaporous sound, a hollow breath that echoed around the pipes like a ghostly thing, and eventually emerged into a space that defied imagination. We'd stumbled into a grotesque parody of civilization buried beneath Los Angeles, a place that defied logic and sanity.

"Fuck, would you look at this place..." Christopher muttered, his voice a fragile thread in the oppressive silence.

I glanced around, my heart pounding. "Jesus, it— it looks like some kind of tent city," I said, my voice raw with disbelief.

"I've never seen a homeless community like this... Where are all the people?" Christopher's words hung in the air, unanswered and unsettling.

Shattered concrete and twisted metal formed the skeletal remains of structures, their outlines jagged and surreal against the murky backdrop. Small fires burned fitfully, casting flickering shadows that danced along the walls in a grotesque ballet. These crude shelters, cobbled together from scavenged materials, stood as grim testaments to the resilience and desperation of those who called this forsaken place home.

The ground underfoot was a slick mosaic of filth and gore, where remnants of past atrocities mingled with the refuse of daily survival. Each step was a reminder of the life abandoned above, now replaced by the grim reality of subterranean existence. The stench of rotting flesh and stagnant water clung to the air, making each breath a torment that challenged our capacity to move forward.

A sickly orange glow bathed the chamber, casting long, sinister shadows that writhed along the slick, grimy walls. The light, a malignant force in itself, seemed to emanate from some unfathomable source buried deep within the labyrinthine recesses of the town. Despite the lanterns and burning barrels scattered around, this glow was something else entirely. It teased, tantalized, daring us to uncover its secrets even as it cloaked itself in impenetrable mystery.

The warped and grotesque structures loomed like forgotten monoliths, silent witnesses to the chaos that had consumed this misplaced mockery of a city. Their jagged outlines etched grotesque silhouettes against the oppressive darkness, as though entropy itself had sculpted a landscape of madness from the ruins of a bygone era.

It felt as though we had stumbled upon a place of eternal damnation. Despite the creeping terror that threatened to paralyze us, a perverse curiosity drove us onward, deeper into this forsaken underworld. Each step felt like a betrayal of our survival instincts, yet the allure of the unknown held us captive, a twisted magnetism pulling us inexorably downward.

My injured hand hung limply by my side, the pain a constant, gnawing companion, infection threatening to end me quicker than the perils that lay ahead of us.

Each footfall grew my sense of unease. The atmosphere conspired against us, its malevolence dragging us further into the depths of a nightmarish abyss.

As we pressed forward, shadows danced and writhed within the feeble illumination of the strange, orange light, their movements fluid and sinister. My breath caught in my throat as I froze, a whisper escaping my lips.

"Chris," I whispered, barely audible, "we're not alone."

"Looks like we've found the people," Christopher responded, his eyes wide with dread.

Slowly, figures emerged from the darkness, their forms distorted by layers of grime and decay. Tattered rags and mismatched clothing hung from their emaciated frames, offering scant protection against the chill. They moved like specters, a zombie apocalypse, their gaunt faces etched with suffering and fear. Some huddled around the fires, their eyes hollow and distant, lost in the flickering flames. Others prowled the edges of the cavern, their movements predatory and furtive, more beast than human. Some quietly picked up makeshift weapons—rusty pipes, broken bottles, and shards of metal—their eyes set on us, while others simply sat in silence, their motionless gazes fixed on some distant, unfathomable point.

They took in Christopher and me with a mix of hunger and suspicion, their movements slow and deliberate as if any sudden action might shatter the fragile equilibrium of their existence.

Amidst this tableau of desolation, a few structures stood out. A gazebo, reinforced with scavenged steel beams and adorned with a tattered banner, seemed to serve as a gathering place. Nearby, a series of cages fashioned from rebar and chain-link fencing hinted at a darker purpose, their interiors stained with old blood and lined with the remains of previous occupants.

Despite the apparent chaos, there was a perverse order here, a hierarchy dictated by strength and survival. The denizens moved with wary awareness, their interactions marked by a tense, almost animalistic undercurrent. Trust seemed like a rare commodity, replaced by constant vigilance born of necessity.

The inhabitants moved with savage grace, their eyes watching, wary, following our every move, oppressive, reminding us of the lurking dangers.

They were a motley assembly of the lost, the condemned, each bearing the scars of the private hell that brought them to this village of the damned. They clung to a semblance of society, trading in whispers and bartered goods, yet suspicion and paranoia tainted every interaction. Camaraderie was a fragile veneer, masking the ever-present fear that gnawed at their souls.

Children, too, were part of this grim tableau, their wide eyes reflecting a world of horrors they should never have had to be part of. They played with makeshift toys—broken dolls and rusted cans—within the protective circles of their families, their laughter a dissonant note in the symphony of misery.

I paused momentarily, lost in the children innocence a gift that would be taken from them slowly, unknowingly, a fragility that would eventually absent itself in this world. In any world. These were the children of the damned.

THE CEILING of the cavern dripped with moisture from some unseen underground river, the occasional drop echoing through the oppressive silence. As Christopher and I navigated this nightmarish landscape, the true horror of our situation became painfully clear. We were intruders in a realm where humanity had been twisted and broken, where the veneer of civilization had been stripped away to reveal the raw, brutal struggle for survival.

More denizens of this makeshift underworld emerged from the shadows, their gaunt faces etched with torment and despair. The earth quivered under the weight of their collective misery. Their hollow gazes, devoid of light or hope, spoke volumes of the torment that gnawed at their souls, a relentless predator stalking its prey.

Clustered in hushed circles, their conversations were fraught with a palpable unease. I couldn't shake the curiosity about the secrets they hoarded, the horrors they bore witness to in the bowels of this subterranean maze. Did they cling to each other out of genuine camaraderie, or was their unity a fragile mask for their own festering fears and insecurities? Suspicion hung heavy in the air, infecting every glance with latent dread.

Beneath the veneer of normalcy they clung to lay the shadows of their deepest desires and darkest terrors, a poison slowly corroding their souls from within. In this underground realm, where reality and nightmare danced in a macabre waltz, denizens existed in a perpetual state of disquiet, casting a pall of foreboding over the murky depths of the sewers.

Christopher's grip on my arm tightened, his nails digging into my flesh in a silent plea for reassurance. His trembling hand mirrored the terror that pulsed through us both. In that instant, I realized the extent of our mutual dependence in this desperate struggle for survival.

"We should get out of here," he whispered urgently, his voice barely audible, raspy in its attempt to express itself through the lack of clean air.

Yet, retreat was not an option. We had no other choice but forward. The familiar cadence of our pursuers' clinking chains was drawing closer, as relentless as the miserable fate of these under-ground dwellers.

The dim light caught the sweat on Christopher's brow, making it glisten, cold fear that oozed from his pores.

"Shit, how are they keeping up with us?" he muttered, urgency lacing his words. His voice seemed to bounce off the walls, distorted and eerie.

"Fucking track stars…" I quipped, shaken. "We gotta find a way to shake 'em loose."

With a silent agreement, we broke into a frantic run. Adrenaline pushed us, our breaths harsh and ragged. Each step felt like a gamble, each turn a potential dead end or our end.

The labyrinthine corridors twisted and turned, an endless maze designed to break the spirit. The echo of chains grew louder, a sinister soundtrack to our flight. The world around us felt surreal, like a nightmare we couldn't wake from. The oppressive atmosphere, the sense of being hunted, the looming dread – it all melded into a terrifying reality.

Erratically, we slipped into the village. We navigated past makeshift structures, praying to blend into the shadows. The inhabitants' gazes pierced through the dimness, eyes glinting with a hunger that transcended mere sustenance. It was a hunger birthed from something darker and more insidious, a void gnawing at their souls. I shuddered under their scrutiny, each glance a chilling reminder of the unseen dangers lurking in the darkness, ready to ensnare the unsuspecting.

They were survivors in the truest sense, bearing scars and fractures from a world that had long forsaken them. Their presence, a haunting echo of desperation, permeated the labyrinthine passages.

"Do you think these people are dangerous?" Christopher's voice sliced through the oppressive silence, his words laced with a mix of curiosity and unease.

I glanced around nervously, the flickering light casting eerie shadows on the jagged walls. "I'm not sure," I whispered, my voice barely audible. "They seem desperate, but not necessarily hostile."

Christopher's grip on my arm tightened, his eyes darting from one huddled figure to another. "Look," he pointed quietly, "some of them might be among the missing. Do you think they're trapped down here too?"

Following his gaze, I observed the worn faces and tattered clothing of the inhabitants. Some sat silently by smoldering fires, their gaunt frames illuminated by the weak glow. Others paced with restless energy, their vacant eyes holding untold stories as deep and twisted as the tunnels around us.

"Maybe they're just trying to survive," I suggested, torn between fear and empathy. "Like us."

Christopher swallowed hard, the air thick with the scent of decay and distant, indistinct whispers. "Or maybe," he ventured softly, "They're with Darren and Misha." His expression darkened, a blend of concern and determination flickering in his eyes.

"Either way, we can't stay here," I declared firmly. "Let's keep moving, but stay alert."

THE TWISTED STREETS seemed to pulse with a life of their own, each turn pulling us deeper into the underbelly of forgotten souls. Uncertainty gnawed at my gut, a persistent itch that couldn't be scratched. These people, these shadows, were they victims of circumstance, or had they become something darker in the sewers' depths? The missing persons posters danced in my mind, specters of a world above that had long since abandoned them.

The inhabitants moved like wary ghosts, their eyes gleaming with a feral mix of survival instinct and curiosity. Some slipped back into the shadows at our approach, while others held their ground, defiance flickering in their eyes, dying embers that sought purchase to remain human. The air was thick with a palpable tension, a silence that felt ready to shatter at the slightest provocation.

And shatter it did. A guttural cry tore through the oppressive quiet, echoing off the cavernous walls. Huddling behind a structure, we froze, hearts pounding, as the sound drew our eyes toward a distant fire's flickering light. There, in the glow, a horrifying spectacle unfolded.

A figure, once human but now a grotesque mockery of life, writhed in agony at the center of a frenzied mob before the gazebo. His body was a canvas of twisted scars, a testament to unspeakable pain.

From the crowd, a familiar laugh cut through the chaos, seething with cruel amusement. Darren stepped forward and onto the platform, his demeanor a blend of charismatic menace and calculating authority. His eyes surveyed the scene with a cold, amused detachment before he began to speak.

"Well, well, look at this," Darren's voice rang out, smooth and dripping with mockery. The mob fell silent, their attention fixed on him. "Seems like we're hosting quite the little send-off party. Don't you just love the atmosphere? It's so... *festive.*"

He gestured lazily at the pleading man, a smirk playing at the corners of his lips. "This poor soul thought he could stick around and still be a player in our grand game. But, as you can see, he's become a bit of a relic. Time for a little... *renovation* of our roster."

Darren's gaze swept over the crowd, his tone growing darker, almost playful. "I gathered each of you here for a reason. Society discarded you, didn't it? The rejects. The outcasts. The lost. I hand-picked you, showed you the ropes, the real deal. You've endured the grind, the pain, the so-called *transformation.* Kudos to you. But here's the kicker: in our world, the rules are brutally simple. The strong seize what they want, and the weak? They become a cautionary tale. And this guy here? He's just the latest exhibit in our little *gallery* of lessons."

Misha stepped forward to join him, Darren's voice dropping to a conspiratorial whisper. "Misha, darling, care to demonstrate what happens when someone's time is up? Let's give them a proper show, shall we?"

Turning back to the crowd, Darren's smile widened, his eyes gleaming with cold amusement. "Remember, in our world, hesitation is a luxury none of us can afford. You either adapt, or you become history. This poor guy," he pointed at the man, "he's not just a reminder; he's a living, breathing example of what happens when you're no longer in the game. Consider it a *public service announcement.*"

With that, Darren faded back into the shadows, his presence lingering like a dark promise. Misha's smile grew as she returned her focus to the broken man at her feet.

"Please, please! What did I do?" He groveled. "Whatever it is, I'll make it right! I can still change! The—the pain! It's getting better, I swear!" His voice was a desperate plea, each word dripping with raw terror.

"Oh, sweetheart," Misha cooed, her tone dripping with mock sympathy, "I'm afraid you're just not on my list anymore. Why keep one servant when I've got two more lined up?" Her laughter was a sharp, cutting melody, slicing through any shred of hope the man might have clung to.

"But I've done everything you asked!" he continued, his shackled arms shaking as he raised them in a futile gesture of supplication. "Please, Michelle, I've always loved you! Even before all this—I had your posters in my room! I admired your every runway—"

"Shush now," Misha interrupted, her voice a smooth but chilling purr. "That woman you adored? She's gone, my dear. She was a fleeting shadow, a whisper in the wind. I am Misha—reborn, beyond your pitiful adoration."

The man's pleas dissolved into whimpers, his face a river of tears as Christopher and I stood frozen, a cocktail of dread and disbelief churning within us. "Please... don't do this. Why settle for two servants when you could have three?"

Misha's voice dripped with mockery, each word a poisoned drop of delight. "Aw, I'm sorry, doll. But three's a crowd. We wouldn't want to overload our little entourage, would we?"

In a frantic gesture, he clung to her feet, desperation etched into every line of his face. "Enough!" Misha's voice thundered, slicing through the tension with brutal finality. With a single, elegant flick of her boot, she sent him sprawling into the crowd of townsfolk gathered below the gazebo. Her laughter echoed like a dark symphony against the stone walls, a chilling refrain.

"Citizens of Tartarus," she drawled, her voice a languid caress of cruelty, "show your devotion to your Masters. You know what must be done." With a casual snap of her fingers, she sealed his fate, the finality of her gesture like the closing of a heavy velvet curtain on a grim spectacle.

The townsfolk, their faces twisted in a grotesque mask of fear and fury, shared a look of hesitant determination before closing in on the unfortunate soul. The scene was a macabre ballet of desperation and doom, a dark dance in the heart of this forsaken place.

Without warning, they descended upon the figure with savage intensity, tearing at flesh and bone with primal ferocity. Limbs were rent from the body, blood spraying in gruesome arcs as screams pierced the air like knives.

"Fuck!" I gasped, my voice barely audible, my breath ragged with shock.

"Well, there's our answer," Chris replied, his tone heavy with resignation.

"Those sick bastards probably tore through the gang..." I continued, my voice sounding foreign in my ears, like an echo from a nightmare.

"Still think these 'missing people' are worth saving?" Chris asked rhetorically.

We stood paralyzed, the chill of horror seeping into our bones as we witnessed the grotesque display unravel before us. The mob's frenzy was a primal roar, a savage tide of elementary instincts unleashed in this forsaken hole. It was a grotesque display of violence, a stark testament to the abyss that churned within the souls of those who called this subterranean realm their home.

As the last echoes of the victim's agonized cries faded into the oppressive gloom, Misha emerged from her shadowed position beneath the decaying gazebo. Her gaze lingered on the mutilated body, a serpentine smile curling at her lips. "How utterly delightful," she purred, her voice a venomous whisper, before she vanished into the darkness, her form slipping away like a wraith.

"Quick, now's our chance," Christopher ordered urgently. "We don't want to be next."

Turning alongside him, my breath caught as my foot collided with a loose stone, sending it skittering across the uneven ground. Heads turned sharply towards the noise, eyes gleaming with a mixture of curiosity and menace, locking onto ours. In that instant, I knew we were no longer mere observers but unwitting participants in this grim theater of desperation and despair.

Christopher's grip tightened on my arm, his voice barely above a whisper. "We have to go," he urged, eyes darting nervously between the silent figures now advancing towards us. "Now!"

Bolting, Christopher and I squeezed through a narrow path between the makeshift structures, our breath echoing the frenetic rhythm of our hearts. But before we could react, a mass of the city's inhabitants blocked our path, their forms shifting like shadows in the dim light.

"Shit," Christopher muttered under his breath, his voice a strained whisper. "We mean no harm," he called out, the words hanging in the air like fragile threads. "We're just passing through."

A low murmur rippled through the crowd, a chorus of indistinct whispers laden with skepticism and suspicion. Faces emerged from the darkness, their features hard and unyielding, yet momentarily softened by the plea in Christopher's voice.

"We're lost," I added quietly, my voice trembling. "Can you help us find a way out?"

Silence greeted our request, broken only by the occasional drip of water from the ceiling, each drop a countdown to an uncertain fate. The tension was palpable, a fragile balance between wary acceptance and imminent danger.

In the bowels of the earth, where darkness reigned like a malevolent king, a harsh, guttural voice erupted, shattering the oppressive silence. The sound sent shivers racing down our spines, as if the very air itself recoiled at the intrusion.

"He bears the scars," it hissed, each syllable dripping with menace, clawing at our nerves. The cavern walls, mute witnesses to this macabre scene, amplified the words, turning them into a sinister symphony.

"He's begun the transformation," murmured another voice from the depths, each word a venomous whisper hanging heavy in the stale air. Slowly, like specters materializing from the abyss, they closed in on us, their intentions shrouded in obscurity.

"They both have," another voice echoed, each word a dagger in the darkness. Figures emerged, their forms wreathed in shadow, moving with an eerie, predatory grace.

"Darren will be pleased," a woman's voice slithered through the gloom, her words like a serpent's tongue. We stood transfixed, our hearts pounding in a frantic rhythm as the realization of our predicament dawned upon us.

Images of past encounters flashed through my mind—each one a grim reminder of our vulnerability in this subterranean realm. I recalled the stories my dad used to tell, horrific tales of battle scenes from Vietnam. Fire. Blood. Ruined cities. Corpses. Those tales now felt like prophetic warnings, echoing in the recesses of my mind as we stood surrounded by living shadows whose minds had been turned. It was clear these beings had no intention of letting us leave unscathed.

As the voices reverberated through the chamber, their source remained shrouded in an unsettling veil of uncertainty. Whispers floated through the air, ethereal and disjointed, like fragments of a forgotten dream. Christopher and I exchanged anxious glances, our senses straining to discern the direction of the murmurs.

"Please," Christopher's voice echoed off the cavern walls, a fragile thread of desperation laced with fear. "We don't want trouble. We just need to get out of here." But our pleas were met with an unyielding silence, the inhabitants' faces devoid of mercy, their expressions carved from stone by some malevolent force that chilled me to the core. They moved like marionettes in a grim puppet show, controlled by invisible strings, leaving us trapped in a living nightmare.

A low, guttural chuckle sliced through the silence, its sinister echo sending shivers down my spine. "Out?" came the mocking reply, dripping with contempt. "You can't leave."

"You belong to us now."

"We must show you our gift."

"Don't be afraid."

"We must complete your transformation."

I glanced at Christopher, our shared apprehension tightening around us like a vice. Cold dread settled in my stomach. We were ensnared, both physically and metaphorically, caught in a web of fate that underscored the fragility of our reality, teetering on the brink of shattering.

"Think we can take them?" I whispered to Christopher, my voice barely audible over the chorus of murmurs. But I knew escape was a distant dream. The town and its labyrinthine tunnels were designed to trap.

Christopher's expression mirrored my unease as he surveyed our surroundings. "Stay close," he urged, his voice trembling with a mix of fear and resolve. "We'll find a way out, no matter what." Yet, as the darkness closed in around us, I feared we were already too late.

CHAPTER 13

STYX

AS THE METAPHORICAL clock's hands lurched forward, each tick seemed to stretch into eternity, and shadows crawled in, serpentine and sinister, tightening around us like a noose. The townsfolk, grotesque and warped, gathered like a twisted carnival of the damned, their presence a mockery of humanity itself. Their stench— a vile mélange of rot and decay—assaulted my senses, an olfactory assault that clawed at my throat, while the rasping symphony of their breath wove a discordant, unsettling melody that moved my nerves erratically.

"On the count of three!" Christopher's voice sliced through the chilling silence, sharp and insistent.

"I... Chris, they're victims too! Brainwashed, maybe—" My voice cracked, betraying my internal struggle.

Their faces, twisted and grotesque, sported grins as jagged as shattered glass, revealing uneven rows of razor-sharp teeth. Cold sweat trickled down my spine as their clammy, predatory hands reached out.

"Their faces, their hands... There's no reasoning with this, Jason!" Christopher's voice was urgent, slicing through the oppressive gloom. "You saw what they did— It's us or them! We have to fight!"

A chill of dread wormed into my bones, every instinct screaming for escape. But we were ensnared, back to back, caught in a futile dance with something so bizarre there was no reckoning.

Unlike Misha and Darren, these figures bore no grotesque piercings. Their scars and wounds told tales of their own suffering, a silent testament to their torment. Christopher and I tightened our grips, fists clenched in futile preparation for the inevitable clash. *There were too many.*

"Damn it, Chris. This isn't right!" My voice trembled, swallowed by the frenzy of the moment.

Their grimy hands were like creeping shadows, dragging at our clothes, their touch a stinging reminder of our grim reality. I felt Christopher's heartbeat thundering against my back—a wild, unrestrained rhythm that seemed to synchronize with my own. Every nerve in me screamed to surrender, to let the enveloping darkness snuff out our fight. But beneath that fear, a fierce ember of defiance flared up—an instinct to claw our way out of this nightmare. Our story would not end here. I glanced back at Christopher, and saw the same stark terror in his eyes, but behind it, an unbreakable resolve. We weren't just battling for survival; we were defying the sinister malevolence that trapped and destroyed lives.

"Fuck it! Three!" I roared, anger crystallizing into a weapon as we wrestled against the writhing mass. Christopher and I were engulfed in a maelstrom of raw adrenaline, our movements raw and primal, Viking berserkers immune to pain, ancient warriors wrestling with the resurrected dead.

With a savage shove, I sent a grotesque figure crashing into a dilapidated shelter, the structure cracking and collapsing, entombing the monstrosity beneath the wreckage. My fingers, raw and splintering, gripped a jagged plank, wielding it with manic energy. Beside me, Christopher matched my frenzy, his strikes a chaotic symphony of controlled rage.

The townsfolk surged forward, their aggression feverish. Their nails were like sharpened razors, ripping through our clothes and drawing blood with each frenzied swipe. I ducked a wild swing and felt the rush of air as it narrowly missed my face. Christopher grunted beside me, engaged in his own brutal skirmish. The townsfolk pressed in, their twisted faces a mask of deranged fervor that froze my blood.

"Come on! Push through!" My voice cut through the din, raw and desperate. We fought like cornered animals. I kicked one attacker away, only to face another, its teeth bared, eyes wild with a hunger that was almost palpable.

We were swamped, encircled by a mass of twisted figures driven by an insatiable hunger. With each passing second, their assault grew more frenzied, their attempts to grab us more violent.

Together, we carved through the throng, each strike a desperate plea to regain the lives we once hated. Yet for every foe we felled, it felt as though ten more sprang from the shadows, relentless in their pursuit. Our struggle seemed as futile as trying to halt the inexorable march of time itself.

In the midst of the chaos, a fleeting glimmer of hope appeared—a fragile thread in the encroaching gloom. "Jason! Over here!" Christopher's voice sliced through the clamor, urgent and sharp. I didn't hesitate, following his lead as our footsteps pounded through the labyrinth of crumbling remnants, the echoes of our pursuers a ghostly chorus behind us.

We raced through the ruins, the darkness swallowing us whole as we reached the end of the chamber. The air was thick with foreboding, shadows lurking like ancient sentinels. The skeletal remains of buildings loomed over us, their empty shelters gaping like the hollow eyes of forgotten gods.

As we reached the chamber's end, no escape lay before us; we found ourselves cornered against an unforgiving wall of concrete, the mob closing in with a hunger that promised nothing but oblivion.

"Hold this!" I barked at Christopher, my voice jagged with panic as the horde pressed in. My hand screamed in agony.

"Got a plan, hotshot?" Christopher's disbelief cut through the chaos, but he swung the makeshift weapon with grim resolve. The creatures, undeterred, closed in on us like a tide of shadow.

In the midst of the madness, I strained my voice, barely recognizable as I screamed, "Doing my best!" My fingers, trembling with a mix of dread and determination, clawed at my shirt, tearing fabric in a frantic bid for survival.

"Quick, give it back!" My voice splintered with urgency as I begged Christopher. His hands moved with frantic precision, tossing the plank back to me. I fumbled with the cloth, binding it around the makeshift weapon. The fire nearby flared, its hungry flames licking up the fabric with a violent, hissing roar. "Stay back!" I howled, wielding the fiery torch like a beacon of defiance. The pain in my hand intensified, blood seeping from fresh cuts as I gripped the torch tightly, the flames a cruel mockery of warmth in the encroaching darkness. "Get the fuck back!"

For a brief moment, the townsfolk hesitated, their advance faltering under the harsh light. But the pause was fleeting; they surged forward, driven by an insatiable primitive need. I swung the torch with desperate force and caught their tattered rags, thick with oily human filth. The flames flared instantly, like throwing kerosene on a cooking fire. They were dressed in layers against the damp and cold; there was no way to tear the fabric from their bodies. They groped and pulled, their hands burning. The acrid stench of blistering flesh sliced through the air—a visceral reminder of our desperate plight.

Their screams, a horrific symphony, echoed through the dark, twisted cavern. I clenched my teeth, struggling to suppress the sickening realization that we had become monsters ourselves.

Amidst their suffering, their faces twisted into grotesque masks of pleasure and pain—a perverse blend of agony and ecstasy for the dark freedom awaited them. A wave of guilt crashed over me, knowing they were mere pawns in Darren's nightmarish game, now deformed beyond recognition.

"Fuck, Jason!" Christopher's voice cracked into raw fragments, caught between disbelief and revulsion. His eyes, wide as saucers, mirrored the grotesque ballet of the flames, a nightmarish choreography that played out in our desperate reality.

In the fractured light of the chamber, they twisted like grotesque phantoms, their writhing forms almost sentient as they closed in.

"Like I had a choice!" My retort sliced through the thick, smoldering tension, its bite swallowed by the relentless crackle of the fire —a chaotic reflection of my own fury.

From the choking darkness emerged still more. I swung the torch with a heavy heart, the fire's hungry maw consuming them with a savage greed. Their screams merged into the chamber's cacophony, an eerie symphony of torment that seemed to bleed from the very stone.

The chamber glowed with the inferno's grotesque beauty, each flicker of flame taunting our enemies' faltering resolve. Yet they pressed on, their thirst for suffering unquenched. Christopher's voice trembled, betraying the terror that tightened around us like a noose.

"They feed on pain— they're conditioned for this! What's our move? We can't fight them all!" His words choked on the smoke, dripping with the weight of our desperation.

I scanned the chamber's dim confines, eyes catching on a slender, elusive glimmer—a tunnel, a fleeting promise of escape amidst the darkness. "There!" My voice cut through the chaos, pointing at our sliver of salvation in the twisted labyrinth. "We make a break for it!"

Christopher's eyes locked onto the tunnel, a silent understanding passing between us. We committed to our last desperate gamble. Each swing of my torch grew wilder, a futile defense against the encroaching dark. As the flame sputtered, casting ghoulish shadows on the walls, panic gnawed at me. "Shit, it's almost out," I muttered, heart racing as I desperately swung the torch, each motion a frantic fight against the swallowing void.

Hesitation clawed at me, my grip on the torch white-knuckled. Letting go of the last flicker of light felt like abandoning our tether to sanity in a world unraveling into madness. With a resigned breath, I knew the end was near. The weight of the lives extinguished by my hand pressed heavily on my soul, a burden that would not lift. I hurled the dying torch to the ground with one final, frantic swing. Its embers sputtered and gasped before being devoured by the abyss.

In that instant, it was more than just light I relinquished—it was our last vestige of sanity in a mad world.

With a heart heavy and resolve forged in desperation, I turned from the dwindling flame, haunted by the flickering images of those we couldn't save. Christopher's hand on my shoulder was a meager comfort; we had crossed a line that blurred the edges of right and wrong. But there was no time for contemplation or atonement or the higher attributes of compassion and empathy. Not now. Not here.

We surged toward the narrow passage, our breaths ragged, racing against the mob that moved tentatively as one. They now seemed hesitant to leave their sanctuary, as though leaving would cause some sort of eternal shift. Salvation flickered ahead, a fragile hope that I dared to believe in. Each step thundered in my ears, drowning out the haunting echoes of the townsfolk's twisted cries.

Then, a voice cut through the chaos with a chilling familiarity. "Let them go!" Darren's words slid through the air, smooth and menacing, like a serpent's whisper. There was a dark, almost hypnotic quality to his tone, making the fear of the townsfolk seem inconsequential. I glanced back to see his smirk, his eyes glinting with a dangerous amusement. "You can't run from what's coming, Jason," he taunted, his voice dripping with a malevolent pleasure. The terror on the townsfolk's faces mirrored the dark fate that awaited us. With one last, defiant glance at the burning town, we pressed on, determined to escape, leaving behind the village and its nightmares in a swirl of smoke and ash.

CHAPTER 14
DEPTHS OF DESPAIR

THE SEWER'S darkness swallowed us whole, a living, breathing entity that pressed down with a suffocating weight. The air was heavy with the acrid bite of ash and decay, a sickly-sweet odor that mingled with the filthy water splashing around our shoes and the monotonous drip-drip that seemed to taunt us.

Chris and I stumbled through the muck, squelching through murky puddles that whispered secrets to the slick, grimy walls. Time felt warped, an endless stretch of shadows and grime.

When we finally slowed, it was like hitting a wall of silence. Our breaths came in ragged gasps, the weight of the oppressive stillness nearly crushing us. Darren was somewhere, as he always was. But when and where he would decide to grace us again was the real terror.

"I need to stop," Chris panted, his voice a hoarse whisper.

I nodded, leaning my back against the damp wall, its coldness seeping through my clothes. My hand ached fiercely, the pain sharp and persistent. I glanced down, watching blood seep from the torn webbing between my fingers, mingling with the sludge. *It shouldn't hurt this much...* but the pain gnawed at me, a reminder of a vulnerability I couldn't afford to have. "I mean– it feels... safe enough." I muttered, the words ragged and breathless. "How're you holding up?"

The silence wrapped around us like a shroud, thick and heavy. The only sound was the distant, persistent drip of water. There were no echoes of pursuit, no disturbing noises from the dark. Just the harsh reality of our own uneven breaths.

"I just need a second," Chris said, his voice trembling as the adrenaline began to drain, leaving him hollow and exhausted.

"I get it," I said, trying to steady myself against the wall. "This whole thing... it's unreal."

Chris's breath hitched, a raw, broken sound escaping him. "I can't stop thinking about Nicole," he choked out, his voice cracking. Tears streaked down his face, mingling with the grime, his shoulders shaking with silent grief. "Her laugh, the way she'd tease me... those moments cut deeper than the pain." He slumped against the wall, gasping for air in the crushing darkness. "She was everything... I can still feel her warmth slipping away." His voice broke into a sob, lost in the suffocating darkness.

My heart twisted, feeling the echo of his pain and my own buried sorrow. Memories of my father's sudden absence surged, a cruel reminder of my own grief. My hand throbbed sharply, each heartbeat intensifying the pain. I clenched my fist, trying to ignore the blood seeping through my fingers. Like my father's illness, it was something I couldn't ignore, but now wasn't the time. "I'm sorry, Chris. I wish there was more we could do—"

"Don't be. We'll find a way out of here," Chris stiffened, trying to regain his composure. His eyes searched the void, clinging to a fragile hope.

My voice cracked as I fought to find comfort in my words. "I'm here, Chris," I whispered, the lump in my throat almost choking me. "We'll get through this."

In that fleeting moment of silence, our shared pain became a palpable force, a dark bond forged in the shadows. The damp walls seemed to absorb our unspoken fears and regrets, creating a fragile sanctuary amidst the chaos.

What I don't understand is why we're not seeing any manhole covers or sewer along the way. Chris slouched against the wall, his frame a marionette tangled in strings of sorrow and defeat. His breath hitched, a quicksilver flash of pain rippling through him. Fists clenched, he fought the tidal wave of grief that threatened to drown him. After an eternity of unspoken words, his voice emerged, raw and unpolished. "My dad... he was killed a few years back. Shot. A junkie wandered into his shop, desperate, wired on something—my dad tried to help him."

His eyes locked on some distant, invisible horizon, as if bracing for another blow. "Then the guy pulled a gun. No warning. Just a flash of metal, a burst of sound. My dad... didn't even get a chance."

The revelation struck me like a hammer, sending tremors through the dim, claustrophobic space. The darkness seemed to coil tighter around us. "I'm so sorry, Chris," I murmured, my voice barely a whisper, struggling to anchor myself in the gravity of his words.

"Yeah," Chris said, his voice trailing off into the void. "Nicole used to say he was 'too trusting for his own good.' When things got worse, when I thought I was at the end of my rope, she was my tether."

A jolt of empathy surged through me, piercing the gloom. Chris's eyes, haunted yet unyielding, spoke of a bond forged in the fires of loss. "She was something else..." I said, my voice soft, reverent. "I keep remembering her laughing, hanging the window of my car. Feels like we've been through this forever. Probably a stupid question, but she was older than you, right?"

Chris nodded, a slow, measured movement that seemed to drag through the sludge of memory. "Yeah, she was. And now... I'm lost. Don't know what I'll do without her."

"Don't sweat the details now. We'll figure it out," I said, trying to pierce through the fog of uncertainty that choked us both. "We're still breathing, and that's something. When we get out of here, maybe I'll just drive us back to NYC, make a clean break."

A shadow of a smile crossed Chris's face, but it was fragile, fractured by the reality pressing in around him. "Thanks, Jason," he whispered, his voice a thread of sound in the oppressive silence. His hand gripped my shoulder, a silent plea for solace in our shared desolation.

"Don't mention it, man. As my dad used to say, 'nothing binds people like a common enemy.'" I met Chris's gaze, my voice dry, attempting to mask the tremor beneath.

Chris's eyes flickered, a hint of recognition sparking in their depths. "You said he got sick, right?"

I drew a shuddering breath. "His name was Jim," I began, each syllable dragging behind it a freight of grief. "Stomach cancer... aggressive as hell. I don't know if it was his pride or—" My voice faltered, tangled in the web of memories. "I never got to say goodbye," I admitted, the words barely escaping, laden with a suffocating regret. "One day he was there, and then... he was just gone."

Chris's expression softened, a quiet empathy washing over his face. In that dark space, our shared agony became a peculiar comfort, a shadowy pleasure in the knowledge that we were not suffering alone. "That sounds rough."

"It was," I murmured, my voice trembling on the brink of silence. "But it was more than just losing him. We... had a fight before he died. He kept his illness a secret. And then he vanished, and I was left with a hollow space where an apology should have been."

"I'm sorry, Jason," Chris said softly, his voice thick with shared sorrow. His hand found mine in the dim light, a muted promise of solidarity.

"I can't escape the regret, Chris. The arguments, the harsh words... I thought there'd be time to mend things. Time to heal, to forgive, to find where pain ends and peace begins." My voice broke under the weight of regret. "But truth is, I was never enough for him."

Chris's eyes, clouded with empathy, shimmered with something like disbelief. "Nah, that can't be true. You're like, the wonder kid."

I managed a rueful chuckle. "Yeah? Well, believe it. There was this one time in high school... He came to all my practices. I fumbled the ball, and he stormed down from the bleachers, in front of everyone—the parents, the team, my coaches. He shoved me, said he 'didn't raise a pansy' and that I was an embarrassment. It was like he couldn't stand who I was. After that, he never came around again. I hoped it was because he was afraid of what people would think, but I knew better. The truth was, he just didn't want to see me. I was never enough." My emotions bubbled over, mixing with the sweat and ash on my face.

"Now, being back in California, every memory of him is like a ghost, a reminder of missed chances, conversations left unfinished. It's like he's haunting me."

Chris squeezed my hand, his grip shaky as he locked eyes with me. "It's okay to feel that way. It's okay to be angry, sad, confused. You don't have to go through it alone."

"He had this vision for me," I continued, feeling the crushing weight of my father's unfulfilled dreams. "He wanted me to follow his path, become an engineer, live a stable life. His dreams were both my burden and my guide. Choosing architecture felt like betrayal."

Chris's eyes reflected a deep understanding. "Sounds like a dad."

"Yeah," I admitted. "That argument... He couldn't grasp why I wanted something different, something... creative. To him, it was a waste of time and money. It seems so stupid now." I turned away, the past closing in on me in a way that left me feeling defeated.

Chris nodded, our bond solidifying with each shared revelation. "He wanted what he thought was best for you."

"Maybe," I murmured, a pang of sorrow gripping my chest. "I lashed out at him. Told him it wasn't just about money. I wanted to make a difference. Architecture, for godsakes. But he couldn't see it. He passed away soon after, and I never got to set things right. Not that I would have changed my mind, but I just wanted him to see some value in what I wanted to do." My voice hitched and I paused. "To see some value in me."

Chris's hand rested on my shoulder. "You can't blame yourself,

Jason. He behaved like an asshole, but he was probably just trying to protect you, in his own messed-up way."

I looked at him, gratitude and sorrow mingling in my eyes. "I appreciate you, Chris," I whispered, the weight of isolation lifting slightly. "Feels like no one really listens anymore. It's always 'party boy Jason,' and nothing more. My girlfriend's great, but even she seems weary of my baggage. Sometimes I wonder if we're only together just because we look good on paper."

Chris nodded, his expression resolute. "We'll get through this, Jason," he said firmly, desperation tinging his voice. "I don't know how to do this without Nicole." His eyes glistened with unshed tears. "But with you... I think I can find a way."

A shadow of a smile crossed my lips, the connection between us solidifying in the mire of our shared suffering. "I feel the same."

Chris's sigh was a heavy exhalation, his posture slumping in the dim light. "Her and I... It's just that we've been through hell together, Jason," he confessed, emotion thick and raw. "She's the reason I'm still breathing. We wanted out of our messed-up lives. Never thought it would lead to... *this*." His gesture encompassed the dank, oppressive walls around us.

He paused, his brow furrowing in deep thought. "Just between us," he said slowly, resignation coloring his tone, "I never truly believed we'd escape. But... I dreamed about it. Dreamed of a life where we could be free, where we could just... be." He sighed deeply. "I just hope we can make it."

Christopher's eyes glazed with distant memories as he retrieved a worn, duct-taped wallet from his pocket. He extracted a folded photograph with meticulous care. It was a filmstrip of him and Nicole, captured in a booth's flickering light. They looked carefree, their faces illuminated with playful joy—Nicole giving the camera a rebellious gesture, their lips meeting in a tender kiss.

The darkness of the sewer pressed in on us, dense and heavy with grief. Every drop of water was a mournful note in the symphony of our despair. In the depths of that darkness, a malevolent pulse still throbbed, and we knew the shadows could burst at any moment with the real live villains, still out there, who would kill us as soon as look at us.

"I already miss her so damn much, Jason," Chris choked out, tears shimmering in his eyes. "It feels like a piece of me is missing... Her laugh, her voice—it's all I see and hear in this hellhole. She believed in me when no one else did, pushed me to be better, to dream bigger." His voice cracked with raw emotion. "And now... she's gone. It's tearing me apart."

A shiver slithered down my spine as I recalled the grim discovery. The blood trail beneath the manhole cover, Nicole's earring catching the dim light... It was all becoming too much. "We're getting out of here, Chris. For Nicole, for our dads, for everyone we've lost. They deserve for us to make it through this. We'll honor their memories," I vowed, still gripping Chris's hand in solidarity. "Their spirits won't die here with us."

Chris nodded, determination carving lines into his features as he peered into the dim, winding passage ahead. He carefully returned the photograph to his wallet, handling it as if it were a fragile relic. "I used to lean on her strength," he admitted. "She was the anchor, the one with the plans and the hope. Without her... I feel adrift. I promised her we'd make it, but without her... I feel lost."

Leaning against the damp wall, I breathed into the encroaching cold. "Kim had this little coffee shop she adored on 3rd Ave," I interjected, memories flickering like restless ghosts. "We'd sit for hours, trying every exotic latte they had. She found joy in the smallest things, made every day an adventure. I miss those moments... they feel so... distant... now. Almost like they never happened."

A fleeting sadness brushed across Chris's face, his lips curling into a melancholic arc. "Nicole had a thing for old diners," he murmured, nostalgia hanging in his tone. "She loved the 'vintage charm,' the feeling of stepping back in time. We used to plan road trips just to visit them."

A soft chuckle escaped me, laced with a bittersweet edge.

"That's... kind of funny," I mused. "It must've been hard for her to protest against me dragging you guys to one. Kim would've clicked with her instantly. Nicole's definitely her kind of girl."

Chris's gaze met mine, curiosity igniting in his eyes like a smoldering ember. "What's she like?" he asked, the glimmer of intrigue cutting through the darkness.

I inhaled deeply, struggling to encapsulate Kim's essence in words. "Kim... she's something else," I began, my voice cracking under the strain of buried emotions. "Her strength—it feels almost supernatural. I carry this gnawing guilt. She's always stood by me, weathered every storm."

Chris leaned closer, his whisper slicing through the heavy silence like a cold draft. "Do you think she's still worrying about you?" His concern mirrored mine, a reflection of our intertwined fates.

I nodded, a wry smirk barely touching my lips. "For all she knows, I'm a ghost. Between her and my mom, I wouldn't be surprised if the National Guard's on alert. Maybe I'm already on one of those 'Missing Persons' billboards." I exhaled slowly, memories of Mike Carnegie bleeding into my thoughts. "Yeah, they're probably losing their minds. But Kim's tough. She'll handle it." My voice steadied, a steel edge of resolve sharpening my words.

A fleeting smile touched Chris's lips, a fragile echo of warmth amidst the cold. "She sounds like someone special," he remarked, admiration tinting his words.

"I'm lucky to have her," I affirmed, the truth of it wavering as I navigated the labyrinth of my emotions. "But I'm not sure if we were built to last."

Chris's hand was a heavy anchor on my shoulder, his eyes cutting through the darkness with an unsettling clarity. "Nah, Jason. It's the other way around," he said, his voice edged with a rare certainty born from our shared nightmare. "She's lucky to have you. Anyone would be. You're an incredible guy, with or without her. Remember that." Then, his brow furrowed as if trying to escape the claustrophobic gloom. "So what the hell do you think is happening here? With everyone?"

I mulled over his question, the unease gnawing at me. It was a thought I'd skirted around but never voiced. "I don't know," I murmured, glancing down the dim, narrow corridor. "It's like... a waking nightmare. People vanishing, these underground fucking towns... Not exactly something you'd throw on a postcard."

"But those people, those *things*... They don't feel pain, and all they want is to inflict more. Not gonna lie, vampires was my guess too, not that I would've ever said it aloud," Christopher chuckled. "You see the look on that guy's face? It's like he never heard that before."

"Well, Darren made it clear—this isn't some cheap horror flick. My guess? An underground cult of sadists. They grab folks from the surface... the homeless, the lost, even high-profile types like Mike and Misha. They torture 'em for kicks. Darren's got this savior complex, convinced them they're better off down here. Some real Sleeping Beauty type shit."

Christopher raised an eyebrow. "I think you mean Beauty and the Beast," he interjected. "Kidnapped and fell in love with the captor and all that. Stockholm syndrome."

"You're telling me you *didn't* graduate high school?" I snorted, amused. "Anyway, from what we saw in that... Hanging Room, or whatever, it looks like they turn those who don't join into their next meal."

Christopher's expression grew contemplative. "How long do you think this has been going on? You think they're the only ones, or is this some kind of nationwide shitshow?"

The thought chilled me to the bone. "Who knows. I've never seen anything like this in New York... but I don't usually spend my time in sewers. As for how long—hell, that town could've been here since the Manson era. Maybe even back to LA's founding. The place looked like the Northridge quake all over again."

Christopher's eyes softened with a hint of camaraderie. "I keep forgetting you're a local."

"And I keep trying to make you forget," I chuckled. "That quake didn't finish me off, and neither will this hellhole. If anything, I refuse to die in California."

"I knew I liked you," Christopher's laugh was tinged with warmth.

For a fleeting moment, the words seemed to crystallize in the thick darkness, fragile beacons of hope. Opening up about my father felt like dropping a heavy shroud, yet a silent understanding passed between us. We sat there, enveloped in our grief, the oppressive darkness pressing in on us. In the silence, amidst our ragged breaths, I felt a faint glimmer of resolve—a vow to honor the memories we held dear.

But just as solace began to seep in, a distant echo shattered the fragile calm—clinking chains, footsteps splashing through the muck, a chilling reminder of the lurking perils.

"Breaktime's over. Ready to run?" I asked, urgency sharpening my voice.

"Like we have a choice?" Christopher's response was edged with grim resolve. With a shared nod, we bolted into the dim.

CHAPTER 15
SLIVER OF SALVATION

THERE WAS no way to keep our footsteps from echoing through the tunnel, making us an easy target for tracking. The only thing in our favor was that we were young, we could move fast. With any luck, faster than our pursuers.

The stench of decay, the mold and mildew, the metallic taste of blood and fear... it all clung to the back of my throat. I was chilled to the bone. The rhythmic drip of water was a haunting reminder of our isolation. Moisture fell from the dank walls, casting an eerie sheen in the faint light that struggled to penetrate the gloom. The low ceiling forced us to hunch over as we moved, the oppressive weight of the earth above pressing down on us.

"Come on, there has to be something," I whispered, urgency sharpening my voice.

"What's our plan if it's another dead end?" Christopher's voice was barely audible over the echoing drip of water. I hesitated, my mind racing through options, each one more improbable than the last in this suffocating darkness.

"We fight," I finally replied, forcing conviction into my tone despite the uncertainty clawing at my resolve. "We'll end this. Or we die trying."

"Sounds like a solid deal to me," Christopher managed a weak smile, a flicker of hope dim but still visible in his eyes. His voice wavered slightly, betraying the strain of our desperate situation. For a moment, I saw beyond his facade of bravery—the raw vulnerability masked by determination. My heart ached with the weight of our predicament, knowing his hope was as fragile as our chances of escape.

As if in defiance to his question, a dim glimmer of light pierced the darkness ahead. Hope surged within us, driving us forward with renewed determination. The light grew brighter, revealing a slim crevice along the tunnel wall—a storm drain. Through the crack, distorted figures moved above, oblivious to the nightmare unfolding beneath their feet.

An old, rusted manhole cover embedded in the tunnel ceiling loomed overhead, scraping against my hair. "Chris—this could be it!" I exclaimed, reaching for the tarnished metal.

I squatted down, pressing my fingers at the edges of the manhole cover as I pushed. It was encrusted with rust and grime, but I dug my fingers in, straining to lift it. The cover didn't yield.

"Fuck, help me out here!" I urged, pushing with all my might.

Christopher joined me, and together we heaved, our muscles straining against the unyielding metal. The cover creaked but remained resolute, embedded in the sidewalk, an immovable object.

"It won't budge!" Christopher choked, his face turning red before letting out a sigh. He pounded the stubborn metal, rust flakes scattering, mingling with the grime on our hands. "Should we try the gap?" His voice cracked, distress breaking through his usual stoicism.

Desperation gripped me. "We got to," I declared, voice steady despite the urgency. "It might be big enough."

I leaned against the grimy, slanted shelf above the floor, trying to force my body through the narrow gap in the storm drain. The abrasive concrete scraped against my skin, but I pressed on, gritting my teeth against the pain. But the gap was too narrow; no matter how much I twisted and turned, I couldn't get my shoulders through.

"It's too tight," I admitted, frustration evident.

Christopher tried next, but he too found the gap impassable. We were trapped, our only hope of escape thwarted by the unyielding concrete.

Christopher's voice was a jagged whisper in the darkness, "We gotta call for help." The desperation in his tone sliced through the silence like a blade.

I threw myself onto the shelf beside him, our shouts ricocheting off the cold, indifferent walls. "Hey! Someone, please!" Our pleas danced in the still air, the silence swallowing them whole. The sound of our voices seemed to dissolve into the void, swallowed by the heavy quiet.

Above, the world continued its indifferent march. Pedestrians hovered on the edge of curiosity but chose to ignore the eerie cries below. Their glances flickered downward, momentarily puzzled by the unsettling echoes. Yet, their steps remained unbroken, a steady drum of apathy that only deepened our despair.

"Help! We're down here!" My voice was raw, scraping against the narrow slit of the storm drain. I shoved my face into the gap, my breath humid in the narrow opening. Distress clawed at my chest as I wriggled, my skin grinding against the rough concrete, but the gap remained unforgiving. I managed to force one arm through, waving it in a frantic, futile dance.

Christopher's cries joined mine, a chorus of desperation that seemed to blend into the darkness. "Please! Someone!" His voice, like the shards of glass and debris that littered the city's roads, was swallowed by relentless apathy. His arm flailed, merging with mine, as the ghosts of pedestrians drifted past, their eyes glazed, their hearts closed off.

The realization crashed over us—a cruel, unyielding tide. *No one's going to be our hero.*

A cascade of memories surged, my father's stern voice cutting through the fog. *Give up now, and you're nothing. I didn't raise a nobody. Get up!* His words echoed, a haunting symphony of resilience. The lessons etched into my soul pushed me to confront the suffocating gloom.

"It's just us," I declared, my voice hardened by the specters of his teachings. "We're the only ones who can pull ourselves out of this."

Our resolve shattered as the relentless footsteps drew nearer, their rhythm a heartbeat of impending doom. Panic surged through us, and in our frantic bid to escape, Christopher's arm was ensnared by the rusted maw of the storm drain. His eyes, wide with terror, mirrored the futility of his struggles against the merciless concrete. "I can't get out!" His voice trembled, a raw cry of dread echoing through the oppressive tunnel.

"Chris, hang on!" My pulse thundered in my ears as I wrestled with his trapped limb, but the concrete's grip was a cruel, unyielding force. Footsteps reverberated closer, a cacophony of despair that twisted around us, squeezing the air from our lungs.

"It's time for the grand finale, my darlings!" Misha's voice slithered through the tunnel, dripping with a velvety malice that promised only suffering. "Are you ready for your final bow?"

"Lose the coat!" My desperation clawed at my throat as I fought against the encroaching terror.

Christopher's eyes brimmed with tears, his vision a blur of panic as he struggled against the choking grip of desperation. With a wrenching effort, he attempted to slip out of the jacket, but his arm remained a captive to the storm drain's jagged maw.

I seized his waist, pulling with a frenzied, reckless abandon until, with a tearing, sickening sound, his arm was wrenched free. The black leather of his coat resisted, but the concrete's cruel teeth had already bitten deep, leaving a savage gash that split his flesh. Raw, bleeding tissue oozed crimson trails, staining the jacket a dark, foreboding red.

We staggered away from the storm drain, the flicker of hope extinguished like a candle snuffed out by a tempest. But we were warriors in this shadowed realm, resolved to claw our way out at any cost.

The footsteps grew louder, their relentless rhythm a chilling reminder of our pursuers. Shadows danced on the walls ahead, their movement a sinister prelude to the terror closing in. Each footfall echoed through the tunnel, a stark reminder that time was slipping away.

Christopher winced, his grip tight on his wounded arm as his jacket trailed behind him like a shroud, but he pressed on, his resolve a flicker in the engulfing darkness. We had no choice but to push forward.

"This way!" I whispered, my finger pointing to a narrow tunnel that beckoned like a siren's call into the abyss. It was our only hope. We hurled ourselves toward it, our footfalls merging with the malevolent pursuit that nipped at our heels.

As we squeezed into the claustrophobic passage, the air turned frigid, and the stench of decay became worse. "Keep moving," I urged, my voice a hushed whisper, unwilling to tempt fate by glancing back. "We'll get out of here. We have to."

THE PASSAGE ABRUPTLY EXPANDED, revealing a claustrophobic vertical shoot, a maintenance shaft from some forgotten industrial era. Pipes snaked up the walls like metal vines, their outlines swallowed by the oppressive blackness above. The shaft seemed to stretch endlessly, a grim reminder of the tangled underworld beneath the city. The air vibrated with the metallic clang and low moan of distant machinery. We halted, trying to steady ourselves, the silence periodically shattered by the menacing scuffs and clinks of our unseen pursuers.

"Quick, we need a way up!" Christopher's voice cut through the noise, eyes darting around the grimy walls. "Scared of heights?"

I swallowed hard, eyes locked on the cavernous space. "Heights? Not even a little," I fibbed, trying to mask the unease creeping through me. "We need a ladder or something—anything to get us out of this hellhole."

The urgency pushed us forward, our movements sharp and desperate.

"There!" I pointed with a burst of relief, my finger trembling toward a rusted metal ladder bolted haphazardly to the wall. It clawed its way up into the shadowy abyss. "Let's just hope it doesn't lead to another nightmare."

We lunged toward the ladder, hope mingling with fear. "You go first," Christopher instructed, throwing on his coat and casting a wary glance behind him. "I'll cover you."

My fingers gripped the ladder, raw and blistered, each rung a fresh assault on my battered hands. Sweat mingled with blood, making my grasp perilous. My heart hammered against my ribs, fear and exhaustion blurring together.

When I reached a landing, I hauled myself onto a narrow platform, its metal surface barely catching what little light filtered through. The platform was a precarious sliver, just enough for us to cling to, suspended within the vertical void. The air here was a touch less stifling, but the threat still loomed large.

I watched Christopher's struggle with a tight knot of anxiety. His pale face was a ghostly mask of pain, blood staining the fabric of his coat in dark, ominous streaks. I extended my hand, trying to anchor him to the precarious safety of the platform. "I got you," I murmured, my voice wavering as I fought to sound assured.

We crammed onto the platform, the darkness swallowing us whole. I dared a glance back down the shaft, half-expecting to see our pursuers' ominous silhouettes emerging from the abyss but there was no sign of them yet.

The ledge ended at a ladder, a cruel reminder that our ascent had to continue.

"Shit, don't look down," I muttered, though the warning was more for my benefit than his.

Christopher's eyes darted downward before snapping back to me, "There's nothing down there I want to see."

We tackled the second ladder, each rung a metal snake coiling around our hands, the coldness seeping into our bones. The climb was an agonizing crawl, the pain in my sliced hand flaring with every shift. Each step felt like dragging my soul through molten iron, but retreat wasn't an option.

Halfway up, I faltered. Tears, raw and searing, tumbled from my eyes. The agony was a relentless beast gnawing at my grip. My heart pounded like a trapped animal, sweat slicking my skin in a cold, clammy sheen. *Come on, Jason. Just a few... more... rungs...* I chanted internally, gripping the ladder with my bleeding hand, trying to drag the rest of me upward.

And then, the inevitable happened.

My fingers, numb and slick, lost their purchase. The rung wrenched free from my grasp. I tried to adjust, but my fingers clawed uselessly at the empty air. A sickening drop followed, and I felt my body jerk as the darkness below swelled.

"Jason!" Christopher's cry was a desperate lifeline, edged with raw fear. He was directly beneath me, eyes wide and reflecting his terror. "Hold on!"

I dangled precariously, the ladder a merciless serpent, its metal bites searing into my palms. My other hand flailed in a futile grasp at the empty air, my muscles tearing like overstrained ropes.

"Come on, you got this!" Christopher's voice, though strained, cut through the suffocating dread. His panic was a fuel, propelling me to fight through the encroaching darkness.

With a final, gut-wrenching effort, I hoisted myself back onto the rung, trembling violently, my vision swimming with sweat and fear. I locked eyes with Christopher, drawing strength from the fierce resolve in his gaze.

"I lied!" I shouted, voice quaking but resolute. "I fucking hate heights!"

Christopher's laugh was a shaky, relieved exhalation. "Now you tell me?!"

As we neared the top, a dim red light filtered through the darkness, a feeble beacon of hope. *Exit.* With every ounce of strength I had left, I pulled myself onto the platform and shoved open a rusted door, collapsing into a narrow hallway. The tiles beneath were a grotesque patchwork of cracked remnants, the sterile air and overhead light feeling like a slap after the sewers' oppressive gloom.

Christopher staggered in after me, exhaustion etched into every line of his face, but his eyes blazed with a determination that mirrored mine.

"We made it," I wheezed, hunched over, gasping for breath.

"Not yet," Christopher responded, placing a hand on my back. "But I have an idea," he finished, his eyes fixed ahead.

We pressed forward, the hallway stretching ahead like a corridor of salvation. The hallway's echoing footfalls were the only sound now, the pursuit's menacing growl receding into silence. Our pace quickened, the end of the hallway a shimmering promise of freedom, tantalizingly close.

CHAPTER 16

PHANTOM'S EMBRACE

THE CORRIDOR STRETCHED AHEAD like a jagged scar. Overhead, the lightbulbs flickered, casting erratic shadows that twitched and pulsed. They wove grotesque patterns on the walls, whispering fragmented, sinister secrets just out of reach. Every footstep we took was swallowed by the cracked and filth-ridden tiles, reverberating through the narrow space like the ticking of a malevolent clock.

Desperation gnawed at my sanity. My heartbeat thundered in my ears, a primal rhythm drowning out reason and replacing it with raw, unchecked fear.

The corridor twisted and contorted, an endless, nightmarish maze dragging us deeper into its bowels. My gaze flitted around, desperate for any hint of escape. Just when it seemed like we would be swallowed by the gloom forever, a door appeared—cracked open slightly, a sliver of light seeping through like a taunting mirage. A worn sign above it, barely legible, read "Service Room."

"I'm telling you, my heart's hammering like a bass drum at a punk show," I joked, my voice trembling despite my attempt at levity. "Where is everyone? Still think this is a part of the 'playground...' or did we stumble onto a horror movie set?"

Christopher shot me a brief glance, a flicker of amusement amidst the fear in his eyes. "Who knows. Maybe your jokes scared 'em away."

"Right, right, my bad for making jokes in the haunted hallway," I mumbled, swallowing the lump of fear that had lodged in my throat. "But seriously, is this whole place abandoned?"

"Well, the lights are on... sort of," Christopher replied, his voice gaining a touch of resolve. "Someone's paying for this place. Let's just hope Darren didn't get to them first."

"I'm with you on that," I said. "All I care about is turning this nightmare into a wicked escape."

We edged closer to the service room, the slight promise of answers or a brief respite flickering in the oppressive darkness. The closer we got, the more the surrounding gloom seemed to recede, as if the room ahead was a fragile hope in the abyss. With a shared nod, we pushed the door open, bracing ourselves for whatever nightmare awaited inside.

The door groaned open, a mournful sound that seemed to drag its last breath into the stifling silence that enveloped us. Each groan and creak from the ancient hinges felt like the whisper of a forgotten curse, echoing the nightmares we'd been running from. The service room was a claustrophobic pit where time seemed to have warped here. It was a chaotic jumble of relics and rust. Pipes clung to the ceiling like skeletal fingers, and tattered tarps draped over forgotten corners whispered of past occupants. The air was heavy with the sickly sweet stench of decay and mildew, each breath a struggle against the thick, oppressive gloom.

Without a moment's hesitation, Christopher reached up, his hand a blur as he grabbed the dangling light cord. His eyes, narrow slits of determination, glinted in the dimness as he yanked. The room was swallowed by darkness in an instant.

I reached out instinctively, grasping the line as though it were a fragile thread linking us to sanity. With a sharp pull, I restored the flickering light. "Hiding? Didn't work before–" My voice barely cut through the choking silence, a mere ghost in the thick air.

In the dim glow, Christopher's eyes, a deep, earthy brown as dark and intense as a forest night, met mine. There was a feverish edge to his gaze, a blend of terror and fierce resolve. "We're not hiding– we're laying a trap," he declared, his voice quaking with a raw edge of desperation.

With a jarring crash, Christopher hurled his arm toward a heap of ancient equipment. Metal cans and broken tools clattered to the floor in a thunderous symphony, their discordant chorus a stark counterpoint to the oppressive quiet. In the aftermath, he spun toward me, clutching a rusted screwdriver with an intensity that bordered on madness. His resolve burned with the frenzied energy of a hunted animal. Despite the gnawing fear inside me, I knew he was right. No more running. No more hiding.

It was time for a showdown.

There was no room for debate, only the raw urgency of survival born from the fiery furnace of desperation.

"Listen," Christopher's voice emerged from the suffocating silence, a ghostly murmur. "You gotta hide in that old storage locker. I'll hide by the entrance, attack 'em from behind. Pray they don't find me first."

"No, Chris," I shook my head, adrenaline coursing like electric currents through my veins. "Your arm's wrecked. You can't defend yourself."

Christopher's gaze flicked to my trembling hand, which I tried to hide behind me. "What, you plan on staying out here?" His voice cut through the tension, sharp yet laced with a deep-seated worry. "Your hand's not just a scratch. I've seen it. You're not in any shape to fight. I'll manage."

I paused, struck by the raw intensity of his determination. "I can't leave you to face this alone," I said quietly, my voice catching like a broken record. The reality of our situation, the sheer enormity of what we were risking, crashed over me like a cold wave.

Christopher's eyes locked onto mine, a storm of resolve and melancholy swirling within them. "Jason, you have to. Save yourself. Kimberly's waiting for you. I don't have anyone waiting for me. Nicole's gone. I've lost everything. But you... you still have a chance."

His words were a punch to the gut, a cruel reminder of what we were about to lose. My heart ached at the thought of abandoning him, yet the gravity of his statement was undeniable. I saw the pain etched in his face, the resigned emptiness of someone who had lost all he once cherished. "I can't just walk away from you," I said, my voice trembling. "You mean everything to me, Chris. More than I can even say. I know this isn't how we wanted things, but there's still time. We can find a way out. Together. There's still a chance if we don't give up."

Christopher's expression softened, a fleeting blur of hope amidst the harsh reality. "Jason..."

"No," I cut him off. "Hell, no. We're both in this. Together, we ride or die." My voice was a blade of determination slicing through the chaos. "We're not finished. I won't let fear or circumstance tear us apart. If there's a way, we'll find it. We have to."

Tears, those treacherous droplets, hovered on the edge of my lashes, threatening to spill over, punctuating our grim reality. Our first encounter, a breath ago but now stretching into an eternal void, replayed in my mind, tainted by the bitter taste of shattered hopes. I clung to those moments, desperate to etch the cadence of his voice into my memory, knowing they slipped away like whispers lost in the wind.

Christopher's eyes, now a tempest of hope and sorrow, met mine. He reached out, grasping my hand with a strength that defied his exhaustion. "Alright. Let's find that way. But you need to hide in the locker. And promise me you'll keep fighting, no matter what."

The thunderous cadence of footsteps echoed through the corridor, each step a ticking clock, time slipping away like sand through clenched fists. Amidst the chaos, our gazes intertwined, a silent pact forged in the crucible of dread. A force beyond comprehension seemed to guide us as we embraced in desperation, fear and respect intermingling amidst the clamor.

"I promise," I said, squeezing him tightly. "We'll get out of this. We'll make it."

"Go," his voice drifted out, a whisper as thin as shadows.

With one final, lingering gaze, I wrenched myself away from him, each step dragging me further into the abyss of uncertainty. I approached the storage locker, fear and determination warring within me. As I opened the locker door and stepped inside, I glanced back at Christopher. His silhouette, stark and resolute against the chaos, was a reminder of what I was fighting for.

Without warning, Christopher moved with a frantic, almost spectral urgency. He seized a rusted metal bookshelf, its groan a metallic wail, and tipped it over. The shelf crashed against the locker door with a resounding clang, wedging it shut and trapping me inside.

"Chris! What—" My voice was muffled by the thick metal, panic surging as I pounded on the door.

Through the narrow crack of light, I saw Christopher's shadow, his face a mask of sorrowful resolve. "Jason, I'm sorry. This is the only way."

"Chris! No! Let me out!" My cries were swallowed by silence, my fists beating against the door with frantic energy, my heart a wild drum.

In an instant, Christopher yanked the cord, morphing into a shadow, a predator in the darkness. Unseen and unheard, he waited for his moment to strike, a spectral figure poised to hunt the unaware.

CHAPTER 17

FREEING PERSEPHONE

THE ROOM LAY IN DARKNESS, with only the faint, feeble light of the hallway filtering in, casting eerie shapes across the walls that confused the eye. It was the kind of darkness that felt alive, creeping into every crevice, swallowing the light whole, like some spine-chilling Halloween night in a cemetery, where shadows danced with the bare winter branches of trees and tombstones. But this was no kids' Halloween party.

I stood there, trapped within the confines of the locker with its musty scent of old books and the stench of sweaty work clothes, a sanctuary that felt both protective and imprisoning. I was in way over my head.

Fuck, Chris! I need to help him.

Drawing in a shaky breath, I attempted to calm the storm of nerves threatening to overwhelm me. *There has to be a way out of here. There's still time. I mean, it's not like there's a creepy figure straight out of my worst nightmares about to come through that door or anything.*

And then she appeared. A nightmare given flesh, emerging from the suffocating shadows like something out of a twisted fever dream. Her silhouette, a grotesque distortion of human form, loomed in the doorway, veiled in darkness that pulsed with malevolent energy. Her presence was so overwhelming that I felt poisoned by her very existence.

A shiver ran down my spine as her figure wavered and warped, the boundaries of reality seeming to strain to contain her. I dared to peek through the narrow slits of the locker, and there she was—her appearance like something out of a sick fantasy. Hooks, cruel and jagged, jutted from her pallid flesh, intertwining with her body in a gruesome display of suffering. Each hook seemed to pulse with a dark energy, as if it were alive, whispering of untold torments.

Her voice slithered through the gloom like a serpent's hiss, its icy tendrils wrapping around my spine. "Come out, little ones..." The words echoed with an otherworldly allure that froze my bones, each syllable a chilling promise of the horrors to come.

Through the narrow crevices of the metal locker, I caught glimpses of her form. She moved with a grace that was hauntingly beautiful and terrifyingly lethal, a sickening mix of ethereal beauty and impending doom.

Then she fixed her gaze on my hiding spot. Her eyes gleamed with a predatory hunger, a look that spoke volumes of the malevolent intent lurking within. With deliberate steps, she moved closer, each step dwindling my hope, fouling my senses, suffocating me.

Shit, think, Jason. I have to make a distraction. What would a distraction do...

With an unsettling elegance, she advanced, defying comprehension, her movements a grotesque ballet of twisted limbs and contorted angles.

"Hey, Elvira! If you're auditioning for a horror movie, you totally nailed it," I said, my voice echoing back to me in the narrow confines of the locker, trying to mask my fear with forced bravado. "But this isn't really the best time for a performance review."

Her voice, smooth and chilling, flowed like a velvet knife through the silence, slicing away any flicker of defiance. "There's no use in hiding, darling. The time for play is over."

I could barely process her words through the overwhelming dread. "Oh, great. Classic villain speech. Can we skip to the part where we fight back, or are you planning to just scare us to death?"

Petrified, I clenched my draining fists, my muscles locked tight in the grip of raw terror. *Why the hell didn't Chris give me a weapon?!*

Her monstrous silhouette loomed large before me, a horrifying figure drawing me into its orbit with a magnetic pull, promising terrors beyond the realm of human comprehension.

"Seriously, is there a manual for dealing with nightmares like you? Because right now, I'm seriously underprepared," I muttered, trying to stay calm as her presence grew more suffocating.

With each heavy step she took, the cavernous silence around me amplified. As she drew nearer, a chill crept through me, and I understood the abyss that awaited, a descent into madness from which there would be no reprieve.

"You'll be exquisite once the transformation is complete," she purred, her voice laced with malevolent delight. "Embrace the agony that binds us, free from the constraints of society."

Her scarlet lips twisted into a wicked smirk, a nauseating parody of a smile as she savored my terror like a connoisseur savoring a fine wine, weaving the promise of a macabre transformation like a spell.

"You know, I think I'm good on the whole 'transformation' thing," I said, trying to sound dismissive even though my voice trembled. "I like my skin just the way it is, thanks."

A stomach-churning foreboding emanated from her, thickening the air with a tangible sense of doom as she approached. "Just you wait, my darling," her words slithered forth, dripping with a sinister hunger, as if she could detect my very essence from miles away. "Darren and I have such plans for you."

My hands trembled as cold sweat trickled down my spine. She, the queen of chaos, ground the metal bookshelf against the floor, the noise screeching in the silence. She gripped the cold metal latch of the locker with fingers of shadow, a symbol of her dominion over the darkness.

Suddenly, the scuffle of footsteps jolted me. Straining to see through the slits, Christopher's silhouette emerged from the darkness, his form edging closer to Misha. My breath caught.

Christopher stepped forward, a beacon of strength amidst the encroaching darkness. But I could see the telltale signs of his injury—his coat, torn and stained with blood. His arm hung awkwardly by his side, the movement a grim testament to the pain he was enduring. Blood seeped through the torn fabric, painting a dark streak down his coat.

Misha's mocking laughter cut through the tension. "Well, well, well. Look who decided to crash the party. Quite the entrance, my dear, but you seem a bit... worse for wear."

Christopher's face was set in grim resolve, his jaw clenched against the pain radiating from his shoulder. Every movement was labored, as if his arm was a weight dragging him down. Despite the agony, his eyes burned with unyielding determination.

"You're right," he said through gritted teeth, his voice strained but steady. "He's in there. I trapped him— just for you."

Panic surged through me, a knife-like twist of betrayal. My hands shook uncontrollably as I clawed at the metal locker, fingers scrabbling desperately. I pounded on the locker's walls, knuckles scraping against the cold metal, but the door stayed stubbornly shut.

"You bastard!" I shouted, my voice cracking with desperation. "You can't do this! We were supposed to be in this together!"

Misha's sinister amusement and Christopher's measured voice were a cruel reminder of my dire situation.

"Christopher, no!" I yelled again, fists hammering against the locker. The metal door groaned in protest but didn't give. I fought to pry it open, but it was as if the locker was fused shut, trapping me in this hellish cage.

Misha's wicked laughter filled the room, a haunting sound that twisted my gut and sent waves of nausea rolling through me. The shadows seemed to tighten, the locker's interior shrinking around me. My mind raced, torn between the horrifying thought that Christopher had betrayed me and the desperate hope that this was some cruel game.

"Ah, *Christopher*. Such a delightful name," Misha cooed, her voice a saccharine poison. "I'll be sure to show my appreciation for this generous gift—"

"All I ask, Misha…" Christopher's voice broke through the pain, a strained growl that resonated with raw determination. "Is that you leave him out of this. Take me instead. I dragged him into this— It's my fault he's here. I'll… do whatever you want." He paused, his breaths ragged and heavy.

"Tempting, my dear. Truly tempting," she purred, her tone like silk over steel. "But, you see, if I don't claim him, someone else will." She turned to my metal cage, her hand curling around the latch. "The time has come, Jason. Embrace your true potential."

In a final, desperate move, Christopher grabbed a heavy book from a nearby shelf. Its weight contrasted sharply with the fragile hope he clung to. He swung it at Misha with a roar of pain and defiance, his injured shoulder screaming. The book struck her, sending her sprawling, but the effort left him gasping, clutching his shoulder as he staggered back.

"You think a book's gonna stop me?" she sneered, contempt lacing her voice.

Christopher's jaw tightened, his resolve unshaken despite the excruciating pain. "No," he growled, voice low and fierce. "But I'll do whatever it takes to keep you away from him."

Misha's taunts echoed through the dimly lit room, each word a blade meant to slice through Christopher's resolve. But he was beyond the reach of her venomous words now, his focus a laser-sharp edge of determination. Every fiber of his being attuned to the moment, the final clash that would decide our fates.

"Look at me, Christopher," she purred, releasing the latch to the locker and turning back to him with predatory grace. "I've broken free from society's chains. These scars? They are my true freedom. Before my transformation, all I cared for was my outward appearance. No one saw who I was, the suffering soul inside. Every red carpet, every PR event... it was the *savior* who changed me. Darren showed me who I can be beyond superficiality... The *mother* of the new world."

Christopher's voice cut through the tension, firm and resolute. "You? You're not free—" he scoffed. "You've just swapped one set of chains for another. Real freedom isn't about running away; it's about outliving your demons."

Misha's laughter filled the room, a chilling sound that reverberated off the walls. "Oh, Christopher, but everyone has their demons. Yours are just more... persistent."

I held my breath, frozen in the shadows as their words danced like phantoms around me. Christopher's bravery sparked a glimmer of hope in the darkness, a resolve that pushed back against the malevolent forces threatening to consume us all.

In the dense shadows, Christopher moved like a phantom, each step a calculated burst of purpose. The darkness writhed around him, whispering secrets in a language only he could hear. The world twisted and bent, a surreal backdrop to his approach.

He was a blur of intent, eyes locked on Misha's twisted silhouette. The pulsating light painted her form in sickly hues as the air crackled with tension. He drew closer, muscles coiled, ready to spring.

Without warning, he erupted in a storm of fury. His roar shattered the silence, a primal force colliding with Misha. His fist flew, aimed straight for her mocking face.

Misha's laughter cut through the chaos, a twisted melody of malice. Blood dripped from her piercings, tracing her scars. "You're lost, Christopher. Just a pawn in a game you don't understand. We're part of something bigger. All we want is to share our gift, let natural selection do the rest."

Christopher's eyes narrowed. "I'm trapped, maybe, but I'm not alone. And I'm not letting you hurt anyone else."

Misha's eyes gleamed with sadistic pleasure. "You can't save anyone, not Nicole, not Jason. And in the end, you can't save yourself."

She lunged, her hooks glinting as they slashed through the air. Christopher dodged with reflexes honed by youth and desperation, every movement a testament to his will to survive. They clashed, a whirlwind of force and fury. Fists met flesh with bone-jarring impact. The room seemed to shrink around them, like a spotlight on a prima ballerina, walls closing in as their fight escalated. Shadows watched, the air thick with the intensity of their struggle. Each strike, each dodge, reverberated through the bowels of this hellish place.

Misha's movements were a blur of predatory elegance. She deflected Christopher's blows with a feral scream, her hooked flesh flashing in the dim light. She retaliated with brutal precision, her strikes a nightmarish dance of violence.

Their battle was a grotesque ballet, a twisted dance of shadows and blood. Flesh tore, bones ground together, the cacophony of their clash echoing through the room. Christopher's focus was relentless, eyes locked on Misha's, seeing his own torment reflected in her gaze.

He dodged a swipe, his movements fluid despite the pain. An uppercut slammed Misha against the wall, but she sneered, wiping blood with a mocking gesture. Debris rained down from a shelf above, scattering across the floor. "Is this truly your best effort? I expected more."

Christopher's chest heaved. "I'm just getting started." He lunged forward, his movements a desperate fight against his deepest fears.

Through the chaos, my heart pounded in my chest. I knew I had to turn the tide. Then, my eyes widened as I saw it. A metallic surface catching in the dim light. A crowbar.

Misha swung viciously, but Christopher evaded with the grace of a predator. He drove a punch into her midsection, eliciting a gasp of surprise.

The fight raged on, a storm of willpower and defiance against evil and malice. Each blow Christopher landed was charged with his struggle for survival, his determination blazing with each strike.

Misha moved with predatory elegance, exploiting his weaknesses with chilling efficiency. Her strikes were a relentless assault, each swipe a cruel reminder of the power she wielded, the supremacy she commanded, the misplaced respect she demanded.

As Christopher gained the upper hand, Misha drove her knee into his stomach, and he gasped, struggling to stay upright.

In a swift, savage motion, Misha drew a blade. Christopher ducked a swipe but was caught off guard as the blade slashed his arm Pain exploded through him.

Misha laughed and pressed her advantage. Her knife slashed with brutal efficiency, leaving Christopher gasping, stumbling back as blood flowed freely from his arm, his thigh, and his shoulder.

"You think you can defy me?" Misha taunted, her blade carving through the air. The force of her next cut sent Christopher sprawling, breath coming in ragged gasps.

Christopher struggled to rise, muscles trembling. His gaze, though blurred by the blood trickling from a wound on his head, remained fiercely determined. But he was on the brink, each heartbeat sapping his strength as he struggled to regain his position.

Misha loomed over him, knife dripping with blood. "You're nothing but a child, fleeing from shadows. Did you really think you could escape?"

Christopher's knees buckled, and he fell again, breathing ragged. Misha's smile was a grotesque reflection of her madness.

"You'll always be a prisoner of your past," she murmured, her tone almost gentle but laced with malice. "Join us, and we'll give you a purpose in the agony. There's beauty in suffering."

As she leaned in, the walls seemed to also, shadows curling him like tendrils.

But his spirit remained unyielding. He lifted his gaze, eyes burning with defiance. "There's nothing you can offer me," he rasped. "I won't be one of you. I'll never let you win."

Misha's twisted laughter rose through the gloom like a funhouse reel. "So brave, yet so foolish. You can't even stand up to me. This is where we say goodbye. There's no place for cowards in the new world."

Her words were cruel blows that hammered at Christopher's resolve. I watched, paralyzed, as she verbally dismantled him with twisted artistry. It was like watching a car crash in slow motion—painful, impossible to look away.

In his eyes, I saw the shadows of his past writhing—abuse, sleepless nights, unending dread. But in the darkness, a flicker of defiance sparked—a blazing fire in the night.

Christopher's gaze hardened, driven by love and unbreakable will. With a guttural roar, he forced himself upright. "I'm no coward. Escaping isn't running away. It's facing fears and fighting for something better. That's freedom. And I'm done being your victim."

In a frantic blur, I scrambled again for the latch. My heart pounded, fingers slick with sweat and blood. With a wrench, the door burst open, and I lunged into the room.

I snatched the crowbar from the debris, my grip tight and desperate.

"Ah, Jason. Nice of you to join us. Tell me, do think you can put up a better fight?" she taunted, spinning with cruel elegance.

"I'm not missing," I growled, blood seeping onto the metal.

Christopher's command cut through the chaos. "Jason, now!"

I swung the crowbar with raw force. The clang of metal against a rusted pipe was deafening, making Misha's smirk falter. *Fuck.*

She charged at me, a blur of rage. I struck again, the crowbar slamming into her hand, knocking the blade from her grasp. She staggered, clutching her empty hand, just as Christopher drove the rusted screwdriver into her knee.

Misha crumpled with a sharp cry. Her legs buckled, and as she struggled to rise, Christopher's relentless stabs kept her down. I moved in, swinging the crowbar with brutal efficiency.

The crowbar crashed into her side, ribs cracking sickeningly. My hand throbbed, but I pressed on, driven by fury and need. A final, vicious blow landed on her shoulder, and each attempt to rise was met with another heavy, punishing strike. The crowbar thudded relentlessly against her back and legs, blood from my hand staining the floor.

Misha's eyes, wide with shock, locked onto mine. Her breath came in ragged gasps, her mocking smile twisting grotesquely. "Is it... too late to savor the grand finale?" she crooned, her voice dripping with twisted anticipation. "Tell me, darling, did you enjoy the show?"

I watched the light fade from her eyes, her defiance ebbing away.

"Sorry, *Doll*. But it's been cancelled," I answered.

Misha's sickly laughter bubbled from her throat, mixed with blood from an internal wound. Her twisted form lay in a heap. Panting heavily, I stood over her, the crowbar gripped tight despite the searing pain. Christopher, beside me, wiped blood and sweat from his brow, his chest heaving. He nodded, his eyes reflecting exhaustion and relief.

I looked at Christopher, our eyes meeting in weary silence. "Christopher...," I began, voice faltering. "Is she—"

Before I could finish, Misha shuddered, her chest falling, letting out a final gasp, her body collapsing in on itself.

"Dead enough for me." Christopher finished, slumping against the wall.

Her eyes drifted shut, holding onto the dark secrets that would never be known.

CHAPTER 18

TIDES OF DESPAIR

AN UNCANNY SILENCE seeped into the void, a thick, suffocating stillness. Stifling tension still gripped my chest as adrenaline sought its release.

My hand pulsed with a relentless, burning pain, blood escaping my desperate efforts to stanch the flow. The world around me constricted, slipping into a narrow tunnel as if my senses were shutting down in denial.

I stumbled toward Christopher, his once imposing presence now reduced to a frail silhouette slumped against the wall. Each step towards him bore the crushing weight of the aftermath. His eyes, dimmed by exhaustion, met mine, a glimmer of recognition flickering amidst the haze of his suffering.

Collapsing beside him, the moment enveloped me like a suffocating shroud. Every breath I drew was labored, weighed down by the twin forces of fatigue and the gnawing guilt and fear festering in my soul. His life now hung precariously on the edge of my actions, a burden too immense to carry. *But carry it I must.*

"Christopher," I croaked, my voice a whisper against the oppressive quiet. "You need to stay with me."

His lips twitched in a ghost of a smile, a feeble attempt at humor.

"You know... you're lucky you're cute," he whispered, struggling against the pain.

"That's my line," I managed, forcing a smile that felt more like a grimace.

Christopher's smile faltered. "I... meant what I said earlier. I... really do... like you." His voice trailed off, the pallor of his face deepening. I clutched his hand, trying to offer what comfort I could amidst our shared nightmare.

"You're bleeding too much," I said, my voice trembling with barely concealed panic. "Save the compliments for later, okay?" But the attempt at humor felt hollow, a desperate stab at breaking through the crushing aftermath of a battle against death.

As if to mock my futile jest, his eyelids drooped with a finality that resonated in the hollow spaces of my heart. Each shallow breath was a dying ember, slipping into the abyss of the unknown. His breaths mirrored the dwindling hope between us, each exhalation a mournful echo of what might never be.

"No, no, you can't leave me now! Not like this!" I pleaded, desperation clawing at my voice. I gripped him firmly, trying to lift him up. "Come on, Christopher, we need to get out of here!"

But he remained inert, his body a dead weight against the wall. His half-closed eyes conveyed a silent plea that was both heart-wrenching and resolute. "I can't... Jason," he whispered, his voice barely a thread in the darkness.

"No!" I insisted, gripping him with renewed urgency. "You got us into this mess, you're getting us out. I don't care if I have to drag you!"

My words were a desperate rebellion against the relentless march of fate. A hollow, humorless smile twisted my lips as I heaved Christopher's limp form onto my trembling shoulders, a burden heavier than anything I had ever known.

THE HEAVENS UNLEASHED their grief in heavy, discordant drops, each one a brutal declaration of our plight, splattering the asphalt above us like dark, vengeful tears. They mingled with the discordant symphony of our struggle, an orchestration of suffering that seemed to mock the fragility of our existence. Tears carved anguished paths down my cheeks, a cold testament to the torment within.

Every step with Christopher felt like dragging a stone anchor through a morass of despair. His failing form weighed heavily on my soul, a relentless pull toward the yawning chasm of our fate. Despite the crushing weight, I held on, summoning every ounce of strength left in my weary body. His diminishing presence pressed down on me like a living gravestone, our connection a stubborn flame flickering in the gathering darkness.

My vision narrowed into a claustrophobic tunnel, the edges of reality blurring into a smothering fog. The pain in my hand pounded relentlessly, a brutal counterpoint to the numbness spreading through my limbs. Christopher's hand clung to my shirt with a ferocity born from pure instinct, each tug a desperate grasp at a fleeting shard of light. In the midst of our shared ordeal, our fates entwined in silent defiance, forming a bond forged in the crucible of our suffering—a flicker of hope in a sea of encroaching shadows.

We plunged onward, each step a brutal confrontation with the relentless despair threatening to swallow us whole.

But in the heart of this oppressive gloom, our spirits refused to break. They burned with a fierce resolve, cutting through the consuming shadows like a defiant beacon.

One foot in front of the other, then another, then another. My footsteps thundered with determination, a raw, primal rhythm against the silence. I stumbled and faltered, yet my will to reach the end of the journey remained unbowed, driven by an unyielding desire to survive, to save my newly made friend, my brother in arms.

As I plodded through the winding corridors, limping and ragged, Christopher draped over my shoulders, my heart hammered with frantic urgency. But I pressed on, inching toward a distant dream, an elusive glimmer of light like a hallucination, diamonds in the sky that beckoned me.

With Christopher's life hanging by a thread, time stretched into an excruciating eternity. The silence was punctuated only by our ragged breaths and the distant, ominous rumble of thunder.

"There's something up ahead. It might be our way out. Hang on, Chris," I urged, my voice strained but resolute, cutting through the exhaustion that clawed at my limbs. The roar of rushing water grew louder, a fierce promise of salvation amid the tempestuous gloom. *It has to lead out. It has to lead somewhere.*

Driven by a renewed sense of urgency, I dragged Christopher toward the sound, each step a deliberate struggle against the relentless pull of fatigue. Pushing past a heavy door, the water's roar guided us down a narrow, slick passageway and the scent of fresh, rain-soaked earth and rot.

As we descended, the sound of water intensified, its icy touch a sharp contrast to the stifling heat and fear. A cool breeze whispered past us, a fleeting caress that seemed to offer a tenuous hope.

"Christopher, we're almost there. Just hold on," I urged, my voice barely breaking through the growing tumult of the stream.

The stream soon became a relentless current, pulling at our legs with a fierce, almost predatory strength. The water rose rapidly, its icy grip climbing to my waist, then my chest. The path had transformed into a treacherous torrent, the current's power an unyielding adversary.

Despite my struggle, the current overpowered us with its violent insistence. We were swept away, the icy water's grip dragging us back into the widening maw of darkness. The pathway gave way to a chaotic rush of water, hurling us into the abyss with a savage, unrelenting force.

THE TUNNEL LOOMED AHEAD. The icy waters clawed at our skin with a predatory chill, each brutal thrust of the current a merciless twist of fate. Darkness coiled around us, a suffocating embrace that seemed to whisper taunts of doom.

My insides were being torn up by fear, gnawing like a ravenous beast intent on dragging me down. Despair pressed like a weight against my chest, a leaden shroud of charging liquid threatening to smother me. Every breath was a struggle, each gasp lost amid the cacophony of the rushing water and the oppressive dark.

I gripped Christopher's form, a desperate lifeline in the abyss. Suddenly the current roared with newfound fury, its strength a monstrous force pushing us, threatening to devour us whole.

Without warning, we were thrust from the depths and hurled into a grim, murky expanse where the water swirled and filled the cavernous space. I choked, the water's acrid taste burning my throat, my lungs screaming in protest. Christopher floated motionless beside me, his body threatening to sink as the relentless water roared past us. I held on hard, my grasp firm on his arm.

It took all my strength to pull him toward a metal platform that loomed just a few yards ahead. Each tug was a titanic effort, the current a cruel adversary, but failure was not an option. Christopher's weight felt like a corpse's burden, but I dragged him on. We had to survive.

I panted, my voice a raw, strained whisper that barely cut through the darkness. "Christopher," I murmured. I watched his chest move. He was alive, but barely.

The metal platform was a cruel contrast—cold, unyielding, a bitter respite from the water's suffocating grip. I hoisted Christopher onto it, my strength dwindling to a thread, but the sight of distant daylight ahead spurred me on.

As I pulled Christopher onto the platform, reality twisted into a startling revelation: the water flowed outward, merging with the vast, indifferent Pacific Ocean. We had escaped, freed from the claustro-phobic depths of the sewer.

"Christopher," I breathed, my voice barely a murmur in the oppressive silence. His eyelids fluttered weakly, a dying moth's final tremors. I sought his hand in the darkness, clasping it with a fervent grip that belied my own weakening resolve. "We're going to make it,"

I whispered, my words a fragile mantra, a feeble charm against the encroaching shadows, meant as much for me as for him.

His eyes, heavy with the weight of exhaustion, opened just enough to offer a faint nod. In the dimness, his resolve glinted like a stubborn ember, refusing to be extinguished. Together, we had navigated the infernal depths, faced unspeakable horrors, and still, amidst the ruins of despair, a stubborn flicker of hope clung to us, refusing to be snuffed out.

I turned back to the water, my heart a frantic drumbeat, each thud amplified by the electric pulse of adrenaline. Without warning, the water erupted in a violent geyser, and Darren emerged, his grotesque form dripping with brackish sludge. With a guttural roar that reverberated through the chamber like a death knell, he lunged at me. "Not so fast, sweetheart!" He slammed my head into the grate. His grip was like iron chains, yanking me back into the water. I flailed desperately, gasping for breath, but his strength was a monstrous reality, an unyielding force that defied nature. His eyes burned with a hellish hunger, promising torments beyond imagination.

I glimpsed Christopher, barely conscious, his face a canvas of agony. His eyes had dimmed to a haunting dusk. Blood pooled ominously beneath him, a grim testament to his fading struggle.

Darren's grip tightened like a vice, pulling me deeper into the suffocating pool of darkness. My limbs felt like lead, the water dragging me down with a malicious grip. Each punch I threw was absorbed by his monstrous form, his laughter a blade slicing through the chaos. It was a sound that mocked my futile efforts with a chilling finality, echoing through the water like a requiem.

Desperation surged through me as I landed a few brutal strikes. Blood and sweat mingled, pain an excruciating symphony, each hit met with Darren's derisive snarls. The relentless pressure of the water was a crushing force, sapping my strength and will. My vision blurred. In a final, desperate surge, I wrenched myself from his death grip and clawed my way toward the metal platform. Darren's roar of frustration was raw, guttural, reverberating through the water as his shadowy form writhed and twisted.

Just as I reached the platform, a cold, sharp edge pressed against my throat. Darren's blade was a cruel promise of death, his breath hot and rancid against my skin. His voice was a dark whisper, dripping with venom. "Well, well, Jason. It seems we're at the end of the line. Your world—crumbling into dust. And me? I'm just here to take what's mine. All your struggles, all your brave little fights—nothing but ashes in the wind. You took my queen. She took your knight. Check. Checkmate."

Despite the pain and terror, I spat out a single phrase, a challenge against the encroaching darkness. "Not if I can help it."

Darren's eyes flashed with a dangerous glint, the blade pressing closer. "Ah, so stubborn. And tragic, really."

He leaned in, his gaze feverish. "You cling to your ideals as if they could cleanse a world so wretched. Society's a festering carcass, a pit of corruption. You and your precious morals are just blind fools in a game you can't win. I see the decay, the rot. I'll set it all ablaze and build something new from the ruins."

Tears of pain mingled with the blood on my face. I glared at him, my voice trembling but resolute. "You're out of your mind. You're not saving anything. You're just another monster thriving on the chaos you create. No better than the society you hate."

Darren's lips curled into a knowing smile. "Monsters, heroes—just pretty little titles. Constructs of a crumbling world justifying its demise. I'm beyond such labels. I am the force of change, the herald of a new era. Only the strong will rise. The weak will be cast aside. And only then will true order be born."

"What about Misha," I choked, "your queen." My Adam's apple bobbed against the blade. "Was she weak?"

Darren's eyes narrowed, cold and unfeeling. "Misha? She was never anything more than a tool. A convenient means to an end. You think her death matters to me? When I found her in that service room, she was just gargling on the floor. A real pity, but I had bigger fish to fry. I had to find *you*, after all. So I left her. It's a small price for what I'm about to achieve. Her loyalty was valuable only as long as she served my purpose. Now, she's just another casualty of the *grand design*."

I stared at him in disbelief. "You really think she didn't matter to you? She was willing to do anything for you. You're telling me you never cared for her?"

His eyes hardened, devoid of remorse. "Her worth was in her usefulness. You took something I utilized, and for that, you'll pay dearly. Her death was a necessary loss. Your defiance, however, is a personal dig."

I shook my head, my voice cracking with emotion. "Your idea of order is just a mask for your cowardice. Using fear and pain isn't strength. It's hiding behind a broken ideology."

His eyes narrowed, a fleeting shadow of doubt crossing his face before being replaced by cold resolve. "Believe what you want, Jason. In the end, your defiance will be your downfall. The world doesn't need saving; it needs a reckoning."

"I've seen pain, death, violence. But that's not all the world has to offer—"

He cut me off, his voice sharp and piercing. "But Jason... that's what makes you so intriguing! You've seen the cracks, *felt* society's failures. Why waste your strength on a world that won't even appreciate your valiant efforts? Embrace the chaos, and you could help shape a new order. Help me bring others into the light. We can rule over the new age, *together*."

His words were a chilling whisper, laced with temptation. "Think about it. No more hiding, no more pretending. *Just the two of us*."

For a moment, the allure was almost overpowering. The idea of ending the struggle, of reshaping the world—it was tempting. But my father's words rang in my ears. *You're going to be somebody, Jason. Don't let others drag you down.*

Darren's face curled into a smirk, his eyes gleaming with a wicked mix of delight and disdain. "Oh, Jason... so earnest. I can see the wheels turning in your head. After all I've done for you, this is how you repay me? Remember it was *me* who saved you. In the tunnel. In Tartarus. I could've ended your life but I spared you, Jason. I even gave your precious *Christopher* a few more moments of life. And do you want to know why? It's because I *like* you. And I don't <u>like</u> anyone! I gave you a front-row seat to the raw, unfiltered truth. And you think you can just waltz away? You're so adorably blind. I crafted this chaos just for you, a twisted little gift wrapped in pandemonium, and you've got the audacity to reject it?!"

His gaze was a blend of playful mockery and dark satisfaction. "Look at what I've offered. A chance to see the world stripped of its illusions. And what do you do? You cling to your pitiful little dreams. How deliciously predictable."

He leaned in closer, his breath a tantalizing whisper against my ear. "You see, Jason, I gave you a rare gift—a ticket to rise above the muck. And now, as everything unravels, you refuse to seize the power I've laid at your feet. It's almost laughable."

I stared at him, feeling the weight of his twisted perspective. As Darren's blade hovered dangerously close, I drew on every ounce of willpower, determined not to let his warped vision break me.

"You're a real letdown, you know that?" Darren sneered, his face contorting into a snarl. With a sudden, violent move, he lifted me high into the air. "I almost forget what I saw in you."

Darren's blade plunged into me, lodging into my ribcage. Pain exploded in me and I reflexively elbowed his throat, sending him crashing into the water.

Instantly, from the murky depths, Misha emerged, a grotesque and spectral figure of raw agony. Her appearance was a nightmarish reflection of her torment—bloodied, battered, and haunted, with eyes wide and hollow. She looked at me, a flicker of recognition and regret in her gaze.

Her rage was a primal storm. "I was your puppet? Your tool?!"

Her scream, a raw, guttural force, seemed to tear at the very fabric of reality as she lunged at Darren. "I'll show you what happens when you toy with people's lives!"

Her movements were a chaotic dance of fury. Darren's eyes widened in a mixture of terror and disbelief as Misha, an embodiment of relentless vengeance, seized him with a supernatural strength, a stark juxtaposition to her battered appearance.

"Misha! What are you—"

"It's nothing personal, *darling*," Misha's voice slithered through the air, a seductive whisper laced with venom. Each syllable dripped with the dark allure of her torment, a twisted promise of retribution. "I'm just what you made me—a monster!"

As Darren writhed, I seized the moment. With a savage twist, I wrenched the blade from my body, agony coursing through me, and drove it into his chest. I pulled upward, slicing through his heart. I yanked it out and manically plunged it into his eye, then his neck, then his heart again, stabbing and stabbing, as though it would make up for all the pain and wounds and lives that came before.

"No! You can't kill me!" Darren's voice was a desperate, ragged plea, his screams reverberating through the chamber. "Don't you know what I am?!"

"Human," I replied coldly, twisting the knife deeper. With a final effort, I shoved him, and Misha dragged him beneath the blood-stained water, their forms vanishing into the abyss.

The water calmed, the stifling weight of Darren's malevolence lifted. I crumpled onto the platform, gasping for air. The agony and exhaustion were overwhelming, but I knew the danger had been vanquished. I had done it. The threat was over.

But I was bleeding. And bleeding badly.

I crawled toward Christopher, my heart drumming a frantic rhythm against my ribs. His breaths came in fragile, shallow gasps, but he was still there. Relief, cold and shivering, washed over me as I touched his face, my voice trembling yet unyielding. "It's over. We did it. Darren's dead."

The chamber hung in a peculiar silence, a darkness retreating into a disturbed calm. Misha's final, haunting act left behind a ghostly echo of her torment, sealing Darren's reign of terror with a bitter finality.

"You're going to be alright, Christopher," I whispered, my voice cracking like fragile glass. "We made it. We got out."

As we lay there, our bodies broken, the crushing weight of our fears began to lift, if only slightly. The darkness closed in around us, oppressive and dense, yet somewhere in that choking void, a distant, flickering hope shone like a lone star in the void.

Clinging to the metal platform like shipwrecked survivors, I knew we couldn't falter. Not after all we'd endured. For Christopher, for myself, for the slender hope of a tomorrow that might yet come.

Fueled by a surge of grim determination, I wrapped my filthy shirt around my waist, attempting to stem the bleeding. I pushed myself to my feet, adrenaline and endorphins numbing the pain that blazed through every inch of me. Ahead, a sliver of light called out, a beacon slicing through the pervasive gloom. Step by cautious step, I moved toward it, my heart a maelstrom of dread and hope. And as I drew closer, the sky, heavy with its bruised clouds, beckoned. We were free—finally breaking free from the sewer's grasp.

Relief surged through me like a tidal wave, lifting my spirits. "Chris, you still with me?" I called, my voice a fragile thread of hope. But when I looked back, my relief turned to icy horror.

Amidst the gloom, a pool of crimson was spread across the floor but Christopher was gone.

I dropped to my knees beside the bloodstain, my fingers trembling as they brushed against the warm, sticky liquid. The scene was a horror show painted in red. My mind raced through dark possibilities. *Who—or what—could've taken him so swiftly? Was Darren truly dead, or had they returned for a final act of vengeance?* The thought sent a cold shiver through my soul.

Tears blurred my vision. "CHRISTOPHER! NOOO..." I screamed into the void, a blood-curdling cry of desperation.

I was alone in this forsaken place, consumed by the gnawing uncertainty of his fate. Fear wrapped around me, tightening with every agonizing second.

Shadows danced mockingly in the dim light, twisting my anguish into cruel, mocking shapes. Burdened by sorrow, I collapsed beside the crimson pool, its surface mirroring the chaos within me.

The metallic scent of blood tainted the air, a bitter reminder of what had transpired. I reached out, seeking solace in the cold pavement beneath me, but found only indifferent stone.

"How did I let this happen?" I muttered, the question clawing at my sanity, leaving behind only fragments of doubt.

Each heartbeat echoed with regret, a relentless cacophony of missed chances. Guilt, heavy and unrelenting, pressed down upon me, threatening to crush me beneath its oppressive weight.

In that moment, I was lost, adrift in a sea of remorse. As I lay there, overwhelmed by my failures, I sobbed deeply. I knew there would be no escaping the depths of my despair.

The searing ache of loss dug into my chest, merciless and unyielding. Its grip squeezed the breath from my lungs, leaving me gasping in the suffocating darkness. Each heartbeat throbbed with grief, threatening to crush me. Tears painted the world in sorrow, a haunting presence I would never escape.

"What ifs" danced in the shadows, taunting me with their cruel reminders of missed chances and unsaid words. I clung to them like a drowning man to driftwood, seeking solace in the echoes of regret. But no redemption could be found in this pit of despair, no absolution for the sins that stained my conscience.

With every ragged breath, I battled against the crushing weight of sorrow, the air thick with the stench of damp earth and decay. Chris' laughter echoed cruelly in my mind, a bitter mockery of the vibrant spirit that had once illuminated my world. I shut my eyes, seeking refuge from the relentless memories that chased me into the darkness, relentless and unforgiving, and there I slept, a deep dreamless sleep of exhaustion.

I woke with a start. The light that had given me hope was gone, swallowed by night, but I could smell the tinge of fresh night air. Collapsed on the wet ground, I pressed my trembling hands against my chest. The anguish that threatened to consume me had returned. But it was futile; the pain was too raw, too all-encompassing.

Yet, amidst the darkness, a spark of resolve ignited. I was determined to defy the encroaching shadows, to fight my way back into the light. I couldn't change the past, couldn't undo my mistakes. But I could honor his memory, carry on his legacy in any way I could. With that thought as my anchor, I wiped the tears from my cheeks with a bloodied hand. The physical pain had come back, but I was determined to leave it where it was and move out, come hell or high water. Both of which had already been and gone. I chuckled inwardly at the irony.

Christopher's sacrifice hung heavily on my shoulders. His memory demanded more than mourning; it called for action.

Standing against the encroaching shadows, my resolve solidified. I took a steady breath, vowing to honor Christopher's legacy and turn his sacrifice into a symbol of resilience.

The pain of loss wove through my soul, a haunting melody from the past. Each note pierced through me, a reminder of the emptiness left in Christopher's wake. Instead of succumbing to its suffocating embrace, I embraced it as my driving force and let it propel me forward. With leaden steps, I rose from the unforgiving ground, the earth clinging to me like a shroud of sorrow.

The sky was now stormy. I could hear thunderous rain pounding the earth outside. There was little light in the chamber, but a flash from a lightning made its way in and glinted off the water. With renewed determination, I stepped into the storm. The wind lashed at my face, and the rain soaked my clothes. With each step I felt a cleansing of my spirit. I defied the despair threatening to consume me. Christopher's memory guided me through the tempest like a flickering flame. He was alive in me.

The rain pounded relentlessly, mirroring the chaos that still raged within me. Gasping for breath, I looked out at the vast expanse of the Pacific Ocean, dark and foreboding. With Christopher's memory as my guide, I prepared to confront whatever lay ahead.

His absence weighed heavily, casting a shadow where his presence once stood.

Amidst the ocean's briny breeze, each step toward the edge felt like a march toward destiny, the abyss below calling with equal parts dread and allure.

I stood there, teetering on the edge, rain-slicked concrete beneath my feet, the ocean's roar drowning out all else. It was a cacophony of chaos mirroring the storm within. Guilt, grief, and the relentless drive to survive pressed down upon me.

Yet, amid the turmoil, a glimmer of defiance flickered. Christopher's memory burned bright, his sacrifice a rallying cry against the encroaching despair. I took a breath, salty and sharp, and glanced at the distant city lights—hazy and indistinct against the harsh reality before me.

But I was ready. Ready to plunge into the depths and emerge anew. With a surge of determination, I leaped into the icy embrace of the ocean, the water swallowing me whole.

CHAPTER 19

THOSE LEFT BEHIND

THE COLD WAS A SHOCK, like a thousand needles piercing my skin all at once. For a moment, everything went dark—the world above, the world below, the very air I had just left behind. The ocean engulfed me, its depths pulling at my limbs with an eerie calm. I kicked hard, trying to push my way back to the surface, my lungs screaming for air.

When I broke through, gasping, the waves hit me with a ferocity I hadn't expected. A wall of saltwater crashed over me, forcing me under again, the weight of it relentless. I fought to stay afloat, kicking, flailing—my arms cutting through the water with desperate strokes. The coastline seemed so far, just a jagged outline of rocks and distant cliffs. I tried to orient myself, but the ocean tugged at me, threatening to pull me back into its endless blue.

Each wave felt like a battle. The current was strong, more than I had anticipated, and I realized too late that I hadn't checked how deep the water was where I'd jumped. It could have been shallow; I could've cracked my skull on hidden rocks beneath the surface. But I didn't care. All that mattered was escape. And that terrifying thought, the recklessness of my dive, fueled me to keep swimming, to keep pushing.

I floated for a moment, letting the waves carry me, my body burning with exhaustion. The salt stung my eyes, my throat, my wounds. I wasn't sure if I was bleeding anymore or if the cold had numbed me entirely. I just knew I had to make it to shore. The jagged granite coastline loomed closer, but with every stroke, the waves seemed to push me back, taunting me.

There were times I thought I wouldn't make it. The pull of the undertow was strong enough to drag me under, and more than once, I felt myself slipping beneath the surface. My arms felt like lead, my legs trembling with exhaustion. But every time the water threatened to take me, I fought back, gasping for air, clinging to that sliver of hope—survival.

Finally, after what felt like an eternity, my hand brushed something solid. The bottom. I was close. I scrambled for footing, the rocks scraping my skin as I staggered forward, half-crawling, half-wading through the shallows. The shore was a cruel welcome—sharp, cold, and unyielding. I collapsed onto the wet sand, every inch of me aching, the wind whipping against my raw skin.

The world had twisted into a smear, a fever dream. The sand scraped my skin like a thousand tiny shards, each grain emphasizing my broken state. The waves seemed distant as they churned in a rhythm of relentless, roaring fury. I gasped for breath. The salt seemed to have stayed my wounds, even if temporarily. My shattered reality spun and swirled, caught in the tempest of my own mind, until the thundering whirr of helicopter blades sliced through the haze. The police airlifted me away, a fragile wisp of humanity amidst the storm of chaos, to a sterile hospital where the slow march of recovery began.

Every scar that marred my body echoed the untold nightmare, etched deep beneath my skin, secrets masked by clothing, the remnants of wounds only partially visible. Each jagged line, every mark, whispered a grim tale of that night's horrors. My memories clung like shadows, vivid and unyielding—Nicole and Christopher's faces, Darren and Misha, the devil's own. Spectral imprints seared into my soul. The physical pain was almost a solace compared to the searing torment of the emotional wounds.

Time slipped by, undeterred by the memories that taunted me, clung to me, played again and again like a horror movie reel, my subconscious fighting to make sense of it all, to keep me sane.

I had told my story. Struggled through tears and disbelief. The police, Kimberly, my mom.

Kim's response: a return to normalcy. Back in New York, our sanctuary was the usual quaint coffee shop on 3rd, where the aroma of fresh beans promised a fleeting balm, a momentary stitch in the tattered quilt of our once-ordered lives. The scent of brewed coffee was a siren call to rebuild the once beautiful existence of young lives, caught in moments of indecision yet innocent. But it was a hollow promise of solace amidst the shards of our broken reality.

The door chimed softly behind us, a gentle whisper swallowed by the chaos of the outside world. We stumbled into the coffee shop, a haven from the relentless storm of life. The scent of coffee, thick and rich, enveloped us like a shroud, wrapping our senses in a hazy embrace that tugged at the fringes of forgotten memories, good memories. Our footsteps traced a path to our usual corner, where the cushions, faded and sagging, had become reluctant witnesses to a parade of lost moments.

I felt our steps were an intrusion as they reverberated through the shop, mingling with the murmured conversations and the clink of porcelain, creating a symphony that oscillated between the mundane and the surreal. The vintage chandelier above us flickered erratically, casting a ghostly light that turned the room into a theater of the bizarre. Faded posters of '70s punk bands, their defiant visages now obscured by layers of dust and disinterest, watched us with vacant eyes, as if they, too, were trapped in a time that had slipped away.

But that was not what I heard and saw. The clinking porcelain cups were rattling chains; the flickering chandelier the random fires in the village of the damned; and on the posters, the faces of Darren and Misha replaced the punk bands.

As we sank into the cushions, the air grew heavy with nostalgia, a thick fog that wrapped around us like an old friend we barely recognized. The coffee, dark and viscous as pitch, seemed to possess an uncanny power, each sip unlocking fragments of buried truths and emotions that wavered on the edge of consciousness. The room felt like a stage set for a drama we couldn't quite place, frozen in an era that had forgotten how to move forward.

I sat there, silently, nothing really to say. My gray eyes were dead and spoke of burdens too heavy to bear. An occasional tear threatened to release itself. Yet, within the murky depths of Kimberly's hazel gaze, a fragile hope flickered, a small, stubborn flame fighting against the darkness that threatened to take me from her. When her hand found mine across the scarred table, her grip was a fierce promise, a silent vow to face the unknown together, even as the room around us seemed to dissolve into a dreamscape of a half-remembered life that could never be recovered.

"Kim, do you ever get the feeling we're just rearranging deck chairs on the Titanic?" My voice was a quiet murmur, tinged with a resigned edge. "It's like we're patching up a sinking ship with a Band-aid."

"That's an odd thing to say." Her grip tightened around her coffee cup, her eyes like steel. "Jason, the world's been going to hell forever. Only now, we had a front row seat to watching it all unravel. But don't mistake the chaos back at the bank for our breaking point. We're tougher than that mess."

I looked at her, my eyes squinted, offense on my face.

"Look. I can't imagine what you've been through without me— the horrors you described. Something clearly happened to you, but I'm here. I'll always be here."

But would she? Always be here? The caffeine seemed to dissolve the shackles around my heart, unleashing a torrent of long-buried emotions and memories. My tears bled out like an open wound, each drop a jagged step toward untangling the chaos inside.

Kimberly's eyes reflected a storm of concern and fierce determination. "Jason, these nightmares, these visions of Christopher and Nicole—they're your mind throwing a tantrum. Trauma has a way of twisting reality into something outlandish."

I met her gaze, feeling the weight of my confessions like a leaden shroud. "But it was real, Kim! And it's like they're still here, like I'm reliving those moments."

She leaned in, her voice steady but carrying a cold truth. "I understand it feels real, but your brain's been through hell. The robbery was a shitshow, and now it's playing tricks on you. Maybe it's just your mind's way of making sense of the chaos."

"But the city— the trap in the sewers. There must've been something—"

Kim interrupted, her voice trembling slightly as she spoke. "The cops did their best. They followed your leads but only found a ghost town of forgotten scraps. They saw it as just another stain on the city's conscience. They didn't dig deeper."

Kim's words were heavy with frustration. "I know it's not the fairy-tale ending you wanted, but maybe it's a sign. We're trying to decode a mess instead of finding something concrete."

"So you still don't believe me," I said, my voice deflated. I stared out the window, watching the oblivious tourists swarm by. "No one does. Not even my mom."

Kim's hand clasped mine across the scarred table, a plea for connection. She hesitated before speaking again, her tone more introspective but edged with sharp insight. "It's a hard sell, Jason. I mean, sewer sadists? It sounds like something you'd see on the cover of a magazine."

She paused, her eyes searching mine. "Honestly, though, meeting your mom without you was like a punch in the gut. She cut through all the bullshit and got to what really mattered. I was worried when you didn't show up, but she told me about you, about what you've been through with your dad, and it was like a slap of reality. And looking at you now, it's clear you're tougher than you think, that you've been through hell and came out the other side."

I nodded, the memory of my mother's wisdom offering a fleeting respite from the storm. "Yeah, I warned you about her," I said, a faint smile barely touching my lips. "I'm just lucky you guys acted. Without you, the cops would've never started looking."

Her eyes narrowed, a spark of defiance igniting. "Jason, luck has nothing to do with it. We were scared. What else would we have done?"

I tried to respond, but she cut me off, her voice rising with intensity. "No, listen. We've... you've been through hell and you're still standing. You've got yourself to thank for that."

I took a deep breath, her fierce energy washing over me. "You're right. It's just... sometimes it feels like I'm drowning in all of this."

She leaned closer, her eyes boring into mine. "Then we claw our way out. One day at a time, one step at a time. And when it gets too much, we lean on each other. You're not alone in this."

But I was.

Her words, soft but unyielding, wrapped around me like a noose. "We face this together, Jason. We tackle these fears head-on and find a way to push through. We can't let this shit tear us apart."

I felt the urge to confess crashing over me like a storm. "Kim, I'm sorry, but I just can't do this. There's more— something I've been hiding from everyone, especially you."

Kim's brow furrowed, concern deepening. "Then spit it out. What's eating at you?"

I took a deep breath, my voice trembling. "It's about us. About this relationship." I paused, avoiding her gaze. "I've been living a lie, trying to fit into a mold that everyone expects from me. But it's not who I am."

Her grip on my hand tightened, her eyes sharp with intensity. "Cut to the chase. Are you unhappy with me?"

"It's not about you, Kim. You've been amazing. But this... facade, it's suffocating me."

She pulled her hand back, her voice dropping to a low, almost guttural growl. "What is it, then? Did you meet someone else?"

"Something like that..." I hesitated, grappling with the weight of my confession. "I've been hiding my feelings. From you, from myself. But I can't do it anymore. I need to face reality, even if it means breaking away from what's expected."

Her voice, though pained, carried a note of reluctant understanding. "Jason, I... I never knew. I thought we were happy, that we had something real—"

"We did... do, in a way. But it was built on a foundation that wasn't true. You deserve someone who can give you their whole heart, and that's not me. I need to find out who I am."

Kimberly took a long pause, her voice firm but resigned. "If that's how you feel, then I get it. It hurts like hell, but I understand. Do what you need to do, Jason. You're going through a lot right now, and we both need to be honest with ourselves."

She pushed herself up from the table, giving me one last glance before stepping into the night.

"As soon as you figure out who you really are, give me a call," Kim said, her voice carrying a mix of finality and an unspoken promise.

As I sipped my bitter coffee, its warmth a small comfort, I found solace in the quiet. Outside, life continued unabated, but within that small shop, time seemed to stand still. My memories were mine alone, pieces of a puzzle that others might never understand. Each encounter, each person from that day, left an indelible mark.

Sitting there, Nicole's ghostly echoes swirled around me. She was a dichotomy. Strong yet vulnerable. Vicious but kind. Deliberate but frail. A roaring kitten who faced down her destructors to the very end. With her unyielding spirit, she had been the catalyst for all this chaos. Her magnetic force, fierce and relentless, had ignited a spark in the darkest abyss. Yet, beneath her blazing exterior, she grappled with demons of her own, her past casting long, sinister shadows. Our fates had diverged, leaving her as just another phantom, a runaway lost in the void, destined to remain elusive.

Misha—Michelle Lopez—her name was a haunting refrain. Her visage, twisted and tormented by her allegiance to Darren, invaded my nightmares. I'd see her face, before all the anguish, before the 'transformation,' on bus stop ads or flickering in a fleeting commercial, fragments of her life before she was consumed. She was a victim, like me, yet her suffering was deeper, her psyche twisted by the grotesque horrors she'd endured. My heart twisted with a bitter sympathy for her, even as her actions wreaked havoc in my life. In another realm, perhaps salvation was within reach, but here, she was lost to the abyss, a living testament to how darkness can corrupt even the purest souls.

And Darren—his shadow loomed omnipresent, a harbinger of malevolence. The scars he etched were more than physical; they were branded on my very essence, the scars of wounds evident on my spirit. He was the epitome of darkness, a blight that devoured everything in its path, leaving me mired in his poisonous influence. His presence was an inescapable poison, staining every corner of my existence, making me question if freedom from his clutches was even possible.

Finally, Christopher—his memory was a bittersweet ache. His courage, his unwavering strength, and his loyalty had been my beacons. His life was extinguished too soon. Now, he was a guiding light; a star in my personal heaven. The guilt of his absence was a relentless reminder of my shortcomings. Yet, within that ache, his memory kindled a flicker of resolve, a reason to push forward, to seek out moments of peace and joy. I imagined he would want me to keep moving, to find solace and embrace life's fragments.

In that dimly lit moment, I shed the weight of the past and the uncertainties of what lay ahead. I found a fragile comfort in the rhythmic cadence of my breath and the unspoken communion that connected me to the shadows of my past and the faint glimmers of hope.

                                · · ·

EMERGING from the subway's dark maw, I was greeted by the moon
—a sickly, spectral orb that hung in the sky like a diseased eye. Its pale
light stretched and twisted shadows into grotesque shapes, writhing
as if alive. The alley leading to my dorm extended out like a mouth,
an abyss that devoured sound and light with a hunger that matched
my own growing dread.

The skyscraper ahead loomed like a monolith of despair, its darkened windows resembling hollow eyes, watching me with a malevolent stare. A passing police cruiser bathed the scene in cobalt and
crimson hues, and a creeping unease slithered across my skin, its icy
fingers whispering of unseen dangers. Each step I took on the cracked
stoop was met with a hollow thud, an echo swallowed by the
encroaching night. The sporadic flicker of the porch light cast jittery
shadows that danced with malevolent intent.

Then, I saw it.

Suspended from the doorknob was a fraternity letter jacket—a
spectral remnant, swaying with an unsettling grace in the night
breeze. My heart pounded in my chest, each beat a reminder of
Christopher's inexplicable vanishing. The jacket's presence seemed
to pull at my very soul, its black leather glinting in the dim light.

With a trembling hand, I reached for the jacket. As I touched it, I
saw a small, jagged tear on the left shoulder—a wound I recognized
from the past. My heart tightened as my fingers traced the rough
edges of the tear. This tear, a raw reminder of our shared suffering
and the violence that had invaded our lives, felt almost alive, pulsing
with the echoes of forgotten pain.

The rustle of the fabric was like the whisper of ghosts, the last
vestige of a life that had been violently torn away. This jacket wasn't
just a piece of clothing; it was a cursed artifact, a link to the past
woven with threads of agony and hope. It beckoned me to confront
the phantoms that lurked within these walls, to unearth the secrets
festering in the dark.

As I glanced back at the engulfing darkness outside, the familiar world seemed to dissolve into obscurity. I stepped into the maw of the unknown, the heavy door slamming shut behind me with a finality that sealed my fate. The darkness within was now my world, a labyrinth of shadows and secrets that awaited my unwelcome return.

THE HALLWAY of my walkup was a maze of shadows and whispers, each door a gateway to unseen terrors that brought me again to the brink of madness. The usual hum of my building had transformed into a low, menacing drone, vibrating with secrets that seemed to writhe and slither just out of sight. The walls themselves seemed to pulse with a life of their own, each flicker of light casting grotesque, twisted shapes that danced with the rhythm of my anxiety. It was as if the building had morphed into a living riddle, torn between the urge to swallow me whole or to expel me into the void.

My heart beat erratically, a wild drum in the throes of a sinister symphony. The familiar creaks and groans of the hallway sounded like the whispers of some dark entity, each one an ominous promise of the unknown. Every shadow seemed to stretch and curl, harboring something malevolent that I could barely comprehend. My breath came in ragged gasps, the oppressive air pressing down on me like a physical force, making each step a battle against the suffocating tension.

I reached my room door, which was ajar just enough to cast a thin, wavering beam of light onto the floor, like a narrow slit into another world. The door's creak as I pushed it open was a groan of ancient wood, sending an icy shiver through my spine.

"...Chris?" My voice was a trembling whisper, swallowed by the cavernous emptiness of the dorm. *There's no way that he...* The silence that answered me was thick and oppressive, filled with an unsettling energy that seemed to pulse and breathe with its own rhythm.

Driven by a frenetic energy, I plunged into the apartment's

depths, tearing through rooms with a frantic, delirious urgency. The walls seemed to close in on me, their angles shifting and distorting, making the familiar space feel alien and hostile. I ripped open closets and searched under my bed, scattering the debris of a forgotten life, each item a fragment of a story I could no longer piece together.

As the night dragged on, the elusive truth slipped further from my grasp, a phantom playing hide and seek. Doubt coiled around me like a constricting serpent, its venom seeping into my thoughts, whispering insidious questions. *Was Christopher really here? Did he make it to New York? Or was it Darren or another one of those beasts taunting me, playing cat and mouse, waiting for the right moment to strike? Someone hung that jacket out there!*

Exhaustion draped itself over me, dragging me toward the sanctuary of my bedroom. I begged for the mercy of sleep and collapsed onto my bed, its worn mattress offering little respite as my weary body sank into its embrace. The relentless search had frayed my nerves, leaving me hollow and spent, my mind a chaotic storm of unanswered questions.

In the murky depths of my fatigue, uncertainty wove its suffocating cocoon around me. Yet, amidst the gloom, a flicker of defiance still burned, a rebellious ember that urged me to continue, to confront the specters that danced just beyond the fringes of my understanding.

My gaze fixated on the cracked mirror in the corner, its splintered surface a chaotic mosaic of my fractured psyche. As I moved closer, a glint among the shards caught my eye—a small, sealed envelope, its presence both a promise and a threat, half-concealed behind the jagged glass.

"JASON," it read, scrawled in an unfamiliar, erratic hand. My heart raced as I pried the envelope from the mirror's edge. My fingers trembled uncontrollably as I tore it open, revealing its contents: a boardwalk photo strip of Christopher and Nicole, their frozen smiles a haunting snapshot of a stolen moment. Beside it, a handwritten note lay like a dark secret.

The note's hurried scrawl seemed to pulse with a life of its own, an unsettling echo from the past. I collapsed onto the bed, the photo and note clutched like a lifeline. My chest tightened, tears welling as I stared at the image of Chris and Nicole, their happiness forever trapped in that moment. *"This is all I have left of her now,"* I thought, his voice reverberating through my mind, mingling with memories I wished to bury. "We'll make it out of this. We have to. For her, and for us." My broken promise gnawed at me, a constant ache.

Then, the note—its scrawl so familiar yet so alien—whispered secrets long buried beneath layers of deceit. Each stroke of the pen seemed to beckon, a siren's call dragging me deeper into the dangerous, all-consuming void of uncertain madness.

My heart pounded like a caged beast. The allure of the unknown, the beckoning abyss, was too potent to ignore. With a shaky breath, I braced myself and began to unravel the tangled web of mysteries that the ink-stained page concealed.

Jason,

Hey, guess who's finally made it to the big city? Yeah, it's me. If you're reading this, it means I finally managed to get my shit together. Not sure if I'm doing this right, but hey, that's par for the course with how screwed up things have been. Dammit, I'm probably already fucking this up.

I wish I could see you again—just to say "hey" and pretend everything's fine. But I needed you to know that I'm still here, in some messed-up way. Those things that took me, they turned me into something else. Saved my life, but it came with a steep price. I'm not the same guy I used to be. Now, they look at me like I'm their leader, mainly because someone wicked witch'd the last one. Yeah, twisted, I know.

I need you to get it—I've become something monstrous. Even though I wish I could be with you, I can't come back.

It's better if I stay out of sight, let you remember me as I was. I'm fighting to hold on to who I was when I first met you with Nicole, but some days are harder than others.

In the end, I need you to know that you made a huge difference in my life. I'm leaving my dad's coat with you as a token of thanks. I want you to know how much you meant to me. No matter how things look, you're never alone. You've got someone out there who cares about you.

Take care, Jason. You've changed my life more than you'll ever know. And even though I might look like a monster, I am who I choose to be.

EPILOGUE: THE SAVIOR EMERGES

That was the last time I ever heard from him. I kept waiting for a sign —a glimpse of him in the subway's flickering lights or a shadow darting through the dank alleys. But he remained a phantom, as if swallowed by the city's very fabric. Whispers began to seep through the streets, spectral murmurs that left an unsettling chill in their wake. Rumors, twisted and grotesque, spread like a malevolent virus, each new tale wrapping itself around the mystery like a shroud.

They spoke of a figure emerging from the darkness—a grotesque apparition, marred by nightmarish scars. He seemed to crawl out of their deepest fears, a harbinger cloaked in shadows, his presence everywhere yet nowhere. Missing people reappeared, their stories suffused with eerie accounts of a savior with unnatural foresight, as if he could sense trouble before it happened. Stories of his ethereal presence seeped through New York, a chilling reminder that reality could stretch into the macabre.

It was Christopher. He bore the weight of that dark day with a strength that seemed almost otherworldly. His scars were a map of our shared struggles, grim illustrations of the horrors we had traversed together.

And as I buried my despair, a glimmer of hope started to grow, like a small flower blooming in the muck, an incandescent water lily that thrived where it should not have. I wore my scars with pride, a testament to the strength we'd found inside us.

With nothing but our raw resolve and the grim understanding that salvation often springs from the unlikeliest of places, we trudged on, Christopher and I, he in his role as the mangled savior, a grim dichotomy who lived in the darkness for the memory of his beloved Nicole. That enigmatic figure, with his haunted visage and battle-scarred form, became the city's symbol of human endurance—a stark reminder that even in the bleakest moments, a glimmer of hope often stubbornly persists.

And me, a dog-eared remnant of a human who persisted in the face of obscurity, unknown and unimportant, making the most of every challenge in honor of my friend. And as we pressed forward, we left a trail of light in our wake, maintaining our defiance and empathy.

In the end, it was our shared humanity that emerged victorious. We'd pushed back the darkness encroaching on unwitting humanity, stayed its hand, and illuminated a path toward a fractured but hopeful dawn.

AFTERWORD

This book is a work of fiction. The characters, events, and settings are products of the author's imagination and are not intended to reflect any real-life individuals, situations, or places. Any resemblance to actual persons, living or dead, is purely coincidental.

A Note on Themes

This story explores complex and, at times, dark subject matter, including violence and the harmful choices some characters make. While these elements are essential to the narrative, they are not meant to glorify or promote destructive behaviors in any way. Instead, they aim to reflect the emotional challenges that many people face and the lasting impact of trauma.

If you or someone you know is struggling with thoughts of self-harm, mental health challenges, or trauma, please seek professional help. There are resources available that can offer support, and no one should face these battles alone. Here are a few organizations that can provide assistance:

- **National Suicide Prevention Lifeline**: 1-800-273-8255

- **Crisis Text Line**: Text HOME to 741741
- **National Alliance on Mental Illness (NAMI)**: nami.org

Thank you for reading, and I hope this story has sparked thought, reflection, and empathy.

ACKNOWLEDGMENTS

A special thanks to these fantastic people who helped make this book possible:

Adri
Bree
Cossy
Jessie
Joanna
Kamran
Keaton
Lee
Mason
Maureen
Mila
Mike
Nadia

ABOUT THE AUTHOR

Author | College Professor | Thriller Enthusiast

Lincoln James, your favorite author's favorite author, is known for his haunting love stories, vintage thrillers, and slow-burn suspense. His characters feel, ache, and bleed, often trapped between the past and the people who won't let them forget it. When he's not writing, James is a Communication and English professor in New York City and cherishes moments with friends and family, proving that the most thrilling tales lie in the love and laughter shared with those closest to us.

www.ingramcontent.com/pod-product-compliance
Lightning Source LLC
Chambersburg PA
CBHW061439150726

47987CB00001B/267